Michael Riddell

Michael Riddell is a writer and s[...] southern hills of Dunedin, wher[...] of Otago. He has a varied background, which includes travel, protest, imprisonment and controversy. A lifelong interest in spirituality has generated many books around the theme. Whenever possible, Michael escapes to the hills of the Taieri Gorge, where he has a 'crib' complete with writing room at Hindon. He is married to Rosemary, a partner in a Dunedin law firm, and is father of Matt, Polly and Kat. His major role in life is walking the family dog, Baxter, beside the wild southern ocean.

By the same author:

Fiction:
  Deep Stuff
  The Insatiable Moon

Non-fiction:
  Godzone
  Threshold of the Future
  Alt.Spirit@Metro.M3
  God's Home Page

MASKS & SHADOWS

MICHAEL RIDDELL

Flamingo
An imprint of HarperCollins*Publishers*

For Matt, who makes things happen with his smile.

Flamingo
An imprint of HarperCollins *Publishers*

First published 2000
HarperCollins *Publishers (New Zealand) Limited*
P.O. Box 1, Auckland

Copyright © Michael Riddell, 2000

ISBN 1 86950 348 1

Designed and typeset by Chris O'Brien
Printed by Griffin Press, South Australia, on 80 gsm
Econoprint

Prologue

This is not the way it happened.

I'm not sure any more how anyone knows if anything happens, let alone how it happens. Actually, there's just me sitting in front of a screen, watching letters scurry across the pristine page. And it's not really a page—just a white rectangle made to look like a page. Most of the time I'm happy to pretend that it's paper, and that the little electronic squiggles are letters. But they're not.

So, you see, there's nothing actually happening. Nor has anything happened in the past that I'm now describing to you. The only events are those which occur in the force field existing somewhere between my imagination and the synaptic precision of my CPU, manufactured in Taiwan.

You're getting annoyed already, aren't you? And we're only a few paragraphs in. You knew, didn't you, when you picked this book up that it was fiction? You weren't expecting a true story, were you? And yet you wanted the illusion of truth. Oh yes, I understand; you wanted to be transported out of the story you're living into another story, and you expected me to help you.

The last thing you want is the author getting in the road of the exercise. Sprawling ego all over the margins like a teenager with no sense of limits. You don't want your boundaries blurred, do you? And I don't blame you. Authors shouldn't presume to intrude on the sacred space created for them. For fiction to succeed, we require *the suspension of disbelief*. Hang it from on high, until dead. Choke it off, strangle it, dangle it, suspend it.

I know I shouldn't show myself at all. I'm not supposed to exist. I've been deconstructed, which is a little like death except that there's nothing to bury. Well, I'm prepared to go along with it.

Have you ever thought that perhaps there are no authors any more? That there's no one and nothing behind the text? That all the time when you think you're deciphering someone else's story, you're actually looking into a mirror? Perhaps the author is a figment of your imagination, which you use as a crutch because you can't bear the reality of your own dreamings. It's possible, isn't it? Perhaps.

Where do shadows fall? What space do they occupy? Are they on the inside or outside? Sometimes I suspect we are incapable of seeing our own shadows until they turn up in other people. If it makes it easier for you, I could write my own shadow into a story, and there you could condemn it. You could hold the author responsible. But it's difficult, isn't it, keeping yourself out of things?

So this may be your story. But if it helps to imagine that someone else is writing it, that the events are somewhere outside of you and actually *happened*, then that's okay. If you want to believe in me as someone outside of you, then I'll play along. Nobody need ever know. As far as anyone else is concerned, you're just reading a book. Written by an author. So be it. All stories are true, after all.

Now, where were we?

Oh yes, this is the way it happened . . .

Chapter One

In the beginning was the ritual. The way of repeating actions so that they mean other things. The nurture of order against insistent emptiness.

Joe arranges his prison cutlery in something of a pattern. Not that anyone else would know. It's *his* pattern, *his* way of arranging them. As a child he'd been called fussy by one of the 'uncles'. And certainly he likes routine, such as can be managed.

He shaves his head because it's a way of keeping neat amid the chaos. There have been times when he's considered putting a crease in his prison-issue jeans.

Three things he knows are important to get you through the lag—space, identity and respect. Lose any one of them and you're screwed. As many have been.

Voices echo and tangle in railway station transience. Concrete walls refuse to yield; splinters of sound ricochet around the dining hall, slicing the air. A prison is made of hard surfaces. The inhabitants adapt.

Blade watches Joe adjusting the position of the fork. He smirks, and blows through his nose. It's a sound of derision, a spontaneous eruption of private mockery. Once it's gone, he can't get it back.

Later the wardens replay the video tape in silent admiration. They'd been watching when it happened, but almost missed it. They wanted the action replay in slow motion.

On the grainy screen you can see the squat figure with the

bald head arranging cutlery in seeming serenity. In one frame Joe is still holding the fork in his right hand. He appears composed and relaxed, placing it with care like a priest arranging communion. There's no sign of trouble. In the next his arm is simply a blur. By the third frame his elbow has reached Blade's larynx, stopping a centimetre short. Blade's eyes are just beginning to open in surprise. Joe's face has turned slightly toward him, and there is the beginning of a smile.

One indistinct video frame sandwiched between habit and violence. That's what they sniff for, the guards. The millisecond in which it all changes, the knife edge of survival.

They argue for a while about whether the blow would have been fatal, had it not been pulled short. The Welshman who talks all the time knows things from the army, and he calls it a killing jolt. In the event they couldn't decide—didn't have to. It was just a gesture, a warning.

'Dangerous bastard,' mutters the one with the silver cap on his tooth. Nobody argues.

Joe has said nothing. Not spoken a word. He simply goes back to making his adjustments, replacing the fork in its proper relation to the other instruments. He allows himself the satisfaction of running a hand across his shaven skull, relishing the hard smoothness.

Respect, that's probably the most important of the three.

A few seconds without a word spoken between them. But it's been seen, observed, analysed, recorded. Some twenty pairs of eyes have registered the challenge and the response. The word will go round. Sometime in the next few days—maybe in the showers, possibly in the workroom—some lesser man will have a go at Blade. Testing himself against the odds. There will be blood, probably. It's the way of things. The stakes are in flux. You're only as good as your last victory.

Joe knows these things as if he's always known them. Bears them deep in the hidden strands of his DNA. He survives, because he understands. And the more he understands, the longer he survives. His rituals carry more than the likes of Blade could ever guess.

beast (biːst) *n* **1** any animal other than man, esp. a large wild quadruped. **2** savage nature or characteristics: *the beast in man*. **3** a brutal, uncivilized, or filthy person.
beast of prey *n* any animal that hunts other animals for food.

it's just silly how people don't look after the world. why would anyone leave a dirty old beer can out here where the trees grow? if i was a tree i'd slap them with a branch. this grass is so soft—like a green fur coat. i love the way it smells. and my skin is all tingly from the sun.

once upon a time there was a fairy princess who lived in a beautiful garden, with blossom trees and bananas growing on vines. and there were lots of birds and some of them had bright colours. all of them could sing and so could all of the children and the grown-ups. but there was a big ugly beer-drinking dwarf who watched football on the sofa all the time. he spoiled everything.

he'd throw his empty beer cans out of the window and they would bounce all the way into the garden of the princess. sometimes she'd come out for a walk in the garden and the birds would sing and she would too. and everyone was happy until she spied the dirty old beer can and she became sad.

one day she saw a can bouncing out of the big ugly dwarf's window and she decided to teach him a lesson. so she cast a spell because she had special powers and the tv set got stuck on nature programmes and wouldn't get anything else. and she made the beer taste even worse than it was, and every time the dwarf drank some it only made him thirstier and thirstier, until he died of thirst. so they buried him in a big hole with all his beer cans and planted trees on top. whenever the sun came out the trees would wave their arms and the birds would sing and the princess was happy again.

oh so happy.

because the sun is shining and the birds are singing and the grass is making patterns on my cheek. and soon it will be time for lunch. oh, go away cloud.

shadow (ˈʃædʊ) *n* **1** a dark image or shape cast on a surface by the interception of light rays by an opaque body. **2** an area of relative darkness. **3** the dark portions of a picture. **4** a threatening influence; blight: *a shadow over one's happiness.* **5** a spectre. **6** an inseparable companion.

Blade has moved by the time Joe gets back with his food. His place is occupied by George, one of the ancient laggers. He's a wizened crow of a man with a hook nose and shrewd eyes. Joe looks out for him.

'See the game?' asks George between mouthfuls.

'Yeah, bloody awful,' says Joe.

'A fookin' disgrace, you ask me. The sooner they drop Willers the better. He squats to piss, that lad does.'

'How's your missus, George?'

'Yeah, okay I think. A bit knocked around from the chemotherapy, like. But the last blood test was good. She has to meet with the quack next week sometime.'

There's a time of quiet while Joe looks at him, chewing slowly and methodically.

'I've got some coffee back in the cell. Come on by later on and we'll have a boil-up, as long as the screws don't get down on my bomb.'

'May the sun shine sweetly on yer arse, Joe, you're a good lad. Now, a word to the wise, like. Keep your eyes on Rollo, you know what I mean? The word is he might be shaping for a bit of action. He's been doing a lot of time in the gym, and he's never got over you stepping him last year. And keep your eyes open for a blade.'

'Rollo? Ear-to-ear bone, nasty little bastard that he is. All right then George, thanks for the tip. I'll be ready.'

'I don't doubt it, lad, I don't doubt it. Here, what's this? It's fookin' baccy, that's what it is. In the mash! Jeez, it gets worse and worse. I like a smoke after the meal, not as a friggin' part of it.'

'Where's Tessa?' she asks him.

'Over by the trees there, lying on the grass. She's all right,

10

don't worry about her.'

Mark watches Elizabeth; the way she brushes her hair off her face, even when it's not there. The hint of a frown hovering behind every smile. She does worry. Not that she's naturally nervous or timid. Just that ever since Tessa was born she's seemed anxious and protective. As if her domain of responsibility has suddenly been stretched to the limits of control. Is that what they mean by maternal instinct? Or aren't we supposed to talk of that any more? I'm sure she was never this jumpy before we had Tessa.

'D'you think we should call her over?' she asks, her eyes narrowing toward her distant child.

'She's okay. She'll be dreaming, knowing her.'

'Yes, well it's almost time for something to eat anyway. I think I'll start getting it organised.'

The day has flaunted itself over Hampstead Heath, and now hangs lazily, waiting for something to happen. There may be some high cloud beyond the faint brown haze; it's difficult to tell. The air smells of old paper bags. There's not much by the way of breeze, just the occasional stirring as the day floats its petticoats. 'Languid' is the word which surfaces amidst the gentle swells of Mark's brain activity.

There are people around, but they are safely on the fringes, and refreshingly free of purpose. On this one gloriously sunny occasion, the day is not a backdrop to human activity; it's the goal of it. The park provides a communal space in which to inhale the ease, to absorb it through the skin, to soak in it until boundaries begin to unravel. Metabolisms have slowed to match the rhythms of the earth. The cruel linear sequence of time is stuttering and beginning to dissolve.

'Here, shift yourself Mark. I want to get this rug spread out properly. Perhaps you could organise the drinks?'

Another 24 hours and it would have gone without trace. Lord knows she's used every form of chemical warfare the pharmacist could provide. But there it is, when you stand close to the mirror under a bright light—the unmistakable remains of a pimple. Nancy resists the temptation to touch it, instead covering it with foundation.

It would have to happen on my birthday. When do you stop getting pimples? I would have thought I was beyond them by now. Eighteen. Amazing. Old enough for . . . well, almost anything.

She tosses her deeply auburn hair away from her face, and practises expressions for the benefit of the mirror. Her smile. Her sympathetic look. Her interested look. Her shy lowering of the eyes. That's the hardest one to get right. It doesn't come naturally. A perfunctory press of the lips together. And the smile again. Perhaps a little more eye shadow.

'Come on Nancy, get a move on. Your father wants a shower before everyone starts arriving.'

Mary is leaning against the door, talking into it. She can picture the scene behind it, with her daughter preening and preparing. Years ago she might have done the same. Now it's all routine, like doing the dishes. Repairing the damage rather than presenting the freshening bloom. Two months past her fortieth birthday, and feeling it keenly.

'Tell Daddy to use the *en suite*—I'll be a bit longer yet.'

'But his shaver's in there. And anyway, you've had the bathroom for an hour already.'

'Oh come on, Mummy. You know what it's like—this is important. I want to be stunning, not just lovely. Another fifteen minutes.'

The confidence of youth. Still, why shouldn't she be? Mary smiles. She is lovely, and the whole of her life before her.

'All right, then. But no longer, mind.'

'Kiss kiss, Mummy. Tell Daddy it's all in a good cause.'

Alex will complain. But he'll accept it. He'd forgive Nancy the earth. He looks at her now the way he used to look at me, with pride. As if he were a better person for being close to beauty. As if he could somehow claim responsibility. And I enjoyed it the same way that Nancy does now.

It all hovers in the middle foreground, as she turns through the nostalgia with a ladle. Not the detail of it—the events and how it grew from a bit of a lark to marriage—no, more that indulgent fug of feeling. The warm treacle of being *wanted*. Alex had always been good with words, even in those days when he was nothing. He noticed me, wooed me, beguiled me with that golden voice of his. I was enchanted.

How it all fades, she thinks, returning to the bedroom to continue reconstruction.

why do sparrows jerk their heads like that? maybe cos they don't like being still. i can understand that. i wish i could fly. i wish i could just spread my arms out like this and take off up into the air. and feel the wind in my face when i swooped down towards the earth. it must be funny to see everything from up above instead of looking sideways at it.

sometimes in my dreams i can fly. i don't have to move my arms or anything. i just think of a place and i'm flying towards it. it feels so lovely and free. waking up is the worst thing. then i feel extra heavy and clumsy.

it's funny how birds don't have to do any work. i suppose it seems like work to them, out looking for crumbs and worms. but they don't have to go to school or do boring things like that. and they always seem to find enough food around to live on.

i love the way they build nests. such warm cosy little homes out of bits of old string and straw that they pick up. and all their little babies with their mouths wide open waiting for food. do they feel lonely when they get left on their own? we once found a dead chick under a tree, and daddy said it must have fallen out of its nest. it was so sad.

> **innocent** ('ɪnəsənt) *adj* **1** not corrupted or tainted with evil or unpleasant emotion; sinless; pure. **2** not guilty of a particular crime; blameless. **3** harmless or innocuous. *n* **4** an innocent person, esp. a young child or ingenuous adult.

She makes her entrance as dramatic as possible. One hand on her hip and the other behind her head. The dress she is wearing is a straight black shift with shoulder straps, cut low. Nancy

13

pouts suggestively in the direction of her father.

His eyes behold her. Gradually the features of his face rear-range themselves from shock to a spreading smile. He holds his breath and savours it. The light sparkles on her dark red hair. She is a vision, truly a vision.

'Well?' she demands. 'Will I do?'

'Nancy, I shouldn't tell you this, but you're beautiful. Where on earth did you get that dress from? I think I should lock you up tonight and keep you away from all those boys.'

'Don't be silly, Daddy; I'll be with Daniel. And don't worry—I borrowed the dress from Amy. It is rather special, though, isn't it?'

'I don't know what to say, Nancy. You must've grown up when we weren't looking. You look radiant. Mary, come and have a look.'

Mary pokes her head round the door of the bathroom. She's wearing a slip, and has a hairclip in the corner of her mouth. Her hands are behind her head, pulling her hair back in prepa-ration. No make-up has been applied yet, and her face is still red from the scrub.

The posing young woman before her evokes a complex re-action. Mary's face creases in an admiring smile. She sees something of her own youth in this lovely daughter. But, unrevealed, there is a darker current surging through the inner channels. Resentment? Jealousy?

'Fabulous,' is all she says, before ducking her head back into the steamy interior. And the face in the mirror is full of regret and the prospect of age.

Joe reaches the last page, and closing the book, lays it aside in reverence. *The Fires of Spring*, by James Michener. A danger-ous book for an inmate to read. No good awakening that which can't be released. Like a cell with a window; seeing things that are beyond reach. He's seen men destroyed by it.

Poor broken-arse bastards, crying themselves to sleep. There's no pity in a prison, nor tolerance of weakness. No al-lowance for hope; only endurance. You get your lag under your belt and you do your time. No looking sideways, no wishing you were somewhere else, no dreaming of the people outside. No mercy and no expectation of it.

So this sort of novel doesn't help. It arouses aspirations which can never be met. Lights fires in a land without water. Creates hunger for that which is forever lost.

He shouldn't have read it. But he's glad he did. Because Joe is one of the strong ones. One of the élite who knows how to do his time. Joe can pace himself. He knows when he's outside the boundaries and what it takes to get back. He reads more than anyone in the block, and it doesn't throw him.

Here's Joe's secret: he has a prison within a prison. An inner vault where he can go and not be found. A secret place which can never be turned over. When he reads, he descends into the cave. If he dreams, or aches, or hopes, or plans, he is careful to leave the longings behind in that place. The books are returned to the prison library. The stories remain hidden within him.

That is where his true life is rooted and guarded. Inviolate, inaccessible, inalienable. As long as the door remains closed.

> **sublimate** (ˈsʌblɪˌmeɪt) *vb* **1** *Psychol.* to direct the energy of (a primitive impulse, esp. a sexual one) into activities that are considered to be socially more acceptable. **2** *(tr)* to make purer; refine.

'Mummy, why didn't I have to wash my hands before eating?'

Elizabeth smiles, Tessa's curious gaze fixed upon her. She leans across and wipes a crumb from the side of her daughter's mouth.

'Golly, we forgot, didn't we? Only this is a sort of a special time, on a picnic. There's not much water around for washing up. So I suppose when we eat outside, away from the bathroom, it's all right to let things slip a bit. It's like the fact that we're sitting on the ground eating, instead of at the table,' she explains. 'Like the way your father's got sauce on his shirt.'

'Like the way your mother's not wearing knickers,' suggests Mark, ducking.

'Mark!' protests Elizabeth, colouring immediately.

'Aren't you, Mummy? Or is Daddy just teasing?'

'Of course I am, darling. Your father's just being vulgar, and I think it's time to give him a good thrashing. Will you help me?'

The two of them pounce and proceed to tickle him until he is helpless with laughter, and rolling along the grass in an attempt to escape.

'You've been naughty,' Tessa explains in amongst the giggling.

Across the way, a plump widow is feeding birds with bread which she carries in her handbag. The commotion attracts her attention, and for a time she watches discreetly as the young couple with the daughter cavort on the ground. Grief turns inside her like a cold fried egg. But there's gratitude as well. At least somewhere there are still families and love.

'Ross can't be here. I can't believe you'd even contemplate giving him permission to stay home,' wails Nancy.

'But it's his home too. What are we supposed to do with him? Throw him out on the street?'

Mary is so tired of these disputes. So wearied with the task of adjudicator. So disappointed that parenthood has turned to this. She preferred the days when the children snuggled against her breast and slept, or looked at her with love rather than this flashing anger.

'He was supposed to be going out to a film. He promised that he'd go out. I just knew he'd find some way to try and gate-crash the party.'

Mary sighs. 'Well his plans have fallen through, and he's promised to stay in the back room with the television all night. Surely he won't do any harm just being in the house?'

'Oh God, you don't believe *that*, do you? You are *so* naïve. It's his big chance to humiliate me in front of all my friends.'

'I'd prefer you didn't call on God when you don't mean it,' cautions Alex, the voice of quiet reason deigning to enter the discussion. With the crinkled corners of his eyes, which Mary has long since decided is an affectation.

'I'm sorry, Daddy, but this is just going to ruin everything. Can't you see that?'

'I'll have a talk with Ross and see if I can't offer him some sort of bribe to make himself scarce. Will that help you to calm down?'

Nancy grimaces by way of conditional acceptance of the terms. Mary determines to avoid Alex's beneficent peacemaker expression. She can't abide smugness.

It happens in the showers. Where there's neither video nor screw to witness.

Joe is under the long line of nozzles, with a lather of soap over his upper body. He is singing, in his cracked voice, a blues song. The sluicing warm water is one of the main pleasures in a barren day. He remembers to appreciate it.

Naked, he is compact rather than muscled. There is no pronounced neck, his bullish head appearing to emerge directly from the thick shoulders. But to look at him, you'd not pick him for what he is. Joe has no time for the body-builders in his block. Steroid queens, he calls them; the only one to get away with it.

On his back at the right shoulder there's a very traditional tattoo of a heart, with the name 'Debbie' under it. He can't quite remember what she looked like.

'She the devil with the midnight eyes . . .' he sings.

There are four others in the showers with him. Shunted through in groups of five, in ten-minute shifts. The steam and concrete make an echoing surreal setting. And then there's the edge, of course. Things happen in the showers. It's one of the few unmonitored sites in the prison.

The administration understands the need for it. There has to be a place for movement in the inmate rankings. A discreet venue where scores can be settled and reputations made and lost. There's a concealed microphone of course, where the screws can hear the start of serious trouble. The peculiar dull thudding of assault on human flesh. Restrained grunting and cursing. Usually they get there before it becomes too serious.

It hasn't escaped Joe's attention that this morning Rollo has joined his shift, apparently to make up for Bainton, who's reported sick. And so his lathered nonchalance masks a state of readiness.

The attack, when it comes, is swift and silent. Rollo has stepped out of the water and reached for his towel. He grips the hem in which he's concealed a teaspoon with a sharpened stem and lunges for Joe's kidneys.

There is this thing which happens for Joe. Colours, noises, smells; everything is intensified. And another sense, not usually available—he can detect movement even when he can't see it. Existence compresses, and time slows to a flickering progression of images.

He becomes pure animal. A human warrior, alert for survival. There is never time for thinking or even processing. It is all instinct and reaction, gut-level violence that only participants know.

Rollo's first step forward is telegraphed to Joe. His assailant is a big man, with movements difficult to disguise. By the time his foot has touched the wet floor, Joe has turned to face him.

The intensity of hatred has distorted Rollo's face. It is ugly and focused. His brow seems to have grown more bulbous, and the eyes beneath it tiny and shark-like. If the strike had been with his will rather than his hand, Joe might have been in trouble. But Joe is now operating in a shifted time zone. He has two moments to his opponent's one. Before he feels his muscles bucking into action, he knows he has it won.

Two wet and naked men in a dance of survival. The bigger of the two all menace, with a thick forearm thrusting forward the rigid edge of a towel. The other smaller, sleeker, faster; clamping down with two hands onto the extended arm, just above the wrist. Turning slightly sideways and pulling to aid the big man's forward momentum.

The other men in the shower have just begun to turn their heads. There has been no sound other than a small release of breath by Rollo as he strikes, like the air brakes on a lorry.

Losing balance, the man with the makeshift knife stabs the air where his victim was. As the big body moves past, Joe raises his knee with deadly accuracy. With his heightened senses, he feels the large fleshy testicles flattening against his kneecap like spongy eggs. The knock and shudder through his leg as it drives hard into pelvic bone.

And then he's completed his one twisting motion, jerking down hard on the arm of his groaning opponent, driving his head firmly into the concrete rear wall. The crack is loud, and together with the cries of pain finally alerts the monitoring guards. On a lesser man the skull might have burst open. As it is only the skin of the scalp tears, sending blood cascading into the drain.

Joe stares down at the collapsed man on the floor. He's aware of a roaring in his ears, and the slight jumpiness caused by adrenaline. There is a flattening moment of transition, as perception drops away and time declutches into normality.

'Too slow, boyo,' he mutters to the blood-pooled and unhearing ear below. 'Too slow by half.'

It's always difficult to find beginnings, isn't it? To sort through the mass of events which impinge on a life and shape it. It's hard to compare your own journey with that of others, because you only know your own experience. I'm not sure how much I've been shaped by circumstances, or if things could have gone some other way.

I don't think of myself as self-reflective. My focus has always been on the horizon, rather than looking back over my shoulder to see the distance already travelled. To be honest, I suspect I'm a little frightened to delve too far.

That's what I want to do, now. I want to be honest. You may think of me as being deceitful, but that would only be because you don't know me. All our lives are complex; mine a little more so than most. But it's always true that the surface of a lake conceals as much as it reveals. I'm trying to let you see the deeper waters, so that you might understand. If that's at all possible.

fear (fɪə) *n* **1** a feeling of distress, apprehension, or alarm

19

caused by impending danger, pain, etc. **2** a cause of this feeling. **3** awe; reverence: *fear of God*. **4** concern; anxiety. **5** possibility; chance.

i like to see mummy and daddy happy. i wish they held hands more often. sometimes i hear them groaning in bed at night, but it's happy noises and mummy seems to be softer after that. she told me once that it was making love. i don't understand how you make love. i asked her if i could make some, but she laughed and hugged me and wouldn't tell me what she was laughing about. they might be making some more tonight.

i wonder what they do with it all? perhaps it's in the hall cupboard with our christmas decorations—stored away for when we need it. it's good to think that we have some love put away for later.

what's that? a squirrel? a squirrelly squirrel! with a question-mark tail. standing still as a gravestone. sniffing and listening. what can you smell, mr squirrel? there's nothing to be frightened of here. nothing at all to be scared of.

Alex and Mary are discreetly sequestered in the back room. Ross, duly paid off, has found another friend to go out with. Alex reads, his glasses perched on the end of his nose. Mary works at her cross-stitch, pausing periodically to give full attention to the Vivaldi which weaves around them. Unfortunately it is underscored by the deeper bass intruding from elsewhere in the house.

The party is under way, and Nancy is undoubtedly the centre of gravity around which it orbits. Alex is content to keep out of the way, despite periodic visits on increasingly dubious pretexts. Nancy is worthy of trust, as much as any teenager can be.

He lays the book aside and closes his eyes. Drifting for a moment on the music, he recalls the day of her birth. The joy and wonder. And now, suddenly as it seems, eighteen years have gone. Good years, most of them.

Tomorrow he will conduct the service at St John's church; his fifteenth year of presiding over the Eucharist. Eighteen in ministry. Nancy a living gauge of his endurance as a priest.

The sermon, as always, is well prepared by Saturday evening. Order outlives enthusiasm; so he was taught and so he has lived. The gospel reading for tomorrow is from the Sermon on the Mount; his favourite section of scripture.

Such a comfort, the familiar voice of the Bible. A place of security in a changing world. The enduring bedrock, shedding transitory human fascinations as a mountain brushes off storms. A quarry of certainty amid the quagmire of contemporary life. An oasis of goodness in a moral desert.

Alex has no time for the liberals with their arrogant criticisms and moral lapses. It churns his stomach to think of the way the church has been weakened through their soppy attempts to be 'relevant'. Falling over themselves to declare themselves gay or play guitar after communion or march in the latest demonstration. Casting about in every direction for some sense of importance, and overlooking the very role which is given them to fulfil.

The priesthood is a calling, a holy vocation, a rare privilege; Alex a priest by conviction as well as circumstance. Set apart by God for the building up of the faithful. A shepherd to the flock, a minister to the ailing, an example to the weak.

Tomorrow, as he dons his robe, he will once again experience the thrill of vocation. As he raises the host, he will be raising his congregation before the living God. A conduit between eternity and the mundane. A clerical lightning rod between humanity and divinity. An actor in the most important drama of all.

A priest of God, and gladly so.

Back in his cell, Joe is deeply tired. He stretches full length on his bed.

There will be a report, but nothing will come of it. The other inmates will testify that Rollo slipped on a piece of soap and hit his head on the wall. Somebody will type it all up, and it will be filed with the other incident reports. Suspicion but no evidence. The unflagging bureaucratic impotence.

Bomber, his cellmate, is rereading a letter. Joe knows which one it is. He could almost quote it himself by now. From the woman who's been visiting with Prisoner Aid, and who's fallen in love. What sort of romance is there about prison that hooks them? A misdirected sympathy? Some sort of urge to mother?

Inmates are experts in psychology. Students of observation, with all the time in the world to indulge themselves. They feed on nuances and hints. The tone of a voice; the flicker of an eye. Looking for weakness or advantage. Skills that no one teaches and everyone learns if they want to survive.

Laggers like Joe can hold a conversation with another of their kind under the nose of a screw with no fear of giving anything away. The words are nothing—props to decorate the stage. The real plot is a dance below the surface; a delicate thing of nudges and blinks and gestures. A good part of it verging on the telepathic.

And so some of them play the visitors as easily as if they were game fish. Reeling them in while they think they're swimming free. It's a challenge, a game, a useful distraction when the end of your lag approaches and you want a warm bed for the night. Joe's seen some good ones. Christian women with the scent of redemption in their nostrils, leaving their husbands to be shagged weary by a prison-horny con. It never lasts. Any apparent love is neurosis by proxy; a creeping tentacle of the sickness of mind and soul which confinement breeds.

But Bomber's got it bad. Seems to have already chosen the dog to put in the kennel for the children to play with. And the woman—Barbara, that's it—is gone for all money. Imagines Bomber as some sort of persecuted and misunderstood martyr, instead of the vicious little bastard that he is. If she'd seen some of the photos presented to the jury after he slashed his last love, she might have taken fright. Or not. Some of them have such a messianic complex that nothing will dissuade them.

Well, good luck to him. Another week and he's out. And then someone new. Bomber's been all right, once I got him sorted. I hate change. It breaks the routine, disturbs the ritual, troubles the order. Reminds you that there's an inside and an outside.

Let's hope it's a lifer.

There are times and seasons. Events, portents, signs. Alignments, conjunctions, disturbances, outbreaks. Shadows creeping in the heart. Moments of coldness in the soul. Shifting patterns drifting across the psyche. Unseen and uninvited. Inevitable? Inescapable? Perhaps.

She lies nestled into the crook of Mark's arm. Warmly and wetly contented. It's a place of safety; a shelter.

'It's been a good day,' she murmurs.

'Fantastic,' he concurs. 'We couldn't have planned it better if we'd tried.'

'It's so easy to let the good days go without being thankful for them. But I enjoyed today—every minute of it. God, I love weekends.'

'I think Tessa had a good day too, don't you? She seemed to enjoy herself.'

'Absolutely. When I put her to bed she was still smiling. I think she might have got a little burned when she had her hat off. But she's sleeping soundly—worn out, I shouldn't wonder.'

Mark leans over and kisses Elizabeth gently on the forehead. She breaks into giggles.

'What?' he asks.

'I didn't tell you, did I? The conversation Tess and I had when I took her to the toilet. I had to stand outside the cubicle as usual, while she did goodness knows what in there. She loves to have these long conversations through the door, which is all right as long as there's no one else around.

'Anyway, we were chatting away about nothing in particular, and then out of the blue she asks me where the sky ends. I said I didn't know—that it didn't really have an end—that it just became outer space. But by this time she's on a roll. She asks me where heaven is. I said something like it wasn't a place at all in the ordinary sense of the word, so it would be hard to say where it was.'

'Did she buy that?'

'Not really. She thought for a while, and then asked me if I really thought there was a heaven. I said yes, which seemed to be the right answer. And then she went silent for a while, and finally said, "It must be like being happy."'

'When I asked her what she meant, she said that happiness wasn't a place either; it was just something that you were. She thought heaven might be something like that—something that you felt rather than a place where you were. I told her I thought that was a pretty good answer.'

'Just as well you didn't get on to hell.' Mark grins in the darkness.

'She told me that she felt the day had been a little bit of heaven.'

'And we just nibbled a big bit to finish it off.'

i'm flying again. down below me the sea is the bluest blue, and there are dolphins jumping. i swoop down and swim with them for a while. then i'm soaring up into the sky again, and the sun is warming my back. i fly over land, and there are beautiful green trees full of birds. and all the birds are looking up at me and thinking how well i'm flying. nothing can touch me up here. i'm as free as can be, and the wind is blowing in my hair. i can fly and fly.

Chapter Two

'In our darkness, there is no darkness with you, O Lord; the darkest night is clear as the day . . .'

An unusual choice for a wedding, Alex is thinking. But lovely, just the same. The choir threads the air with harmony, weaving a complex cloth of beauty. White robes reflect a mosaic of colour as the sun beams through the stained-glass windows and lights upon them. Pungent incense melds with the softer fragrance of summer blooms. Bride and groom nervously resplendent. And presiding over it all, Alex.

Life as it should be, he considers. The conjunction of eternity and human transience, steeped in the wisdom of the Church. A joining of man and woman, of God and humanity, of purpose and chance, of commitment and love. The binding with ancient symbols, full of mystery and grace: the ring, the cup, the promises, the blessing. How could anyone miss the essential *dignity* of the ceremony?

'In our darkness, there is no darkness . . .'

A very old man sits on a park bench. Two buttons of his flies remain undone, because he finds it difficult to make his eyes focus. No trouble seeing things far away, however. He prides himself on still being able to read street signs.

The sun is shining on his creased face, and he's glad of the warmth of it. This sunlight knows of other times. It whispers of wheatfields and his broad strong back, of mornings with joy as sharp as the light, of white-tiled rooms in Bombay. It knows of youth and passion and hope. These things the sun recalls, with no memory of cloud. The old man is content to give himself to it.

He opens his eyes and is satisfied. The trees still hold a little of that lime-greenness of spring. The grass is thick and luxuriant. This may be my last day, he reminds himself. My only day.

There's a small girl over against the fence of the rabbit enclosure. Dark-haired. She's wearing a white blouse over bright-yellow leggings. On her feet she has some sort of sneakers. She seems to be talking to the rabbits.

You lose control when you age. Emotion, bladder, senses—they all betray you. This little girl, what can she know of these things?

There is a shadow attached to the girl's heels. They're hard to escape from, shadows.

'Control to unit 426.'

'426 here.'

'You still up Oldfield Road?'

'Just about to leave. You got something else for us?'

'Had a report of a prowler outside 53 Chesholm—can you go and have a look?'

'Will do. We'll let you know. Oh, and Julie? See if Durney can get my lunch order right this time, there's a good girl. Out.'

come on chaser—i've got a carrot for you look. that's right, there's nothing to be scared of. and you greyskin, you can have some too. not so fast, now—you'll be eating my fingers.

i wonder where queenie's got to? oh there she is, over behind the pipe. what are you hiding from, missis rabbit? you're usually the first one over to say hello. yes, come on—i've kept some for you as well. what's happened to your ear? it looks like someone's been chewing it. i hope it wasn't you, chaser. i've told you to leave her alone.

look at those two climbing all over each other. i think that's nancy underneath, isn't it? yes and bounder on top of her. well

26

if you want to miss out on the food then that's your lookout.

do you know, rabbits, what i've been thinking about? i've been thinking that one day mummy and daddy might let me have a rabbit of my own. we could put a cage out the back and i'd take such good care of it. i don't think i'd be allowed one of you, and anyway you'd miss the park here. but i could get a special lead for my rabbit and bring it for walks to visit you and say hello. wouldn't that be fun? i hope you won't be jealous if i do. it won't be because i love you all any less—it's just that it would be so much fun if i could cuddle a bunny of my very own.

yes, all right nancy, i might have something for you now that you've finished. just let me get it out of my bag. everything comes to those who wait.

He pauses for a moment before beginning his homily. Ostensibly to allow the gospel reading to sink in; but in equal part to provide a little anticipation before he begins to speak.

Alex looks out over the faces of the congregation. Only a few are known to him. He senses their dis-ease; the uncertainty over what to expect. A smile to reassure them.

It is the moment in the sermon which brings the most pleasure to him—the space before a word is spoken. The uplifted eyes, the gathered souls, the awaiting ears. From their nothingness, he will create meaning. Into their void, he will speak order. Over their anxiety, he will pronounce blessing.

The silence gathers like a summer thunderhead.

'Love is much misunderstood.'

Another eloquent pause, as he allows the mellifluous voice to work its magic. In adolescence the gift descended. His parents looked at him in astonishment when he spoke. A rich warm resonance rising so easily and convincingly within him. You could be a hypnotist, his mother once told him.

'We imagine it as something over which we have no power. A force which seizes us, a wave which sweeps over us, a state like drunkenness which we may fall into. Love, as it were, lies in wait for us. When we stumble upon it, we are helpless to

27

save ourselves. Love is the emotional equivalent of gravity. We fall, brothers and sisters, do we not? We fall.'

He is pleased with the cadence of the repetition.

'Thomas and Madeline are here because they have "fallen" in love. When they look at one another, they feel that they are caught up in something greater than themselves.'

A smile of acknowledgement directed at the couple, bestowing approval with those crinkling eyes.

'Which is as it should be. They are young, they are full of life, and they have fallen in love. Why should they not imagine that this state will last for ever?'

A frown to indicate a change in rhetorical direction.

'Sadly, my friends—and I say sadly with all the grief of one who walks amidst the rubble of relationships—that which is fallen into can equally easily be fallen out of. Scandalous as it may be to speak of such a thing on a wedding day, those who have been carried along by the tide of love can wake to find themselves washed up on the shores of disillusionment.

'"Love never ends," says the apostle Paul. How can he possibly talk such rot? Does he not know what it's like to face someone across the breakfast table and feel not so much as a flicker of love? Is he unaware of the way that domesticity and routine erode passion until all that is left is a faintly disguised resentment? Might he be ignorant of the familiarity which turns lovers into enemies? Has he not consulted the divorce statistics? How can he possibly hold that "love never ends"?

'The answer, of course, is that he understands all too well what love is. Primarily, that it is not a feeling at all. It is not something that can be fallen into or out of. It is not an emotion or a force or a tide. Love, as Paul understands, is an act of the will. It is a choice, a decision, a way of life. Love should not be confused with the hormonal rush which often sweeps couples into marriage. In fact, it is not until that tumultuous rush subsides that love even becomes necessary. Precisely at the point when the bloom fades, the romance wilts and the devotion stutters; precisely at that point does love begin to be called upon.

'Thomas and Madeline know nothing of these things as yet. Nor should they. But when the day comes—as it will, as it will—then they will need to look back on this their wedding not as the day on which they *felt* certain things, but as the day on which they *decided* certain things. This is a day of promising and commitment, of covenanting and betrothing.

'Love is as love does. These two have promised to each other that they will stay together whatever may come. Whatever may come. And what of we who witness their promise? Are we upholders of such a promise? Do we believe in love, as the apostle Paul names it? If not, let us become such. Let us believe and act out a love which never ends. And in so doing, let us add our blessing not only to Thomas and Madeline, but to every couple who undertake the vows of matrimony.'

Alex is pleased with the ringing oratory of his concluding paragraph. He would have been delighted had he not noticed his wife's face among the congregation. There is a slight frown on her brow, and a wistful look in her eye. Almost as if she were disappointed.

rabbits have holes
in which to hide
all warm and cosy
tucked up inside
birds have nests
woven with string
all snugly enough
to make them sing
when i was a baby
i had a womb
and now that i'm bigger
i sleep in a room
so if god still lives
way up in the sky
why can't i see him
when i go there to fly?

*

'Unit 426 to base, over.'

'Come in, Harry.'

'Just been round to that Chesholm Road prowler alert. Nothing much doing. Young lady getting dressed on the first floor reckoned there was someone in the garden. We've had a good scout round and can't find anyone, but we did find a footprint in the garden. Might be an idea to get a photo of it.'

'Roger, Harry. Will do. Number 53, wasn't it?'

'Roger that. We're coming in for lunch, if there's nothing else.'

'See you soon. Out.'

I've always had two conflicting impulses within me; to create and destroy. It may be that they're different sides of the same force.

Once, as a child, I collected matchsticks. I'd seen a friend's model of a fort made entirely out of matches glued together. I wanted to do something similar. I thought I'd build a bridge. I needed thousands of used matches, and I collected them wherever I went. An ashtray was the equivalent of a treasure-chest to me.

I had a plan, and ever so slowly the bridge began to take shape. I spent hours gluing them together and checking they were in the right place. After six months, I'd almost finished. I was more proud of that construction than anything else in my life.

And then, on an afternoon, I smashed it to pieces. Not in anger, or even in a hurry. I simply broke it apart until the floor was littered with small fragments of matchwood. I told my mother that I'd tripped and fallen on it, though I suspect she guessed the truth.

I got as much pleasure, if not more, from shattering that delicate structure as I had in making it. It seemed right, in a strange sort of way.

Deep in the silence, Joe breathes. He is nothing but his breath, rising and falling with it. The stillness is complete. He is a single head of wheat in the early-morning freshness, awaiting the light of the sun to rise upon it.

Some moments pass in basking. Gradually, gently, carefully, he surfaces. Opening his eyes to the familiar concrete wall.

Spending a few moments in transition, as a different set of senses takes over.

He's grateful that Bomber has gone, with his heavy and distracting sighs. A rare interlude to have the cell to himself.

Joe has taught himself meditation, from books and practice. Nothing that he likes to talk about. But another strategy in the plan of survival. Something the screws can't monitor. Zen and the art of inmate endurance.

Parole hearings demand concentration. Tricky little bastards, trying to catch you out. Like jackals circling, alert to any vulnerability. Pushing for some outburst; a few angry retorts to write down on the record. You have to stay calm, stay above it. Give them nothing they can use against you. It requires focus and serenity. That's why they're out to get me, he muses. Because I know the rules, and I know how to play.

I'll be ready for them. He runs his hands across his newly shaved scalp, as if to smooth the hair which is no longer there.

'Where's Tessa?' Mark wants to know.

'You need to ask?'

'Up at the park, talking to the rabbits. I might wander up and meet her there.'

'I'm still not sure about letting her go up there on her own. I'd feel terrible if anything happened.'

'You have to let her be a kid some of the time, Lizzy. You know how much she loves it up there. And she can't come to much harm in Clissold Park in broad daylight. Anyway, I'll go up and find her and bring something good back for lunch. Okay?'

'Okay. I'm sorry—I'm being neurotic, I know. I wish I could change but I can't.'

'See you shortly.'

Stoke Newington is still uneasy about her transformation. Like an elderly smoker being instructed in the benefits of a healthy lifestyle, she grimaces at the pain of transition. Easy enough to paint a new face on her trendy bars, but lungs still coated in tar

31

are congested and straining to keep up.

Even so, the yellow sun washes her brick complexion with a cheery disposition. There's a buzz on the streets as the ragbag of residents spills out into the day. Colours, languages, ages, faces, gender variations, garments; an urban potpourri of humanity. Gathered in the cupped hands of the streets, and presented as an offering.

Immigrants, all of them, in one way or another. Even those born there find themselves in a new community. It's a strange place in which to find exuberance. As if an ancient broken oak should begin to send forth exotic shoots. As if a fresh wind should blow through a graveyard, unsettling the resident ghosts.

'Joe Bailey,' announces the superintendent, opening the fat file before him. He wears glasses with thick black frames, and smells of bay rum.

Around the table there is a corresponding shuffling of papers and files as the board members prepare themselves for the next candidate. To the superintendent's right is the minutes secretary. Next to her is the staff representative, a fat Welshman with a scar on his brow. Beside him a woman with gold earrings and a long neck, a magistrate. Across from them the prison chaplain, Rev. Anders, and the Prisoner Aid representative—a small man with a friendly face and round rimless glasses. The far end of the table holds an empty chair, awaiting an occupant.

'What do we know of him, chief?' The woman magistrate is chair of the board, but in customary practice defers to the superintendent.

'One of our regulars. Been in and out of custodial care since borstal at the age of 15. Mostly burglary and assault, though this time he's in for rape. Current term seven years, of which he's served two. First appearance on this round, so we're really just getting him on the books.'

'And how's he been behaving himself?'

'Been cited in five incident reports, but never any supporting evidence. He's a tough one, is Joe. No one's going to nark on him in a hurry. Fairly quiet, keeps to himself a lot of the time. Most of the trouble comes from younger inmates having a go at him, trying to knock him off his perch. By and large he's one of the old school, content to put his head down and do his time. He needs keeping an eye on, just the same.'

'Psych report?'

'Just the initial pre-admission one done for the trial. Let's have a look now. Hmmm . . . Relatively stable presenting personality, repressed anger periodically erupting in violent outbursts, little evidence of remorse for offending. Usual bullshit about inadequate parenting—no resident father—few support networks, bit of a loner. Some suspicion of sexual abuse but unconfirmed. Rape uncharacteristic and unlikely to reoffend, though deep hostility to powerful women.'

'Anyone got anything to add? Padre?'

Kevin Anders is startled from some private reverie. He scratches his eyebrow to gain a little time. A few small flakes of dandruff fall onto the open file before him.

'No, I can't say I really know the man. I had one conversation after he was admitted, but we didn't get beyond pleasantries. He does read pretty widely, judging by what he gets out of the library.'

'He's fast, he is, that boyo,' the Welshman contributes.

'At reading?' asks the long-necked magistrate, puzzled.

'No, no; with his hands. You got to watch him, like, or he can do a lot of damage in not very much time. The lads are all a bit wary of him.'

'Quite,' sighs madam chair. She detests the machismo undercurrents of prison life. The officers as much a part of it as the inmates.

'Let's have him in then, shall we?'

The empty building is still rich with the atmosphere of transcendence. The incense and candle wax pervade the air as a proximate odour of sacrality. The silence is anything but vacant. Alex spends a few moments bathing in it. He sits on a pew and makes the sign of the cross.

After a time he notices that the altar candles are still burning. An oversight which sometimes happens at a wedding. Their pure flames are perfectly formed—without flicker to evidence their consumption. Such a rich symbol of the purity of God, considers Alex. The soft and single light.

There are shadows cast on the wall behind the altar.

Eventually he rises and extinguishes the candles. He hears a noise in the vestry and goes to investigate.

It's the choirmaster, Donald. He looks up from his buttons as Alex comes in.

'Splendid service, Alex. Top-notch sermon as always.'

'Thank you Donald. The choir did us proud as well.'

'I say, Alex. You wouldn't have a few minutes for a bit of a chat, would you?'

'Give me five minutes and come to the office. I have to be away by four, but that gives us half an hour or so. Okay?'

'Splendid, splendid.'

the man in the shop keeps looking at me as if i'm going to steal something. he's got an ugly big nose that's all red and blotchy. just because i don't have any money doesn't mean i can't come and look through his books. they're second-hand anyway so it's not like they haven't been opened before.

i love books. i love the smell of them, specially the ones that have been shut up in cupboards for years. they soak up the lives of the people who own them, so that when you sniff you can smell all the years and things that've happened. i love the words huddled together and fenced in on the page. big flocks of them, waiting to be set free. the best are poetry books with the words dancing all over the place, like they've settled down for a bit but could take off again at any minute. i love to touch the pages—the sandy feel of the paper under your thumb. and sometimes there are coffee stains or dead insects squashed into them like signs to show where somebody has left a bit of themselves.

i love the magic of stories that can take you away from where you are to a different place. just like flying—just like the flying i do in my dreams. every book's like a magic doorway. you open it up and step through and you're somewhere new, somewhere you haven't been before. There are new people there to meet and things to watch and listen for. if it gets scary or dark you can just step back through the door again and be on the outside.

i wish i had some money to buy some more. but i suppose i don't need to own them when i can just come here and be with them. apart from old ugly-nose over there.

T he heart fears.
The heart senses what the mind cannot hold. Long before the surface is troubled, there is a murmur in the deep. A nothingness. The rattling of a lock. The stirring in a vault. A hint of dead air rising on the breeze. The breath of putrefaction. The passing of a shadow.
The heart fears.

'Welcome, Mr Bailey. Please take a seat. You know the routine, I imagine?'

Joe looks at her from deep within his cavern. He notes the supercilious smile; the polite mask over her disdain; the edge of insecurity beneath it. All this comes to him unbidden.

'I've been through it before,' he says.

'Very well. Perhaps you'd like to begin by telling us how you think you're doing so far. After, how long is it? Twenty-seven months?'

'Give or take eleven days. I'm doing well.'

'Come now, Mr Bailey. I hope I don't have to remind you that the parole board is for your benefit rather than ours. You may need to be a little more expansive in your answers if you want our co-operation.'

It is the beginning of engagement. The first threat, issued with perfect vowels over unblemished teeth. Joe feels the anger tremble in its chasm, and breathes deeply to subdue it. A long way to go yet.

'I've settled into my lag. I'm keeping my nose clean—haven't been put on charge at all since being here. I work out regularly at the gym and keep myself healthy. No problems from my end. I just want to do my time without sweating it.'

'No charges, but five incident reports? How do you explain that?'

Joe observes that there is a slight imperfection in her upper lip. Almost obscured by lipstick, but still visible. He takes it as a point of reference for focus.

'Nothing to them, obviously. Otherwise I would've been charged. You know how it is in prisons. Always someone making things up.'

The super smiles. He and Joe are two of a kind. A dying breed. Survivors who understand the unwritten rules and are happy to abide by them. No place for it in the new regime, where there's always an expert who knows better.

The Welshman is still looking down at his expansive belly when he speaks.

'Fancy yourself with your hands, do you lad?'

'I don't know what you're talking about.'

'Consider yourself a bit of a standover man, do you?'

'I've kept myself out of trouble as best I can.'

'We hear things about you, lad. Things that go on in the showers and so on. People seem to have accidents all around you, like.'

'People can be clumsy.'

'Oh yes, that they can, lad, that they can. Mind you, officers get clumsy too, now and again. Now and again; not often.'

The long neck arches.

'I'm not sure this line of questioning is helpful. Now tell me, Mr Bailey, how you feel after a few years reflection on the rape.'

Several pairs of eyes turn to look at her. The super wonders what she's up to. She knows better than to rake over the crime. It's a fundamental violation of the prison code. Joe keeps his attention fixed on her lip. He clamps down on the rage, and maintains calm.

'Read the file.'

'I beg your pardon?'

'All the details of my conviction are in the file. I imagine you have that in front of you. If you want to know about my getting sent down, it's all there.'

'I'm asking you.'

'With all respect,'—Joe smiles—'I don't want to talk about it.'

'You don't like women?'

'I don't want to talk about it.'

'You must have something against women. To rape. It's an act of aggression, really, isn't it? An act of power. Weak men who feel threatened are the ones who rape. Is that what you are, Mr Bailey, a weak man?'

The calm is sliding away as a cold mass rises steadily from the deep. Joe looks sideways to the super for support. He reads the answer there—disturbed, but not willing to intervene.

There's a cough from the other side of the table. Kevin Anders makes an attempt to derail the interrogation.

'I imagine there's . . .'

'I've asked Mr Bailey a question, chaplain, and I'm waiting for an answer. Are you a weak man? A rapist?'

The Welshman sees that Joe's knuckles are white and the tips of his ears red. He shifts his chair back slightly, just in case.

Joe closes his eyes for a moment. When they open, he's staring at her.

'I must be,' he says slowly. 'It's in my file.'

'Control to unit 426.'

'426 here.'

'Just thought I'd let you know, Harry, we got a report back from forensic on that footprint in Chesholm Road.'

'What about it, then?'

'It matches one that we took from a peeper report last Wednesday, just round the road from there. Looks like we might have a live one.'

'We'll keep an eye out then. Anything else to go on?'

'Nothing so far, sorry.'

'Okay. Thanks, love. Out.'

*

'Come in, Donald, take a seat. I'll just close this file and I'll be right with you.'

Alex finishes at the computer and moves from behind the desk to sit opposite the choirmaster. A florid man, with fading red hair and large cheeks latticed with broken blood vessels.

They exchange the ritual conversational rallies before Donald feels ready to broach his purpose.

'I've come to you as my pastor, so this is nothing to do with the choir—well, not exactly, anyway.'

Alex has been in the game long enough to know that silence is the best aid to encouraging hesitant starts. He nods sympathetically, and carefully avoids looking at the clock. He had been hoping to catch the end of the game.

'I'm not sure how to begin, now I've got here. It's just that I've been living with this for a long time, and I need to get it off my chest, you see. I've got myself into a bit of a mess. I just can't get a handle on the rights and wrongs of it. I thought to myself, I'll have a chat with the vicar, that's what I'll do. So here I am.'

'I'm listening, Donald.'

'It's my wife, Edna, you see. Well, it's not exactly her—it's me—but she's the cause of it. She won't . . . She doesn't . . . I don't know how to put this rightly, Alex, but we're not having marital relations any more.'

'Your wife doesn't want a sexual relationship?'

'Yes, by George, yes—that's it exactly. Couldn't have said it better myself. That's the nub of the problem.'

'And have you talked to her about this?'

'Ah, sort of. In a roundabout sort of a way, if you know what I mean. We've had some terrible rows.'

'About the sex?'

'Not exactly. About the roses.'

'The roses?'

'Yes. I've told her not to pick them when they're blooming, but she will insist. It's not good enough, and I told her so.'

'Don't you think it might be an idea to talk to Edna about what's really troubling you?'

'Edna?'

'Yes. If you can pluck up the courage to talk to me about it, I'm sure you can do the same with her.'

'But I can't, vicar, I can't. She's my wife, dash it all—you can't just talk about sex with your wife! And anyway that's only the half of it.'

Alex is happy to ride the silence. The truth will come, given a chance.

'I've been . . . ah, I sometimes . . . Oh God, this is so humiliating. I've been pulling myself off, Alex. That's what it's about.'

The silence continues.

'Going off into the lavatory and flogging myself like a schoolboy. I feel so dirty afterwards. I wash my hands, but I can't get rid of the smell. We've been going through a lot of soap—I'm sure Edna's aware that something's going on. It's such a mess, such a mess. And the worst part of it is, when I do it, I imagine myself with Melissa Brown.'

'The soprano? She's young enough to be your daughter.'

'I know, God forgive me, I know. I've tried to stop, but I just can't help myself. I don't know what to do—that's why I've come to you, Alex.'

'Well I'm glad you have. That's the right thing to do—to nip this in the bud before it gets any worse. You're aware that it's sinful in more than one respect, I suppose?'

'Is it? I mean I knew it was a sin, but I wasn't sure how big a sin it was.'

'It's not just the masturbation, is it now Donald? Yes, let's call it what it is, masturbation. There's also the lusting after a woman who's not your wife, which according to Our Lord is as good as adultery. And then there's the violation of your responsibilities as choirmaster.'

'I haven't touched Melissa, or even spoken out of turn . . .'

'Nevertheless, you can see where all this might lead if it was left to run its natural course. That experience of feeling dirty afterwards, you know what that is? It's the voice of the Spirit, convicting you in your heart. Light and darkness don't mix,

Donald. The one will destroy the other. Do you understand that?'

'Well, yes . . .'

'There's only one thing to do with sin. You have to excise it. Rip it out like a rotten tooth and be rid of it. Self-control, Donald, is a fruit of the Spirit. Self-control. You're a servant of Christ, a leader in the Church. This won't do at all. I'm afraid I'll have to relieve you of your formal duties for a few weeks, while you get yourself sorted out. I'm sorry if it seems harsh, but sometimes we need to endure pain for the good of our souls. Have a talk with Edna, take control of yourself, and for goodness' sake, man, leave yourself alone.'

'I'm sorry, Alex. I've let you down.'

'It's God you've disappointed, Donald, which is altogether a more serious matter. Now down on your knees while I ask God's mercy for you. We're going to pray.'

Like a light shining in the darkness, thinks Alex, a candle burning in the gloom.

The sweat is dripping off the back of his neck. He can feel it trickling its way down his backbone. It's a form of purgation. Joe has been pounding at the punching bag for fifteen minutes now without stopping. His vision is beginning to blur.

With each blow a small aggressive cry explodes from him. It's like siphoning out the pressure from a boiler. And still the furnace seethes, hot and threatening to blow. He needs to get it back under control, get himself back into balance.

He focuses once more on that small imperfection on a scarlet lip, as his fist hammers into the bag again. The shudder causes a little satisfaction, but not enough.

The old man with the bottle is sitting on the steps of the library. He watches the people coming and going. He was one of them once, with things to do. A part of the team. A member of the community. Now he watches from the sidelines.

Stoke Newington is the most faithful of his friends, in that she's still there. After all her changes and moods, she abides. With her faintly ridiculous ties to Daniel Defoe and the Booths.

The famous dead, mocked by the infamous living. And the others buried now—Margaret, of course, and Ted and Alfie and George—all gone. Making no impression on the landscape.

He remembers the post-war years. The council housing. The immigration. Black faces and startling white teeth. How he hated them when they first arrived. Hated their laughter and their sleek bodies. Hated their food and their singing. Turks it was now. A regular bleeding United Nations. And this new lot. Parking their BMWs on the footpath. Filling up dump bins with rotting window frames.

But the old girl was still there, her bones showing under all the alterations. A man can remember, if he sits in the sun for a few moments, and lets it all come back.

The teacher looks up from her desk to see Tessa still there. Busy writing in her book. She smiles and wanders over, sitting on a nearby chair.

'Sorry, Miss, I won't be long. I just wanted to finish writing something.'

'That's all right, Tess. There's no hurry. Is it poetry you're writing?'

Tessa self-consciously covers the page with her hand.

'Yes Miss.'

'I liked your poem about the rabbits and birds. Do you write a lot of poems, then?'

'Sometimes,' admits Tessa, a little defensively.

'I wouldn't mind seeing some more one day, if you felt like showing me. I like poetry as well.'

'Do you write some, Miss?'

'Not much these days, I'm afraid. But I read a lot. I've got some lovely books of poetry you could borrow if you like. What are you writing about now, or is it a secret?'

''Course not.' Tessa smiles. 'It's about tigers. I watched a programme on the telly about tigers with my Dad. I've never seen a real one though, have you?'

'I rather think I have, in a zoo somewhere. Do you like tigers?'

41

'I like them and I'm scared of them, Miss. They're terribly fierce and proud. I think they're beautiful with all that fur, but they're *very* dangerous as well. I wouldn't want one as a pet, I don't think. I'd rather have a rabbit. I don't think a rabbit would want to eat you.'

'No,' Tessa's teacher laughs. 'You need to be able to tell the difference between a rabbit and a tiger.'

He's walking down a hallway lined with windows. Behind every window is a face. The eyes follow him; the expressions severe. The passage stretches on and on into the distance. He stumbles. The carpet beneath his feet has turned to mud. It becomes thicker and thicker, until it's an effort to lift each foot free of the sucking bog. Still he staggers on, under the gaze of the witnesses.

And then, quite suddenly, the walls retreat, and he's standing alone in a gigantic hall. He can only just see the beams of the roof, high above him. The vast arena is empty, apart from a desk in the very centre, at which a man sits writing. The man wears a robe with a hood. His face is concealed inside it. Alex approaches the desk. Every footstep echoes into the distance.

He stands waiting. The hooded man continues writing, and the dry scratching of the nib is deafening. Eventually he pauses, and the head comes up.

'Yes?' the man enquires.

'I've come to see,' says Alex.

'Are you sure that's what you want?'

'Yes; that's why I've come all this way.'

'There's a long way ahead of you yet,' the man warns.

He reaches into a drawer in the desk and withdraws a large iron key, which he presents to Alex. He gestures over his shoulder, towards a door on the far side of the hall.

Alex makes his way through the echoes to the door. He fits the key in the lock, and turns it. The door opens. Inside there is a small dark room. In one corner is an armchair, and seated on it is a naked girl. She has shiny black hair, and her eyes are unusually shaped. There is blood running from the corner of her mouth, and more down the inside of her thigh. She stares up at him.

'Who are you?' he asks.

'Don't you know who I am, Alex? I've been waiting for you.'

Her voice bears a strange accent. She rises from the chair and comes toward him.

'No,' he murmurs, 'please no.'

'Oh come on,' she says. 'One little kiss won't hurt.'

And she raises her bloodied lips towards him, drawing his head down with her hand. Her lips brush his, and suddenly he is falling, falling into the endless blackness. The never-ending night; falling, falling. And crying out.

'Alex, Alex, wake up. What's the matter?'

'Mmmph,' is all he can manage. The room looks strangely sinister under the thrall of his dreamworld.

'It's all right, darling. You've had a bad dream, I shouldn't wonder. Here, I'll turn on the light.'

Joe falls onto his cot, exhausted. In the distance are the usual sounds; the nightlife of the prison jungle. Tapping, catcalling, and the occasional groan.

He blanks his mind, and takes a deep breath. Another day, and I have survived. It is his last thought as consciousness ebbs.

> the tiger prowls
> the tiger roars
> the tiger shows
> his awful claws
>
> his fur is soft
> his teeth are white
> all men fear him
> in the night
>
> be careful when
> he creeps around
> for he can move
> without a sound

i want a bunny
that can leap
a tiger isn't
safe to keep

Chapter Three

Have you ever stood and looked at yourself in the mirror, and tried to peer beneath the surface? Gazing into your own eyes, searching for what lies beyond them? Straining to catch sight of your soul?

And have you ever felt just a little uneasy while doing it? As if there were something unexpected there, some unrecognised phantom? Just a flicker, no more. Like the passing of a shadow over the retina.

It's hard to maintain for very long. Because you begin to wonder, 'What if there's something in here that I'm not aware of?' If you know yourself only partially, what could possibly be in the place that's kept secret? And who's responsible for keeping the secret?

No, it's best to look away.

It's Chromefang who does the unlock. With his silver smile and mock jollity.

'Good news for you today, Joe. A new partner for you. Someone to share the long lonely nights.'

'Fuck you,' scowls Joe.

'No, on the contrary, fuck *you*, Mr Bailey. I insist.'

'Who is it?'

'Ah, that would be telling, wouldn't it now? Let's just say that it's not one of our regulars. Now, if you don't mind, I've another client awaiting my professional services. Have a nice day.'

*

'Control to unit 426.'

'426 responding.'

'Harry, we've had a call-up from the mother of two young lads. She says they've been playing down Abney Park Cemetery and they've seen a body there.'

'Well, that wouldn't exactly be surprising, would it? They've probably been into one of the crypts and found a coffin.'

'She said they reckoned it was a little girl. You'd better check it out.'

'Okay, we're on our way. Whereabouts exactly?'

'The mother's going to meet you by the High Street entrance—she's on her way already.'

'Have you told Homicide?'

'Not yet—I thought we should just confirm it first, in case it's a false alarm. But tread carefully, and call it in straightaway if there's anything there.'

'All right love, 426 out.'

'. . . and so all the villagers gathered in the square to cheer Magic Girl as she came home. There was peace in the valley for another thousand years, and currant buns on Tuesdays.'

Elizabeth lays the book aside and smiles down at her daughter, who is staring out beyond the ceiling.

'That's the end, I'm afraid darling. Time for sleep now.'

'What happened after the thousand years, then?'

'I don't know, Tessa—the story doesn't say.'

'Well the story hasn't ended, then, has it? We don't know what happens in the end.'

'The story might go on, but the book has come to an end. There needs to be space to tell another story later.'

'Do you know how the story ends, Mummy?'

'Not this one, no. I only know as much as you do about Magic Girl.'

Tessa closes her eyes for a few moments. Her brow is slightly furrowed. Elizabeth, contemplating her, can hardly believe that this little angel is hers.

'Did God make tigers?'

'Yes dear, God made everything.'

'And God made goats?'

'Come on, it's time you were going to sleep.'

'Then why did God make it so that tigers eat goats? Doesn't he like goats?'

'There are no tigers in England, Tessa.'

'No, but there are foxes, aren't there?'

'A few, but not as many as there used to be.'

'So why do foxes eat rabbits, then? They do, don't they?'

'Sometimes they do. When they're hungry.'

'I can't believe that God doesn't like rabbits. Why doesn't he stop the foxes eating them, then? It's not fair, is it? The rabbits don't hurt anyone.'

'Oh Tessa, it's just the way the world is. Foxes need to eat to stay alive, and they've been made so that they sometimes kill rabbits. It's not because foxes are nasty or hate rabbits, anymore than we hate chickens because we had chicken for dinner to-night. Some things die in order to keep others alive.'

'It's God's fault, then, isn't it?'

'Why do you say that?'

'Well if God made everything in the world, then he made it so that foxes kill rabbits. He could have made it so that they ate grass or leaves or something.'

'I suppose so.'

'But you said that God was good. If he was good and loved everything, then rabbits wouldn't have to get eaten, would they? He could stop it if he wanted to.'

'God is good, Tessa. Don't ever doubt that. It's just that, well . . . the world is more complicated than you can understand yet. God has a lot of things to worry about, and even though we can't always understand what happens, it doesn't mean he doesn't love us or rabbits or chickens. But you don't have any-thing to worry about, except getting to sleep. So close your eyes and we'll pray, and we can talk about all this another day.'

A fragment of verse from the lectionary reading stands out to him like a glint of light on bright metal.

'. . . the Lord raises up those bowed down.'

Alex lays the Prayer Book aside and considers it; lodges it in his imagination and sucks on it for some time. How far he has come. Full circle, geographically. A journey of ascent by any other measure. He recalls the dark and difficult days of his childhood, here in Stoke Newington.

The dinginess of poverty. In all his memories of the house, it's full of gloom. Climbing the stairs always with foreboding. And damp; still the fetid smell of rotting timber can plunge him into despair.

His father consumed by an inner rage beyond memory of cause. A bullying, sadistic despot, scrupulous in his search for disobedience or offence. The hard bright eyes of hatred raking his brood for evidence of dissent. His heavy bricklayer's hands clenching themselves into vengeance. All this contained within the walls of the house, with no one ever suspecting. Though a teacher did once ask Alex about the bruising.

He'd lie there at night, hearing the terrible and ominous thumps, and his mother's muffled cries. Trying to stop it, screwing up his eyes and willing the noise to cease. Praying for God to intervene. When it did cease, he was never sure if he'd contributed or not. The next morning his mother would do her best to smile through split lips.

She was a Christian woman, trying always to see everything in a positive light. Holding her martyrdom like a lamp in a dark room, desperately wanting everyone to be good. Alex remembered her simple prayers beside his bed at night, and the way she would twist the hem of the sheet between her fingers as she prayed.

Little wonder she was nervous, neurotic. No surprise that she had given up on her life and vested hope in her children. Like burying her treasure in the depths of their less polluted humanity. Placing herself as a shield between them and the cold currents of violence which drove her husband. Hoping against hope that something or someone might survive, might escape.

In the event, only Alex had made it. Alex Thomas Hanson, her youngest and final attempt. The others had fallen at the hurdles, hobbled by the bitterness which seared all legacy of innocence from their souls. Rosalind an alcoholic; Anne somewhere in a housing estate after a string of abortions and miscarriages; Peter a petty thief with a habit. He retained little affection for or sense of connection with his siblings.

Only Alex, born at home during a power cut, with the midwife cursing the poor light of the candles. Holding him, and inhaling the sweet freshness of his newborn skin, his mother had kept her hopes alive.

And here he was now, saved by the strength of his intellect as much as his mother's prayers. Surprised and delighted that he had this power, these gifts, which marked him out. The careful rational ticking of his mind. Inaccessible to his oxen father, mystifying to his fawning mother, encouraged by his appreciative teachers. A grappling line with which to scale the walls of poverty. And of course, the voice.

All the rest had followed. The scholarship to St Giles, the success in rugby, becoming a prefect. Faith, of course, was not a legacy of intelligence. It was given; a discovery. The one thing perhaps his mother could claim credit for. But even so, his incisive powers of reasoning had helped him along the path. Certainly lifted him from the bunch at Ridley College. Mary had admired him for many things, his keen mind among them.

By that stage he was utterly free. He looked back on his earlier upbringing as might a child raised in a foreign land. It was distant, strange, and no longer of any relevance. He had pragmatically divorced himself from his parents, made easier when they moved to Leicester. The correspondence with his mother, even, was now a matter of duty more than gratitude.

From there the course had been relatively untroubled. A lovely wife, good grades and a reputation for powerful preaching. Three years at St Jerome's in Campden, doing his curacy mostly among the young people of the parish. His two children—one of each. And then, ironically, the appointment to St John's. A return to his roots in Stoke Newington.

He had been nervous about coming back at first; as if still vulnerable to his hidden past. But gradually he came to see it as destiny. It was his final victory over all that had sought to destroy him. The homecoming of the conqueror. He had routed the ghosts of childhood; put them to flight like the spectres they were. The forces of darkness had been engaged and overcome, through the sheer application of intellect. And with the help of God.

Who raises up those bowed down. Blessed be He for ever.

'Unit 426 to control.'

'Come in, 426.'

'Request switch to emergency channel. Code 401.'

'Hold on a moment. Switching channels. Go ahead.'

'You'd better get Homicide down here. It's a little girl all right. Looks like she's been interfered with before being killed. We've secured the area and will wait for the big boys to arrive.'

'Understood, 426. They'll be there as soon as. You okay, Harry?'

'No, and I don't want to talk about it. Just get things moving, will you love?'

'Wilco. Stay on this channel. Control out.'

'Aaaaah.'

Elizabeth closes her eyes and savours the thick undercurrents of the cabernet. It is her favourite part of the day, the lacuna between Tessa's sleep and her own. Mark looks up from his book.

'All right?' he asks, a gesture of affection more than a question.

'She got me again,' laughs Elizabeth. 'Somehow or other we got from Magic Girl to why God allows suffering in the world, all in the space of five minutes. I don't know how she does it.'

'Her mother's daughter.' He grins.

'I swear she'll turn us all into vegetarians before long.'

'Just so long as it's not teetotallers.'

'Where does it all come from, d'you think? This fascination with God? Neither of us is particularly religious.'

50

'We went to church for Easter. *And* I made a point of talking to the vicar. What more can you ask for?'

'I wonder if we shouldn't send her to Sunday school. What d'you think?'

Mark glances down at his book again before answering. It's something that's never occurred to him.

'Can't do any harm, I suppose. So long as we don't have to *take* her to church. We could go out for breakfast instead.'

'Mmmm. Though the vicar is rather yummy, isn't he? And not a bad sort of preacher, either.'

'And here's me thinking all that time it was religious ecstasy you had, when all along you were just lusting after the cleric. Oh God, I imagine we'll have to go with her the first time, won't we?'

'Jenny's daughter goes—I'll ask her about it. I think it'd be good for Tess. Any more of that wine, or have you quaffed it all?'

He can hear them coming down the runway, and guesses what it is. The new man. A chorus of jibes accompanies the procession, which comes to a halt outside Joe's cell.

Joe, lying on his cot, puts his book aside and regards his prospective companion. He looks as green as they come. Fortyish, clean-cut, average build, good-looking. A wife-murderer, has to be. Standing stiffly and uncomfortably in the prison issue. You can smell the fear on him. Never mind. Rather train a new boy than have to play power games with a crim.

Chromefang wears his perpetual smirk.

'This here's your groom,' he says to the new man. 'He'll be your live-in partner for the next little while. I wish you all the best for your married life, and do let us know if there's anything we can do to make you more comfortable.'

Pleased with his own sarcasm, the guard propels the inmate into the cell with a quick shove in the small of the back. His kit falls to the floor. Joe rises and picks it up, tossing it onto the top bunk.

'Joe,' he announces, extending a hand.

51

The new man stares blankly for a while, as if this is a custom he's never encountered before. Finally he takes Joe's hand and shakes it, nervously.

'Tom,' he offers.

'Right, well that's your cot up there, Tom. Okay?'

'Yes, yes, I see. Only I thought I'd be here on my own, you see.'

'I'm sorry, all the single rooms are taken at the moment. Only the share-twin available. There seems to be quite a demand for accommodation. 'Course, you make enough mayhem they'll fix you up with a nice little room on your own. Not quite as well appointed as this one, unfortunately. Just get on your fucking cot and shut up, will you?'

The new man flinches as if he's been struck already. That should sort out the chain of command fairly quickly, thinks Joe.

i fly down into a field that has huge trees round the outside. one minute i'm flying and the next i'm standing on the grass, looking all around me. i can see something white moving on the ground, so i go across to have a look. it's a rabbit, a big one like bounder, with its head poking out of a burrow.

he looks up at me with those big eyes, and i can hear what's going on in his head. he's frightened, but he doesn't think i look too dangerous. i pick him up by the scruff of the neck and cuddle him. i rub my face in his soft white fur. he's all warm.

and then i see something out of the corner of my eye, and it's a fox coming out of the trees. its fur is sort of reddy-brown, and it looks quite beautiful with the sun shining on it. but i can see its sharp white teeth flashing in its mouth as it moves across the grass towards us.

'what d'you want?' i ask, and i know the fox can understand me too.

'i'm hungry,' it says. 'i've come for the rabbit.'

i hold my bunny tightly to my chest. 'you can't have the rabbit,' i tell the fox. 'i'm going to look after it.'

the fox begins to walk in circles round us, and dribbles long strings of spit. 'very well,' it says, 'i'll have to eat the both of you.'

my rabbit is trembling, but he looks up at me and says, 'let me go. it's right that foxes should eat rabbits, but not that they should kill little girls.'

i hold him even tighter to let him know that i'll never give him to the fox. instead i lift my head to the sky and cry out, 'god, come here this instant! i want you to make this fox go away and leave the rabbit alone.'

a big voice booms out, shaking the ground. 'it's just the way things are, tessa. i can't do anything about it.' and then there is silence.

the fox seems to be grinning at me. 'don't ask for help where there's none,' he says. 'none of us like this, but we've all got our jobs to do.'

so i throw the rabbit as far away as i can, to give him a head start, and i grab the fox by the tail. it turns toward me, and those sharp white teeth are snapping at my face.

and then i'm awake. it's just me in my bedroom and everything's all right.

I'm not an angry man. Things have been done to me in the past that I'd have cause to be angry about, but I don't let them get on top of me. I get on with things, and put the past behind me.

There have been incidents, of course. But no more than that—isolated incidents. Enough to frighten some people, but perfectly understandable. There's always been some reason for my rage, at least from my point of view. It's just that once I get to the point of anger, I have trouble keeping it under control. It blows through me like a storm, and occasionally there's damage in its wake.

That makes me sound dangerous, doesn't it? Whereas I'm not at all, so long as people play by the rules. Once the boundaries are crossed, then anything becomes fair game, doesn't it? But by and large we keep life inside the playing field, and there's nothing to be worried about.

It's a tranquil setting among the trees. The glory of Abney Park Cemetery may be faded, but its wild peacefulness abides. A cacophony of green gentles the sunlight, the result of a largely unplanned mix of sycamore, ash and bramble. Even the immigrants are represented by Japanese knotweed.

The mock Egyptian entranceway bears a hieroglyphic legend announcing 'The gates of the abode of the mortal part of man.' It is the mortal part of a small girl which mars the beauty on this day.

Pain is not unknown by the non-conformist dead who lie in the cemetery. Nor misunderstanding and rejection. They have had their share of suffering. But this vile deed has fouled the spiritual waters. There is turbulence beneath the surface of Stoke Newington.

A thin plastic streamer announces a police line of demarcation. Tourists are offended that their progress is blocked. They have come to visit the dead, and death has prevented them.

From a low scrubby bush, a thin white leg protrudes.

Mary sits on the side of the bed, wearing her silk pyjamas. She is removing her earrings. From the corner of her eye, she notices in the mirror the rumour of a wrinkle on the side of her neck. She fingers it with apprehension.

Alex enters and begins to disrobe. A muffled wail rises through the floor. It's Ross practising on his guitar. Alex frowns, and shakes his head.

'You bought him the amplifier,' Mary reminds him.

'He said he wanted to play in the youth group band,' growls Alex. 'As it is, he hasn't been near the youth group for the past month.'

'He's just a teenage boy, Alex. Weren't you the same when you were his age?'

'I honestly don't think I was. Mind you, it's getting a lot of years to cast my mind back over.'

Alex smiles ruefully. He's anticipating sex tonight and doesn't want to disturb the delicate emotional balance. Unfortunately Mary is already disturbed. She slips into bed beside him. He turns toward her, but her eyes are staring far beyond what is immediately visible.

'That wedding sermon about love,' she says.

'Mmm?'

Alex begins stroking her forehead softly with his fingers.

'Is that what you really think? That love has nothing to do with feelings? That it's all about promising and so on?'

'I'm not sure that I said it has nothing to do with feelings. And it's not what I think that's important—it's what scripture says. Romantic love is a Hollywood invention.'

He feels the prickling of frustration building. A philosophical discussion isn't what he came to bed for. Already he can feel the mood turning away from him, dissipating like tendrils of smoke.

'The hell with scripture, Alex. I'm sick of it. Why do you always have to be appealing to the Bible? You don't need to preach to me—I'm your wife, not your congregation. I don't want to know what the apostle Paul has to say about love. I want to know what you think.'

Alex withdraws his hand and sighs deeply. There is a clenching in the pit of his stomach.

'I don't like it when you speak disrespectfully of Scripture. I'm sorry if the Bible intrudes on what I say and think, but then I'm a minister, so perhaps it's not surprising. I believe it contains the guidelines by which I choose to live. As you used to.'

'Oh don't get pompous with me, I can't bear it. If I've grown cynical, it's because of what I've seen in the church. You're a human being, Alex, beneath all that religious posturing. When I ask you about love, I want to know what's stirring in your heart, not what the latest Church of England missive has to say.'

'I don't think you're being fair. I can't separate myself from my vocation. It's not something I do for a job, like being a teacher or something. It's a calling, a way of life. You can't just take it on and off like a robe. Is that what you think? That when I'm preaching I'm putting on some sort of religious mask that's not really me? That I don't really believe the things I say? I would've hoped you knew me better than that by now.'

There is an interlude of strained silence. Mary has turned

her head away from him, and is considering what she might say. Alex feels the cold rage creeping up the lining of his belly. There is a strange pressure at the base of his skull.

'I'm not sure what I think any more,' she says quietly. 'I want to be loved because you love me, not because you consider it part of your goddam Christian duty. I want to be normal. I want to see some softness in your eyes. I want to get just a little of that devotion you lavish on God. I want to be let in, Alex. Do you have any idea what I'm talking about?'

'Yes,' he answers, 'I do. You're jealous of God. And that's nothing that I wish to take responsibility for.'

Judging by the amount of movement on the top bunk, Tom is getting restless. He's not used to being with people without speaking, thinks Joe. He'll do it hard, this one. There should be some sort of school for doing a lag, a sort of pre-entry course. But there's only the hard way.

Joe stands, and begins rolling himself a cigarette.

'Smoke?' He waves his pouch by way of invitation.

'No thanks, I don't.'

'Soon will,' predicts Joe.

'What are you in for?' asks the man on the bunk, propped up on one elbow.

The movement is not sudden. It's fast, certainly, but almost casual. Joe's right hand has somehow found its way to Tom's collar. He pulls the startled inmate over the edge of the bunk, until he's in danger of falling. And then Joe's face is only centimetres away.

'Lesson one,' he says. 'You don't *ever* ask anyone what their crime is. You understand? That's their business. If they want to tell you, they will. You go talking like that round the block, and you'll wind up with a screwdriver up your arse if you're lucky. You understand?'

Tom nods. He's not totally cowed, Joe observes. A good sign. There might be some resistance in him. Joe releases his grip and shoves the new man back where he was.

'It's just that, you see, I shouldn't be here,' explains Tom.

'I'm innocent.'

'Well, you've come to the right place, then, haven't you?'

'How's that?'

'They're all innocent in here; every one. It's just that they've been caught.'

It is the time of gathering.

The time of photographing, observing, detailing, measuring, searching, inspecting, sifting, uncovering.

And it is the time of recoiling.

She is completely naked. No shoes, no knickers. Her hands are tied behind her, bound with masking tape. There are many bruises on her small body. Around her throat, the upper part of her arms, and the inside of her thighs. There is heavy bruising around her vaginal area.

Police officers find a way of coping, of bracketing their reactions. They concentrate on the detail. One small area of concern at a time. Fragmentation is the key to containment. Focus on the observation, the measurement. Vomit at home, later.

And so this dark-haired broken doll forms the centre of a web. And yet she remains undiscovered.

> **sacrifice** (ˈsækrɪˌfaɪs) *n* **1** a surrender of something of value as a means of gaining something more desirable or of preventing some evil. **2** a ritual killing of a person or animal with the intention of propitiating or pleasing a deity. **3** the person, animal, or object surrendered, destroyed, killed or offered. **4** loss entailed by giving up or selling something at less than its value.

Deeply tired. Soul weary. Harry has been in the force too long. His shield is disintegrating. He can't get the picture out of his head.

The DI continues his briefing, and Harry struggles to concentrate. He has a job to do.

'It looks like the rape and murder were committed elsewhere, and the body disposed of in the cemetery. We've found blood smears on the perimeter wall near Church Street, and there's a couple of indistinct footprints there. So we're looking for vehicles, sightings around that area. Door-to-door foot-slogging I'm afraid.

'Cause of death was asphyxiation. A lot of force used in the attack—quite frenzied according to the pathologist. So we could be looking for a nutter, but keep an open mind.'

All Harry can see is that pale, smudged body.

The new girl, Tessa, seems to be enjoying herself. She's certainly enthusiastic.

Miss Bates is a veteran of the Sunday school trenches. Fifteen years in service, five of those as superintendent. Most of the time she likes it. Had things been different, she might have had children of her own. She has a niece in Liverpool, but it's not the same.

She prefers the younger children, before they become too sullen and rebellious. It's a contribution she can make, retelling the stories of the faith. You can never tell when it might make a difference.

'. . . and then an angel came to the men in the furnace,' she continues, tugging at the hem of her skirt to make sure it covers her knees.

'Please, Miss, what's an angel?'

It's Tessa, with her curious eyes and her hand raised in the air.

'An angel is a servant of God, a sort of messenger,' Miss Bates explains, perplexed.

'And they're all white and they have wings and that,' adds Malcolm, who likes to know the answers.

'Angels look after people, Tessa. This one came to save Daniel from King Nebuchadnezzar. Some people think that we all have our own angel to look after us and keep us safe.'

'Do rabbits have angels, Miss?'

'I don't know, I'm sure. Not many rabbits turn up in the Bible, I'm afraid.' And she turns the page quickly to get back to the familiar ground of the story.

*

He hates writing. He knows that the spelling's all over the place, but he can't quite see it. They didn't pick up the dyslexia until it was too late. There's only his mother to write to now, and that's ordeal enough.

Each sentence ground out from a constipated will. Old tart that she is. Why would anyone bother? Well, she stuck around at least. That's something.

Memories are not part of Joe's regime. Unless he's deep within his private vault, where there's no time.

She did what she could with a bad lot. On the streets from the age of fifteen, trying to make a go of things. Funny thing was her old man was a preacher of sorts. I never did find out why she took off. Lots of kids in the family and no dosh to feed them with. One thing about it, it put her off the church for good. Any door-knockers were seen off with her tongue-lashing following them down the stairs.

Never had much of a chance, did she? Hard for a woman on her own in those days. Joe always suspected she might have been on the game for a while, but she'd never admitted it. Got herself into hairdressing, though, and made a reasonable go of it.

Knocked up by that bastard Bob. Alkie scumbag. She'd told him the story one night, after a few drinks. How she'd lived with him for a few weeks after, before finding out she was pregnant. She was set for an abortion. Had some money stashed away for emergencies, she told him. And then came home to find the place turned over, and both Bob and her money gone. I suppose I should be grateful to him. He saved me from the bucket.

Joe had grown up with just his mum, and whatever man she took on for company. He hated them all, and especially the ones who tried to sleaze up to him. Though he'd take their money when it was offered. She was always around, old Pat, and she did her best for me.

Gave me my career, she did. Teaching me to shoplift. We made a good team the two of us. Always seemed a bit of a lark to me. You got to survive, she'd say, you got to beat the bastards. Not that she ever did, not really. What was she now? A

59

sharp-tongued old biddy in a council flat, with her smokes and regrets. Tough old bird, though.

Never forgave herself for that night with the whisky. But we won't go there.

He'd turned up once, Bob. Near Joe's tenth birthday. Drunk. Said he wanted to see his boy. Pat had followed him down the stairs, banging the back of his head with a cast-iron frying pan. Joe never spoke to him. Just watched the sad old prick, and tried to see if there was any sense of connection. He couldn't make any.

Bob was dead now, of course. Pat had heard from some friend of hers. Buried God knows where. Sometimes Joe wondered about him, what his background had been. But not often.

It was his mum who'd gone the distance, hard old bitch that she was. The only constant.

it's not fair how the grown-ups all get to line up for a drink and the children aren't allowed to. not that there's much to drink anyway, by the looks of things. and what is it they get to eat? looks like crisps.

the candles are quite pretty, and the coloured windows. but the songs are awfully dreary. they could all do with cheering up a bit. the man nailed up there, he doesn't look too happy. a bit spooky really.

these seats are hard. wish i could sit on the floor. i was hoping god might have been here, so that i could ask some of my questions. but no sign of him so far, though they keep talking about him. the man up at the front with the dress thingy on, he seems quite nice. i like the way he smiles. he does talk a lot, but no one seems to mind.

i might go and see the rabbits on the way home, though i haven't got anything to give them. greyskin was looking a bit sad yesterday. probably rabbits should be running free, not put in cages. but i'm glad they're there, really, or i wouldn't have got to know them.

the sun makes that old lady's hair look purple—oh, it's the colour of the window. isn't it lovely how the sun goes different colours depending what it's shining through? and then if you stand in it you go that colour too. except for black. light doesn't shine through black at all. it just sort of gets stuck there.

oh good—it looks like we get to stand again.

He's well liked by parishioners. As he holds his arms aloft for the blessing, he can sense their willingness. They want his words of peace; want his assurance of God's loving presence in their fractured lives.

And it's more than just a ritual. Alex feels the surge of spiritual power. The words are charged with something not of his making. They pour over the bowed heads like soothing oil. They come again and again, these people, because it makes a difference. Their hearts are strengthened, their minds uplifted, their faith deepened. It's the only work I ever wanted to do, he thinks.

In his priestly role, he is complete. Something that Mary can't understand. Everything else is peripheral, subservient. To know God and to do his will—that's what counts. To watch over this flock and feed it with the bread of life. To speak the words of truth even in the face of opposition. It's the highest calling.

Joe sits with him at the dining table, against his better judgement. Still, someone's got to look out for him.

Tom looks on as Joe arranges his cutlery according to his pattern, and wonders if this is something he should imitate. But no one else seems to be following suit, and the grim concentration on his cellmate's face scares him off doing anything without prompting.

George wanders past and nods at Joe.

'Here George—this is Tom. Come to join our establishment. Keep an eye out for him—he's likely to have a few teething problems.'

'Hello there, Tom. You could've done a lot worse than end up with old Joe here.'

Tom makes to extend his hand, before realising that there's

none offered. He nods instead. There's too much to take in. Altogether too much.

Rollo's sitting at the next table.

'I see Joe's got himself a new nancy boy,' he announces to no one in particular.

He's the only one who smirks. The others keep their eyes on their plates, bracing themselves in case. But Joe simply smiles broadly.

'Had to find someone, Rollo. What you tried to slip me in the shower wasn't quite to my liking, you know what I mean? And by the way, if you're having trouble swallowing, it's because your nuts are still somewhere up around your throat.'

A few snickers escape. Rollo searches desperately for a comeback, but there's nothing there. The moment's passed, though Joe won't forget it.

'Keep your eyes open for that one,' he warns Tom.

Harry doesn't like taking orders from Homicide. Doesn't want to be on the case at all, truth be told. You wear a uniform, they all assume you're thick. Give you instructions three times over.

It's his patch, and he doesn't like intruders trampling all over it. He knows some of them—you run into a few over the years. That young chap with the sandy hair—he lives out this way now. One of the weekend renovators. But they don't know the area.

This one has a funny smell, he thinks. Nothing he can put his finger on. But there's something unusual about it. Not that anyone cares what he thinks.

Sunday nights have a feel all of their own. Elizabeth hates them—Mark quite likes them. So they've reached an arrangement. She goes out somewhere—usually to a film—and he stays home with Tessa. Watches telly, drinks a beer, lets the weekend slide over him and linger.

He likes his job more than she likes hers. Marketing manager sounds good, though he's the only one who does the marketing. Not a hard ask, with the constant roll-over of technology driving the demand for the computer hardware they deal in. Popular at work, where he's always got time for the small talk.

As it happens, Elizabeth earns more than he does. She's good at what she does, and systems analysts are still in short supply. Most of it's on contract, though, and that's what she doesn't like. Working with new people all the time doesn't suit her. She likes a steady base. Still and all, the world's her oyster. She could leave any time she chose. They gave her a year off when Tessa was born, which is probably why she's stuck with them.

He pulls at the tab of another can, enjoying the soft sigh of its opening, and tours the channels again.

Tessa is lying stretched out on the floor, writing in her book. He watches her for a time, smiling.

'So how was church, chooky? Did you enjoy it?'

Her face settles into seriousness as she contemplates an answer.

'It was mostly fun,' she decides. 'I liked the Sunday school best, 'cos we got to make things. And there was a good story. But the church part was mostly for grown-ups, I think.'

She looks up at her father with a new thought.

'Why don't you go to church, Daddy?'

'I do, sometimes. Not all the time though. I guess I'm just lazy.'

'You're not lazy really, though, are you? You work awfully hard during the week. So it must be some other reason.'

'I'm not sure that I believe in God,' he says, frowning.

'Oh Daddy,' she laughs. 'What a funny thing to say. Everyone believes in God, don't they?'

In another part of the city, a man looks into the mirror, and sees nothing.

Chapter Four

The old man sits at the bar, clutching his half pint as if it gives him a handhold on a rock-face. There aren't many in at this time of the day, and none that want to talk to him.

He suffers a tiredness that has nothing to do with lack of sleep. His eyes, if there were anyone to look into them, are glazed and disengaged. Even with failing sight, you can end up seeing too much. Gates of the soul, perhaps. Gates which have allowed through too much traffic.

It's time to close the door. Time to move on to whatever comes next. I've overstayed my welcome. Outlived my capacity for hope. Exhausted my supplies.

He takes a small sip of the beer. It has lost its taste. In the flat surface he sees the reflection of his own face. It seems to belong to a stranger.

I've been where I don't want to be; seen what I never wanted to see. I wish there were something I could feel.

Flowers are such a cliché, but even clichés have their place. At least this bouquet is suitably spectacular. Alex is glad to get them home, having carried them rather self-consciously up Stoke Newington High Street.

Unfortunately his first encounter is with Ross, who sneers in the superior mockery and silence of adolescence. Alex's brow descends, but his mood is resilient enough to endure ridicule.

Mary is in the lounge, where the air is laced with Bach, and a stray shaft of light is choosing books from the shelf. With

Alex's entry she starts, a little resentful at being disturbed.

He presents the flowers like a trophy, allowing them to work their own magic. Mary adopts a rueful smile and inhales the summer fragrance. She looks up at Alex questioningly, not yet ready to concede too much.

'I'm sorry,' he confesses. 'I've been a prig. I do love you, and I don't mean just in the biblical sense.' He grins. 'I get distracted by my work at times. Much as I hate to admit it, you're right.'

'Oh, Alex, I hate it when we fight. I don't resent your work so much as what it does to you. I'm sometimes scared that I'm losing you, in amongst all the prayers and performances. I worry that there's a part of you that's been destroyed by ministry.'

Alex bites back the temptation to defend himself. Instead he bends down and kisses his wife on the cheek.

'I'm sorry,' is all he says. And who can doubt his sincerity when it is carried on the rich timbre of that rumbling voice? Like syrup on pancakes, Mary once described it. Irresistible.

'Control to 426.'

'426 receiving.'

'Harry, you remember that prowler we had at Chesholm Road a few weeks back? Where you found the footprint?'

'Yes, the university student—what about it?'

'Well we've just had a phone call from her. She thinks she's seen the man. Pop round and check it out—she's at home now. You've got it because you did the first interview, but Homicide want a report as soon as you've finished.'

'Okay, understood. We're on our way. 426 out.'

His eyes are constantly sliding sideways. Joe hates visits, even if he looks forward to them at the same time. Doesn't do a lot for your rep to have your mother coming to see you. And so he's watching the other inmates in the room, brooding over any reactions which might signal mockery.

It's a delicate dance, the visiting. You have to strain into the unknown, searching for memories of life on the outside. They come from a different order, these people with their breezy chat and lack of guile. There's a whole universe out there where people are human and sociable and occasionally even kind. Or so it seems.

So you do your best to accommodate them, to draw deep on reserves of whatever it is that drives life on the outside. You bracket out the jungle instincts of prison life, where confrontation is the starting point of encounter. And for the sake of your visitor, you let your guard down. Lower the shutters. Joe finds it almost unbearable to feel vulnerable under the gaze of screws and other inmates. Like releasing a butterfly into a furnace. Little wonder his eyes skitter.

He endures it for the sake of his mother. Wouldn't be right to shut her out just to preserve face. But every time you show a little weakness, you have to go out there and win back what you've lost.

Still and all, she keeps coming. And she brings a few smokes. He grins at her.

'You're looking good, Pat. Must be doing something right.'

'Looking good my arse. I 'aven't looked good for thirty years or more, and even then it wasn't me face that was me best asset. But thanks anyway. I need all the encouragement I can get, lad. How're you doing?'

'Not too bad, Pat. Pacing myself, you know.'

'You could always look after yourself all right, even when you was little. Had to, mind you, with a mother like me.'

'Leave it out. You've always been a good mum to me. I've got no regrets, and neither should you have.'

'Still, I can't help wondering how it might have been if you'd had a better start, you know. You've got a good brain on you— all them books you read—who knows where you might have ended up?'

'Yeah, could have been a better class of prison, I suppose. Listen, Pat, I've made my own way in this life, and I'm big enough to live with it. You've stuck by me all the way through, and I couldn't ask for more than that. So stow it, you old bag, before you start me feeling guilty for having you here.'

'Right enough, lad, right enough.'

She gives a hefty sniff. Joe knows it will have been noticed, even though not an eye in the room is looking in their direction. Like everything that happens, it will have to be accounted for.

It's the first time Tom's been left alone in this cell. He lies on the bunk, staring up at the ceiling, two feet away from his face. Once more, he tries blinking his eyes. The ceiling remains obdurately present.

There's a terrible consuming hollowness in the pit of his stomach; a bilious mixture of outrage and defeat. The sense of injustice writhes like a snake in his soul. This is England, for God's sake. They'll come for me soon, and be apologising...

But the weariness of spirit presses with crushing persistence. In the depths of his bowel there's a seeping corrosive undercurrent which announces to him that it's over. The trial has been held and the verdict given. Now he's cut off from everything and everyone—deleted from public sympathy as casually as last week's race results. There are no campaigns to free him, no band of supporters to stand with him in fury at the conviction.

That's the eviscerating part of it all. Not that a system he has trusted and served all his life should turn against him, but that he's alone. That he should be given up to his fate by those who were his own, flesh of his flesh. Betrayal and abandonment.

And now there is nothing but the proximate silence, and the cold, grey concrete which resists every assault. An emptiness; a womb of cramping pain. Which is not likely to open.

i like the smell of the wind on these summer days. it carries all sorts of secrets i can't name but i still know. sometimes it seems like it blows in through my nose and out through the back of my head somewhere. and it messes up my hair as if someone's stroking it with their fingers. maybe it's god's fingers. or an angel.

when you stand on your head like this the whole world looks different. you've got the sky beneath your feet and the grass over your head. and in the middle there's this funny little narrow band where people are. i wonder why it seems bigger when you're up the right way?

i could be walking on the clouds. oops—it's hard to keep your balance when you move your feet. that's better, though now i'm seeing little bright stars dancing around. i suppose it's better to have them in the sky than in the grass.

i wonder why you can't see the real stars during the day? you can see the moon sometimes, even if it's white and thin. maybe it's because it's not dark enough during the day to see them. they're such delicate little things that they get painted over by the sun. isn't it funny that something so beautiful should only come out in the dark? like hedgehogs.

i love breathing. i want to get as much of this air inside me as i can. i hope this summer will go on for ever and for ever.

From her place in the back pew, surrounded by the youth group, Nancy watches her father. Daniel's sitting near her, but not next to her. That would be too unbelievably naff. She's pleased that she doesn't have to explain that to him.

It's a weird mixture of feelings that compete within her. She wants to be cool and diffident and whatever. Nancy feels she has some sort of responsibility to despise her parents. And yet, as she watches him up there, the surge of love and pride threatens to bring tears to her eyes.

There are so few truly good people in the world. And Daddy is one of them. A man who not only preaches the faith, but does his best to live it out. If it weren't for him, I don't know if I'd believe at all. What a terrible thing to think, though it's true just the same. Even when things get tough, I have faith in *him*.

I don't think he even knows how wonderful he is. He's so hard on himself, more aware of his faults than his gifts. And yet he's *brilliant*. I need to tell him sometime. Dear God, thank you for the father you've given me. Look after him, and let other people love him as much as I do.

*

'Unit 426 to control.'

'Control here.'

'We're just on our way back in. We've got Rachel with us, the young lady who phoned in. She's got a very good description of this man for us. Maybe you can get hold of DI Thompson and have him ready to meet us when we get there.'

'Okay, will do. He's in a meeting at the moment but I don't think he'll mind being pulled out for this.'

'A bit early to say if there's a connection as yet, but it's the best lead we've got so far.'

'Absolutely. Well done, Harry. See you shortly. Control out.'

You get tunnel vision after a while. Staring into the screen as if there were some hidden depths to it. Elizabeth pushes her chair back and shakes her head. An involuntary shudder passes through her; a cold dank chill falling fleetingly across her soul. A small gasp escapes.

'All right, love?' asks the balding man at the adjacent work station, his eyes never leaving the VDU.

'Yes, fine,' she says. 'I just need a break. A slight caffeine deficiency, I shouldn't wonder.'

She welcomes the slow return of equilibrium. But an edge of apprehension lingers, as if a chasm has opened under her feet and she can no longer be sure of the ground on which she walks. It will pass.

I didn't do very well with girls. For a time I wondered if I had homosexual tendencies. I did a little experimenting with some boys from my school, but it was all adolescent anxiety and lack of other avenues.

I remember taking a girl to the pictures. I must have been thirteen, I suppose. She seemed to like me well enough. In the darkness, I slid my arm across the back of her seat, and very gently held her by the shoulder. She seemed to accept it. And then, screwing up my courage, I leaned across to kiss her. It was clumsy, and I half missed her mouth the first time. But she responded enthusiastically enough. It was so exciting, that kiss. I'd never felt anything like the giddy rush of pleasure going through my body.

My heart was beating frantically as I took things to the next stage. With my free hand, I reached out for her breast. She squirmed a little under the touch. To this day, I'm not sure if she was uncomfortable with it, or just moving to get into a better position. Whatever she intended, in my fragile and fumbling libido, it was interpreted as rejection. I've never known emotions to turn from roaring passion to granite coolness in such an instant. I withdrew from her altogether, apart from my arm round her shoulder, and watched the rest of the film with my heart in shreds.

She was as confused as I was, and we never went out together after that. I wanted her so badly that I still had an erection. But I hated her for humiliating me like that.

Alex reaches the midpoint of his sermon, and with the finishing line in sight, begins to pick up the pace and enthusiasm of his delivery.

There is an exhilaration in preaching that nothing else brings; the feeling that this is what he was born to. It's the meeting place between the hungry and dislocated hearts before him, and the resounding word of God which heals and enlivens them. And where do the two meet? In him, in the person of the preacher. In his sanctified but equally broken humanity. In his groping imagination, which gathers ripening words to give birth to the intangible divine tenderness. In his educated theological mind. Where the hammer meets the anvil, and smoke rises.

'Paul tells us there is no more condemnation for those in the house of faith. But how do we reconcile that with our experience? Are we not condemned on every side?

'Every time we watch television, we discover that we are too young or too old, too plain or too dull, too fat but never too slim. A flick through a few magazines will make us feel inadequate at the way our house plants die, our quiches fall, our hair falls out and our love lives fail to sizzle. In our work we are confronted with performance reviews and output quotas. We face the twin dangers of unemployment on the one hand and burnout on the other. We discover that we don't exercise enough, that we eat the wrong kinds of food, that our cholesterol levels are too high and blood-sugar levels too low. Economists tell us we don't save enough, we don't spend enough, and we have altogether too much credit. And to top it all off, we're probably all carrying emotional blocks inherited from our dysfunctional families.

'Whichever way we turn, we are condemned. The message is simple and sustained: "You are not good enough. You are a substandard, inadequate, unhealthy, poorly adjusted, incompetent, unproductive and emotionally stunted individual." And these messages are not just beamed at us from the outside world, are they? They have become part of our interior soundscape as well. We have taken them into ourselves. We believe the worst. We truly are inferior specimens; a fact that is confirmed every time we look into the mirror.

'In the face of this, Paul's assertion is a distant whisper; the faint scratching of chalk on a forgotten blackboard. Oh, it may be the word of God, but how do we hear it among the contrary facts? Friends, we can't hear unless we make some attempt to listen. We need to create some sort of space in our lives where we turn off the noises around us, and wait in quiet to hear what God has to say to us. This is what we are doing here today, in part. Coming again and again to renew ourselves in the story of the gospel. Turning aside from the clatter of contemporary clichés, so that we may instead be transformed by truth.

'And what is it that we hear? As we listen from our place of self-loathing and rejection, as we cower behind masks in secret knowledge of our failings? As we believe ourselves beyond hope, beyond acceptance by the people who matter? As we accept the world's judgement upon us in resigned despair?

'The Bible tells us, "There is no condemnation." No condemnation. No blame. No censure. No reproach. No judgement. No criticism. No punishment. No rejection. Nothing. "Yes, but . . ." we're tempted to say. But nothing. Do you want to argue with the word of God? When God declares you innocent, do you want to claim guilt for yourself? When God declares you free, do you want to insist on captivity? When God declares you accepted and loved and treasured, do you want to hang back in shame and defiance?

'No condemnation. None. This is not some time in the future we're talking about, when all our problems have been solved and our blemishes removed. This is here and now, where we are, on this morning in St John's Church in Stoke Newington. No condemnation. There is nothing that you need to become. Nothing you need to change. Nothing you need to give up. No condemnation. God loves you now. God accepts you now. God welcomes you now. We come to the Eucharist with one voice ringing in our ears, defying all others: "There is no condemnation." Nor has there been. Nor will there be. No condemnation.'

There is an unnatural quietness over the congregation. Even the children are reluctant to move lest they disturb it. It is not the absence of sound, so much as the presence of peace. Alex breathes it in, gratitude flooding him. The word of God.

Thompson has allowed Harry to stay in for the interview—not strictly necessary but something of a courtesy and a concession. This is the third time he's heard the story now, and it remains substantially unchanged. A bright girl this, with good keen memory. Not like some they get.

It's the place she saw him that triggers something in the recesses of his mind. In the newsagent's on Church Sreet. That and the description. Red hair is unusual, especially in an older man. Something is nagging, raising its voice in the forgotten corridors of discarded files.

Think of something else, he tells himself. Immediately the picture is before him: those awfully thin limbs poking out from among the bushes. No, not that. The cricket? What was it they scored in the first innings? A hundred and fifty-six? Or a hundred and sixty-five?

And then suddenly it's there, pretending it always has been. A burglary, about a year ago, on Oldfield Road. They broke the glass in the front door, and made off with the silver and jewellery while the owners were at church. Bit of a stuffy old boy he was, moaning that the police were never around when you wanted them. Mid-fifties, perhaps.

And with fading red hair.

'Excuse me, inspector,' he interrupts, 'do you mind if I just have a quick word with you outside?'

At first glance Joe thinks the new bloke has taken one of his books. And then he remembers returning it to the library a couple of weeks back. He unclenches his fists.

'Enjoying that, then?' he asks.

'Sorry? Oh, the book. No, not really. I can't concentrate. I keep losing the thread of it.'

'You take my advice, you'll learn to concentrate bloody hard,' advises Joe. 'You have to practise it.'

Tom looks at him as if he's made an improper suggestion.

'You never done time before, have you? You've got a lot to take on board, and not much time to do it.'

'I shouldn't be here. I . . .'

'Don't give me that bollocks,' snaps Joe. 'You think anyone here gives a fuck about the rights and wrongs of your case? The fact is you're here, and you're not moving in a hurry. Once you start going soft you've had it, see? You'll end up topping yourself or getting screwed up the arse by some gorilla. Here's the ground rules for survival. No weakness ever. No talk about innocence. No thinking about people outside. No remembering how things used to be. No wishing you were out. No socialising with the screws. No picking a fight you don't know you can win. Got that so far?'

Tom simply stares, with his mouth slightly agape.

'Remember what's written over the gate of Dante's Inferno? "Abandon hope, all you who enter here"? Well that's not bad advice in pokey, Tom. Not bad at all.'

hello god. are you listening? i never know if you are or not. i suppose you do always. or do you get your angels to do it for you, and only tell you the important things? i imagine that would be easier. though you never seem to do things the easy way, do you? never mind, i like the things you've made anyway.

please look after mummy and daddy. they have so many things they have to worry about like bills and work. i don't always understand what the problems are, but i'm sure you do and you could fix it up for them, couldn't you? daddy says he might not believe in you but i think he's only being silly with me. just the same, you may want to do something special to cheer him up.

and i pray for all the rabbits in the whole wide world and most of the tigers and foxes. though i think it would be better if they all just got on and stopped eating each other. i expect i'm not supposed to tell you what to do—it's just a suggestion, really.

look after me when i'm asleep and guard my dreams. i do love you and when i grow up i'll tell lots of people about you and make them happy. though if they'd just look around they wouldn't need telling in the first place.

The small bodies always look out of place on the table. A pathologist learns objectivity or perishes. But there's something about children that threatens to penetrate your defences.

At least the flesh changes colour and texture—there's that much of a demarcation line between the living and the dead. And his responsibility is to do as thorough a job as he can. If he's going to help, than that's what he has to offer.

I just wish she wasn't quite so brutalised.

'Nice roses,' comments Harry, admiring the arrangement in the vase.

'Yes. Well they were at least. Before they were cut. I don't like cut flowers,' Donald explains.

He looks at the policeman with lowering brow. Thank God Edna's out playing bridge. Did they have to park their blasted car in plain view?

'I dare say you're wondering what this is about,' suggests Harry, watching the big man's face.

'Well I assume it's something to do with that burglary. It

was you I dealt with then, wasn't it?'

'Indeed it was, Mr Evans, indeed it was. But unfortunately this is a separate matter. Quite a different kettle of fish altogether.'

Harry takes a sip of the tea and savours it. He learned a long time ago the intimidating nature of pauses. Yes, definite signs of anxiety.

'I don't suppose you'd like to tell us where you might have been on the fifth of this month? It was a Tuesday from memory. Mid-morning in particular we're interested in.'

'Well I don't know, I'm sure. Tuesday, you say? I expect I would have been here—I work from home you see. Importing.'

'Anybody here with you who could confirm that for us?'

'No, my wife goes out on Tuesdays. She helps at the arts centre. For goodness sake, what's all this about? Anyone would think I was the confounded criminal.'

But Harry has apparently found something interesting in his notes which he studies. The moments tick by. When Harry looks up, he notes a single bead of sweat has emerged on Donald's brow.

'So you wouldn't have been anywhere near Chesholm Road?'

'Chesholm Road? No, I don't think so. Why would I be? I was at home, I tell you.'

'It's just that we've got a report of a man standing in a garden watching a young lass getting undressed. And we've got a good footprint. You wouldn't mind, I dare say, if we had a quick look at your shoes? Nothing for you to worry about, of course, if you were at home.'

Harry watches the man sag. All the bluster wheezing out of him as if he's sprung a leak. There's something pathetic about it.

'Oh my God; oh my God,' is all that Donald can say.

It's one of his favourite spots to think. You'd hardly know you were still in the city. The greenery blocks out the noise, and there's enough space to find a corner where you can be on your own. The peace of the dead, thinks Alex. If you have to be buried somewhere, then this wouldn't be a bad spot to end up. He likes to come here on his day off, wearing old clothes to remain incognito. You can walk a long way exploring the paths.

Some of the gravestones are like old friends now. They mark his progress, give him stations to stop and pray at. He has his favourite bench, which he's developed a sense of ownership about. If ever there's someone sitting on it when he arrives, he feels tempted to tell them they're trespassing.

But sitting there today he allows the quiet to wash over him. Looking down, he notices blood on his trousers. And then the source—skinned knuckles. He must have done it coming over the wall. It's a stupid thing for a grown man to do, but it saves the long walk round to the High Street. When it's your day off, you like to do things out of character. Climbing the wall is his little act of independence; a sign that not all of him belongs to the church.

He casts his mind back over Mary's accusations. Has he lost something of himself in the vocation? Is he in danger of sacrificing wife and family for the sake of ministry? It's a danger, and one he's prided himself on avoiding. You can't escape the tension, of course. The gospel of Christ is all consuming. It's one area where the Catholics have an advantage with their celibate priesthood. No conflict with domestic duties.

But it's a false escape in many ways. You don't solve a tension by simply eliminating it. You have to position yourself somewhere in the polar force field. And from time to time make adjustments. Life is a process of balancing; a singular trek on a rather narrow path bounded by ravines. With any luck, you don't fall too often.

> **tragedy** ('trædʒɪdɪ) *n pl* **-dies. 1** a play in which the protagonist ... falls to disaster through the combination of a personal failing and circumstances with which he cannot deal. **2** a shocking or sad event; disaster.

'Can I speak to Detective Inspector Thompson please?'
'Putting you through now.'

'Thompson here.'

'Mullins, from the lab. That blood sample we got off the wall of the cemetery: it's not the girl's.'

'Certain?'

'Absolutely—no chance. Looks like it might be from the perp.'

'Thanks Mullins. That's good news.'

What's the difference between fate and the will of God in the end? Events slide and twist past each other, setting up patterns and causal chains like amoebae writhing under a microscope. Slithering in a constantly churning soup of happenstance. Is there any force guiding them? Any tide of purpose tugging circumstances into line? Or is it we who imagine connection, for the sake of our own significance? Seeing meaning where there is none?

If it were entirely random, what would we lose? Why the need to cajole and plead and protest, as if we had some influence on it all? Are we scared of dissolving in the soup?

Blind fate or the will of God? How do you tell them apart? Why do you need to? Who would you blame if there were no God?

There are some advantages in prison chaplaincy. As a rule, your parishioners don't hound you at night. When you walk out of the gate, you leave it all behind in a way that's not possible in a church. And the expectations are low. Nobody whinges about the colour of the carpet or lapses in the liturgy.

It suits Kevin. Good with people; an absolute failure at ecclesiastical politics. His time in the parish was a disaster; he crashed and burned. After three months out, the bishop suggested chaplaincy. It was an inspired move, all things considered.

Not that you'd call it easy. You have to make your own job. The inmates are suspicious. In prison, there are only two sides—us and them, inmates and staff, crims and screws. You're on our side or you're the enemy. No middle ground. No place for someone who claims to straddle the divide. You're either for us or against us—that was the message, even if never in so many words. And the staff treat you as a bumbling idiot. A sort of Victorian relic, like the gallows. Some of them are friendly in private, but in groups they are generally guarded.

They try to keep the underside of the prison a secret from him. The beatings, the smuggling, the pornography—as if it would corrupt him. Understandable perhaps; they want to maintain the veneer of civilisation which marks them out from the inmates. He is an intruder, a potential spy from the outside in their midst. His presence breaches the separation between the two worlds; threatens the divide between family life and the jungle of prison. And that division needs to be maintained for their own sanity and sense of decency.

Kevin understands it as only a clergyman can. How is it possible to live in a world of filth and violence on a daily basis, and then change out of your uniform to go home to domesticity? To beat a man senseless with a rubber truncheon, and a few hours later cuddle your child? Only by a strict separation of the two. Only by making the prison gate a door between different dimensions, where different rules apply and humanity ceases to be generic.

It's how you deal with conscience in a situation where you are forced to routinely violate it. By splitting. By operating on two levels. By keeping the unpleasant concealed. Men prefer the darkness to the light, because their deeds are evil.

Kevin knows all of this and understands it and forgives it. He is a dealer in the commodity of sin. He needs to know his product. Prison removes illusions, that's all. Strips away the delicate skin of sophisticated life like boiling water on a baby. To reveal the full horror of the raw and putrid interior of human life. To expose the truth.

Oh yes, there's the weariness and cynicism. But there's also the satisfaction of confronting reality. Here in this cesspool, where every vestige of morality has failed—here is where the gospel either stands or falls. Where it means something or nothing.

*

The big man is slumped on the sofa. He looks to Harry like a collapsed inflatable dummy. They've been over the territory a few times now. He folded without resistance. Confessed not only to the two incidents they have the prints for, but also to another which has never been reported.

Pathetic really. An ageing man creeping round the bushes and jacking himself off. Why didn't he just go to a brothel?

But he won't budge on the child. Claims he's never been near the cemetery. Even when I mentioned we had footprints from there as well. I'm tempted to believe him. You can never tell. Wouldn't be the first time I've been surprised.

We'll have to turn him over, anyway. Poor bastard. That'll put paid to what's left of his marriage, I shouldn't wonder.

Slowly the fragments are collected. A cotton thread. The blood sample. A vague footprint. The masking tape that bound her.

But some of the vital ingredients are missing. No witness statements of any help. No tyre marks anywhere near. And most disappointing of all, no sperm. The cunning bastard must have used a condom, and taken it with him.

A regular? Could be, though with all the publicity about DNA nowadays, anyone could have anticipated it.

Motive? In these cases you never bother looking for one. What motive could possibly be sufficient?

It was a bit of a lark at first, joining the debating club. Joe would never have considered it if he hadn't been asked. He knew nothing about it. Still, it was a night out from the cells, and sometimes they had women come in on the opposing team.

He made a lot of mistakes first time up. But he watched and listened and learned. Twice now he'd been elected captain, and done a fair job of it. It was all a bit of a wank really, but good fun just the same. They held it in the gymnasium, rustling up one of the blocks as an audience.

Tonight's moot was 'Bars do not a prison make', and the inmates took the affirmative. Joe was speaking second. The opposition lead was brilliant—funny, incisive and convincing—

a mile ahead of their own effort, which opened the session. As Joe rises he knows he has a task ahead of him.

'Ladies, gentlemen, and Block G. The spiv in a suit who just spoke would have you believe that because we're meeting inside locked doors tonight, we're all prisoners. He thinks that because he can walk out of the door and we can't, that he's free and we're in captivity. He imagines himself more fortunate than we poor inmates.'

'Well better equipped, at least, by the sound of things,' comes the interjection.

'You seem to be familiar with handling your own equipment, I'll give you that,' retorts Joe. 'I've always thought self-abuse a poor line of argument, and essentially unproductive. But to get back to matters in hand, as our colleagues often do, I want to suggest that it's our visitors who're flogging a dead argument. I suspect they're more accustomed to debating in groups.

'Let's ask ourselves, then, what these mass debaters return to when they step outside of this establishment. They go back to their mortgages, their credit-card bills, their nagging wives, their slave-driving employers, their domestic duties, their suburban neuroses, their flatulent children, their whining relatives and their endless responsibilities.

'By comparison, we inmates have food provided for us, guaranteed shelter with no cost of upkeep, our laundry done for us, a gymnasium provided, films twice a week, and a welcome absence of wives, relatives, children and duties. Ask yourself, who are the free?

'We live in physical containment, but our minds and souls are liberated. We can read, we can think, we can talk, we can write and we can dream. These pitiful men, on the other hand, have freedom of movement but captivity of the spirit. They are too busy to talk, too preoccupied to read, too tired to think, too confused to write and too stressed to dream. Who would choose that?

'We may have bars, but they serve to keep distractions out. For hundreds of years men and women chose to enter cells like

80

ours for their spiritual development. They knew something. And now we have been personally selected by the government to...'

There's a commotion in the back rows of the audience. Some quick harsh shouting, and the screws are running. And there's a man on the floor with blood spurting from a gash in his neck.

Elizabeth has been having trouble concentrating all afternoon. She jumps when the phone rings.

'Hello?'

'It's Beryl here, Elizabeth. Sorry to disturb you at work, but Tessa hasn't turned up at the centre. I wondered if she was ill or something?'

'Tessa? No, she should be there—what's the time? Yes, she should definitely be there by now. You haven't heard anything from school?'

'No, I rang them first and they said she left there all right. I didn't want to worry you unnecessarily. You don't have any idea where she is, then? Her father didn't pick her up by any chance?'

'Not that I know of—I'll check. Oh God, I don't know what to do. Can you start looking for her around there? I'll come over straightaway. She is a bit of a dreamer, but we've always stressed going straight to the centre, and she's never let us down before . . .'

'She wouldn't be at a friend's place or anything? Only we've had that before with children, stopping in to see a toy or something. I wouldn't start worrying too much yet. Though perhaps I should inform the police.'

'The police? Why . . . Oh God, oh God.'

'Just to be on the safe side, like. You get hold of your husband, and we'll start organising a bit of a search. And then we'll see you here just as soon as you can arrive. I'm sorry, Elizabeth, I know what a worry it is. But she's probably okay.'

'Is she? I mean . . . I don't know. I'll see you soon.'

For a few minutes she sits there with the phone in her hand, staring off into the impenetrable distance.

'Tessa,' she whispers.

Chapter Five

See how easily a hole forms in the fabric of time. How it tears; how the interlocking stitches rip asunder, revealing the waiting darkness. So easy, on a summer's afternoon, for normality to be gashed with a terrible wound.

You think it will never happen. Childhood dread subsides, and the mindless terror of the night becomes subdued by reason. Perhaps it disappears; or perhaps it is simply banished into hiding. People assure you that your fears are baseless, that civilisation has driven out the demons. You begin to believe them. Perhaps it is needless anxiety; the product of primal shadows on the collective unconscious. You have nothing to fear but fear itself. You laugh at yourself, and look to the smiling faces of your friends.

And then, without warning, the world falls in on itself. In the space of a few sentences—thirty beats of the heart—it is all gone. Tumbling away into the hole which has opened at your feet. As you look down, there is nothing but darkness. It is the substance of your fears. The reality which your imagination sketched in vain. The gaping chasm which nothing will heal.

What did you expect? Did you think your routines and appliances and insurances would protect you? Did you? Did you imagine that you were safe in your restored Victorian semi-detached? Could you have been so naïve as to believe that a gloss of civility made you immune?

Ah no. When the axe falls, the blade cuts. Yes, my friend. The blade cuts.

*

Elizabeth reaches out a hand for the wall as her knees buckle under her. She's aware of nothing but falling, falling.

Mark sees her dropping slowly to the floor, and reaches out. But his arm moves no more than a few inches, as if protesting the futility. There is no way he has of evaluating any more whether it is normal or not for people to fall to the floor.

She has slumped to her knees, where an unholy sound is gurgling up from the depths of her belly. There are no tears on her face.

The policewoman moves to hold the stricken mother by the shoulders. Harry stays where he is, locked in the muteness and immobility of his role. What should a man be doing? The husband is watching him, looking for some clue as to what's expected of him. Some lifeline in a sea of dreadful confusion. Nothing comes.

It's a frozen tableau, like an amateurish nativity scene. Except there's no baby. No child. No Tessa.

'What . . .' begins Mark, flailing for comprehension. But the act of opening his mouth releases a gigantic bubble of pain which surges up within him and renders him incapable of speech, thought, breath.

'I'm afraid there's still the formal identification to do, Mr Bromley.' Harry despises himself, his work, his existence. His ridiculous fucking duty.

Mark looks at his wife in the posture of prayer, and wonders at the groaning which continues to bleed from her mouth. Nothing is registering. Nothing.

'Yes,' he says. 'I see.'

> **grief** (griːf) *n* **1** deep or intense sorrow or distress, esp. at the death of someone. **2** something that causes keen distress or suffering. **3 come to grief** *Informal.* to end unsuccessfully or disastrously.

He's looking for some envelopes in the dog's-breakfast drawer. There's a roll of tape in the front. Alex picks it up and studies it.

'Where did this come from?' he calls to Mary, who's ironing.

'What is it?' she asks.

'A half-used roll of masking tape. I didn't buy it.'

'Well, me neither. Probably something Ross has picked up out of a dump bin—he's always scouting round them looking for treasures.'

'Hmmm . . . A pity—I was wanting masking tape a few weeks ago and I couldn't find any. Still, it'll come in handy I dare say.'

The old boy's pulled through. Joe's eyes narrowed in fury when he saw that it was George lying in a pool of blood on the gymnasium floor; thought he was done for. But somehow the main artery had been missed, and they patched him up. Tough old bird that he is.

It was Blade. They've got him on the video, dead to rights. Joe would've picked him anyway, whether it'd been proved or not. As it happens, now it means revenge will have to wait a while for Blade to emerge from solitary. Everything finds its level. And every action has an equal and opposite reaction.

George is grinning at him from the bed in the hospital cell-block.

'Not bad in here, Joe. Not bad at all. Food's good. You want to try it sometime.'

'You tell me if they don't treat you right, George, and I'll see to it. They told your wife?'

'Told her I had a fall. She'll know, lad. Probably hoping they'd of done me proper, so's she could get the insurance.'

'I doubt it. By the way, I've got this covered.'

'Nah, leave it out, Joe. Drop it now. I can fix it meself.'

'No you can't. Nothing more to be said; I've got it covered, I told you.'

George ponders this and smiles again.

'When's he back?'

'Three weeks.'

'Okay, lad, okay.'

i expect when i grow up i'll be famous, though i don't know how. i might have my own television show, or be a writer or

84

something. one time i dreamed that i was a space explorer, and that i went out of the spaceship to look at the stars. i was tied on with a long rope, and i was just floating around looking at how beautiful everything was. and then suddenly something happened and the rope broke, and i was floating off into outer space. it wasn't as scary as you might think.

daddy says i'm famous already, because i'm his daughter, but i think he's just teasing. he does like to play games a lot. i told him he'd be famous because he's my father, and we laughed together. he says he doesn't care whether he's famous or not, so long as i love him. of course i love him. i might make him a card tonight to tell him.

there's a boy at school who has one leg longer than the other. he wears this funny thing on the bottom of his shoe to balance him up and make sure he doesn't fall over. it's a pity he wasn't born on a mountain 'cos then he would have just the right sort of legs to stand up straight. except that he could only face one way, i suppose, or it would make things worse.

it makes me wonder what sort of special things i've been born with. daddy says everyone has at least one important thing to do in their life, and i haven't found out what mine is yet. it might not even be something you're good at, he says. it's like throwing pooh sticks in the river—you can't ever tell before-hand which one will go furthest. i don't mind too much. i'm just going to jump in and see where i end up. the river can do what it likes with me.

It's not right. These things should not be happening, are not happening. The car trip is like visiting another planet, where people go about their business, not realising they are already doomed. A plague city where the inhabitants ignore the spots on their hands. Mark watches through the wrong end of the binoculars.

He is dwelling in a strangely insulated realm, a lobotomised silence. Words and images pass across his space but do not con-nect. There is someone next to him; a policeman. Why am I in a police car? What has happened? I don't want to be here.

Perhaps he has said something by mistake. The policeman turns to look at him. The car seems to be gliding above the ground, as if by magic.

They stop outside a concrete building. Mark waits, floating in his womb of formaldehyde. People are moving and talking. They lead him from the car; the policeman on one side and a man in a white coat on the other. They pass through swinging doors and down a corridor. The policeman's boots are echoing. It's like a dream which Mark has had. Perhaps it is a dream. I'll wake soon. Yes, soon.

They're in a white room with bright lights. Somebody has asked him if he's all right. He strains against the inertia to find an answer. Am I? How do I know? What is there to compare with?

'Yes,' he answers, and the word balloons out of his mouth into the whiteness. The others look at him as if he has cursed.

There's a shape on the trolley in front of him. A small shape. Draped in white like an angel. It seems to be the centre of attention.

The man in the white coat reaches down to the white cloth. Why is everything in white? Why is it so quiet? The cloth is pulled back.

It's the face of a small girl, a child. She is so very very beautiful. So innocent. So angelic, with her black hair. But there seem to be smudges all over her, as if someone has touched her with inky fingers . . .

Something shifts. Deep and massive; somewhere inside so that Mark cries out. It's like a split image which gradually comes into focus as the lens is turned. And then the images merge, and a word screams across the surface of his psyche.

Tessa!

His entrails are crushed between two giant steel slabs. Black bile rises and jams in his throat, which has constricted in terror. There is no space to contain the anguish, and so it explodes outwards through orifices and the pores of his skin. It shreds his bowel and his cortex, until there is nothing but a raw pulped mass of pain.

86

He staggers sideways into the policeman. There is nowhere to hide.

He nods. He betrays her with a nod. Silences her, kills her, slays her, extinguishes her; with a nod.

Tessa!

That's the trouble with facts. You can't change them. And the facts are that there's no shoes in the choirmaster's house that match the prints in the cemetery. To make matters worse, it seems that his alibi for the time period has been backed up. His blood's the wrong type as well.

Thompson sighs. Routine police work; the highs and lows. Just when you think it's breaking, it comes to a dead end. Maybe we'll do a little more digging, just in case. He's the only live one we've got.

He flicks through the photos from the crime scene again, and furrows his brow in distaste. We've got to get this bastard.

There's a man in a dark suit sitting in their lounge. He's asking them something. Elizabeth stares at him, trying to remember what he's doing there.

'I'm sorry?' she says.

'Woodgrain or white, Mrs Bromley? We recommend white with young children, but she wasn't quite a child . . .'

'White,' insists Mark. 'It must be white.'

'Very well. And the handles?'

'What?'

'There's a variety of options for handles . . . I can show you the range in this book.' He reaches into his briefcase and extracts another folder.

Elizabeth stares at him in incomprehension. He is speaking a foreign language. There is no possible connection between him and . . . him and . . .

She heaves again; a great, wracking, silent convulsion which buckles her nearly in half.

'For God's sake, man,' shouts Mark. 'What's the point? Handles? We don't give a shit about handles. Just do it—do whatever it takes.'

'I'm sorry, Mr Bromley, I'm almost finished. The celebrant?'

'What did you say?'

'The celebrant—the person to take the funeral. Do you have a minister?'

'Do we?' he asks Elizabeth, terrified of meeting her eyes.

'Reverend Hanson,' she manages. 'St John's.'

'Ah yes,' approves the funeral director. 'Very good.'

Is this how it happens then? Bureaucrats filling in forms and ticking options? Is this what it comes to? That evil should be tidied away? The life of a little girl measured in satin shrouds and coffin handles? God save our miserable little souls.

The old man is following the sun. He sits opposite a street sign and contemplates it. Defoe Road. Named for Stoke Newington's most famous resident, Daniel Defoe. A dissenter and a writer. A wordsmith and a satirist, carving deep into English sensibilities.

His father was a butcher.

It was in Stoke Newington that he composed the curious work *The Political History of the Devil*. What was he thinking of? Why the interest in demonology?

Do writers sometimes encounter darkness in their explorations of the interior vaults? Does it frighten them or intrigue them? Are there shadows on the walls of the cave? Was Defoe unbalanced by something he saw? Or did it just spring from the ferment of his religious imagination?

These are not questions for an old man petrifying in the sun. He is not a writer, but an observer. A witness, if you like.

> **witness** ('wɪtnɪs) *n* **1** a person who has seen or can give first-hand evidence of some event.   *vb* **2** *(tr.)* to see, be present at, or know at first hand. **3** *(tr.)* to give or serve as evidence (of).

i'm getting to like church better and better. even some of the songs are all right once you get used to them. i love the smell of the smoky stuff they burn up at the front, and the waxy smell after the candles have been snuffed out. there are some children who help out up at the front, passing things and holding things. i wonder if i could be one of those? i expect you have to be very good to be allowed to.

on sunday the minister man talked about why things go wrong for people. i didn't quite understand. he was saying something about the will of god. i thought a will was something you left behind when you were dead, but that doesn't seem to make sense. he told a story about when his wife was having her first baby, and how the baby was very sick. they thought she might die. and how he prayed to god and didn't know if the baby would live or die. but the baby did live, only he wasn't sure whether that was because of god or the doctors. now his little girl has grown up and is lovely. she was sitting there, and i looked at her. she was a bit red in the face, but smiling as well.

i think he was still hurt about it, because he looked like he might cry. so on the way out, he was standing there like a bus conductor, shaking everyone's hand. i said to him that i thought god loved him and his daughter, and wanted them to be happy. he smiled and said he expected that i was right, and asked me where my mummy and daddy were. i told him they were going out for a breakfast because it was a good chance for them. he asked me my name and shook my hand. i forgot to ask him his name.

it's very hard to know what things god does and doesn't do. i think he should make some things a bit more obvious than he does, and then people wouldn't worry so much.

Alex pauses for a moment outside the door. Stilling himself, breathing deeply, summoning whatever resources he can find in a sort of prayer. As he raises the knocker, he's aware of beginning something that cannot be easily ended.

Mark opens the door, standing there not seeing. He steps aside without speaking, allowing the priest to enter. All of these strangers entering his house, at the one time when all he wants in the world is to be alone in the dark. Alex lays a hand on Mark's shoulder as he passes, a gesture of solidarity.

As he enters the lounge, Mary is holding a fluffy toy to her cheek and weeping. It appears to be a rabbit.

Even now, even here, the dictates of convention draw her to her feet, and she is tempted to smile. Only her unsteadiness prevents her. She stands there, stooped. Mark hovers in the background. No one has spoken.

He has worn his collar. It's a marker, a symbol, a badge of continuity in a season of dissolution. Vicars deal with death as bakers with yeast. They are the midwives of grief. They understand its ways.

Because of this Alex reaches out to embrace the woman he hardly knows. She is a social stranger, but a sister in human anguish. He holds her, feeling her wet cheek on his collar. She shudders against him in a strange parody of the sexual act.

His embrace is the first encircling of flesh she has experienced in the five thousand years since she knew for certain. Mark would have held her but for his own tsunami of pain. The warmth and steadiness of Alex is more than she can bear. Now the sobs begin; the rhythmic gulping of air where there should be sound, and is none.

Mark looks on at a scene which is no less strange than any of the others. He is dumb of spirit. Nothing connects with anything else.

From somewhere there come the beginnings of a high-pitched wail; an ungodly keening which waxes in the terrified air. Alex continues to hold her in silence, closing his eyes against the sound.

'You bastard! You bastard! You fucking bastard!' she rails, pulling back from him and raining ineffectual blows on his shoulders. 'Don't bring your filthy God into my house! Don't talk to me about goodness or God or love! I hate you and your God—you've taken everything that I have and now you come wanting more. Well you can't have it! You've taken my little girl, my little girl, my Tessa . . .'

And now she is incoherent again, words dissolving in the flood of pain. Still he holds her, absorbing the blows.

'Elizabeth . . .' mutters Mark, roused from his disconnection.

But Alex turns toward him, and shakes his head.

'Let her be,' he says. 'Let her be.'

Spring would have been the time for a clean-out, but it passed by. Like so many things, thinks Mary, like so many things. She pauses for a moment in her relentless pursuit of order in the wardrobe, and sits on the edge of the bed.

There was a time when everything was beginning. Somewhere, imperceptibly, it changed. Now it is fadings and endings. When was the balance point, and how did I miss it? Surely there must have been a climax? A high point from which to pause and look down?

It's not so much regret as an underlying sadness that I can't seem to shake. A maggot of discontent buried in my soul. I have so many things to be thankful for, and none of them work. I seem to remember a time when it felt different.

She picks a battered sports shoe of Alex's from the floor and contemplates it. It's worn through at the toe, and the laces are hopelessly frayed. She tosses it in the plastic bag reserved for discards. Once things are past their best, there's no use in hanging on to them. Ah, there's its mate.

Alex will complain. If he notices. She sucks the inside of her lip, and stares into the hidden depths of the wall. For no particular reason, she remembers a bird which became trapped in the house when she was a child. They tried to catch it, but eventually it battered itself to death against the window pane in its attempt to escape.

The new man is keeping himself apart from the others. Kevin has noticed. He keeps a special eye out for the new ones. Not that they have any interest in the chaplain, by and large. But they're vulnerable in these early weeks, especially first-timers. Suicide or attack; a lot of them do it hard during the entry process.

And this one's as green as they come by the look of him. Trouble waiting to happen.

Kevin finds him in the gym, where he's sitting on a bench

after pressing weights. His cheeks are red and there appear to be blisters on his hands.

'Kevin Anders,' he offers. 'I'm one of the chaplains.'

'Tom,' is the guarded response. The sweaty eyes have narrowed in suspicion.

'Settling in okay?' asks Kevin, as if he were the concierge of a luxury hotel.

But the man simply stares at him, apparently trying to evaluate something.

'The thing is, Tom, that most inmates find it tough in the first few weeks. Adjusting to the routine, learning the ropes, that sort of thing. And the separation from family, if you have any, that takes it out of you. So if you want to talk at any time, or if I can help out with anything, just let me know. I'm not going to ram religion down your throat, you know what I mean? The offer's there; you can take it or leave it. Some of the others have found it helpful—you can check me out with them if you like.'

'I used to believe,' says Tom quietly. 'I used to think there was a God, and that he looked after people, but I can't anymore. I've lost it all now.'

It takes Kevin a few moments to recover. Faith is the one thing he seldom discusses in prison. Sometimes, when he knows an inmate well, or after a suicide, conversation may drift briefly in a theological direction. He's unprepared for this direct approach.

'Do you want to talk about it?' he asks, immediately regretting the banality of the response.

'I don't think there's anything left to talk about. I've been betrayed, that's all. Have you ever trusted in something or someone with all that you have, and then been let down? That's what's happened to me. For the first time in my life, I understand Job's wife. God's a sick bastard. It's best to curse him and die. Best to have nothing to do with him. If I had, I might not be in here.'

So that's it, thinks Kevin. Another persecuted innocent. Perhaps I'd better have a look through his file. I'd be interested in the psych report on this one. It must have been borderline where they sent him.

Thompson attends the funeral as a matter of course. He has a man above the shop across the road, with a video camera. They'll scan the faces of the crowd later to see who's turned up. You just never know with this sort of case. A dog returning to its vomit.

He studies the order sheet for the service. On the front cover there's a picture of the little girl. Thompson's mouth turns down in distaste. Over-familiarity, that's the trouble with the church these days. Trying to make God chummy. Ridiculous.

The building itself is traditional enough, thank goodness. He notes with pleasure the absence of a projection screen in the sanctuary. If I want a screen, I'll go to the cinema.

The organ is growling something suitably sombre. The mood is sedate and museum-like, with a faint lisp of whispers creeping round the walls. People arriving are cautious and uncertain, checking out of the corner of their eyes to confirm their choice of attire is in keeping with the code. And they are overly apologetic to all and sundry.

As if somehow they shared the responsibility for that white coffin at the front. An oblong obscenity in the mouth of God. A sacrilege against the backdrop of the altar. Something akin to an offering, considers Thompson.

In the front row, the parents sit slumped amid their respective parents. From time to time an arriving mourner approaches to extend them sympathy. Mark bears the burden of acknowledgement, muttering indistinct words. Elizabeth gazes into the distance, alarmingly passive. They do not lean against each other. Their only partnership is that of pain, and somewhere there has been tacit mutual understanding that touch will only deepen it. Isolation becomes a rough haven of anaesthesia.

You can't help wondering, thinks Thompson, if the killer is among us.

*

93

Some of the incidents look more significant in retrospect. But that's a view that only comes after the event. I found them to be aberrations in an otherwise normal life. They're only given meaning by later developments.

But yes, I can see now. Certain points at which things might have gone a different way. Opportunities for change, if you like. I could have decided otherwise than I did, and I might have become a different person. It's a little late to alter the course of history now.

I spent a lot of time masturbating. Shut in the toilet with a sweaty hand and my imagination. I think that was fairly normal. It's often difficult to know what's 'normal' or not, isn't it? During a war it's normal to kill people. But certainly most of the other boys of my age were doing it as well. Not that we talked about it a great deal. We were ashamed of ourselves, I suspect. We felt inadequate because we didn't have girls to be with.

We went through enormous quantities of soap. My mother could never understand where it all went to. But I wanted to get rid of that smell on my hand. It was a giveaway, and I was sure that it marked me out everywhere I went. So I scrubbed and scrubbed to get rid of it.

I was miserable most of the time, though no one would have guessed it. I learned how to present the image which people wanted. Looking back, I may have done better to reveal the truth.

There's nothing sophisticated about the revenge when it comes. Violence seldom needs embellishment. It explains itself adequately to those who know its grammar.

Joe hasn't planned anything other than to commit himself to respond. It's more a case of being in a constant state of readiness; fostering the deadly instincts. He once watched a panther prowling its enclosure at the zoo, and recognised everything at a glance.

Blade knows that something is coming. He's seen the way Joe watches him at meal times. And the word is out for him to watch his step.

In the event it's as sudden as a snakebite, and with as little time to anticipate. Your concentration lapses, no matter how you try to maintain a constant state of alertness. It wears you down, the threat, until you blink. And in that millisecond it happens.

Even for Joe, it comes upon him as if he were the one being attacked. One sweep of his eyes while walking along the corridor does it. It's all there, laid out before him: Blade, walking towards him; the certainty that they will pass in the blind spot directly under the video camera; the recognition that there are no screws within sight. The moment is anchored in still-frame at the back of his eyes, as he feels the time continuum grind down through the gears.

There's so much time as Blade takes another two steps toward Joe, only now beginning to lift his head and catch sight of his nemesis approaching. Even in the instant his eyes are beginning to dilate, Joe has sprung silently off the balls of his feet, an outstretched arm tracking the advancing throat. The impact is jarring and deadly. Blade drops immediately to the concrete walkway, with Joe collapsing on top of the felled inmate, a knee to his sternum.

'Leave George alone,' is all he grunts as he takes Blade's hand in his. And then he has the index finger and is bending it further and further back. Joe knows how hard it is to break a bone even as small as a finger bone. You have to get it under tension and then apply a little flick to get the break. The first time he tried it, it didn't work, and he ended up being humiliating. But now he has the knack.

There's a gratifying crack as the bone goes, and a strangulated cry from his opponent, who's still trying to discover what's happening. The finger becomes loose in Joe's grip, but he keeps on twisting. The sharp end of the fracture tears through the flesh and skin to emerge as a white shard protruding grotesquely from Blade's finger. And then, with steady controlled fury, Joe begins to bend it back the other way.

No good doing only half a job. You need to leave them with something to think about. He's never seen Blade with tears in his eyes before.

Thank God for the liturgy. Alex is already a good way through the service, with the entire congregation borne along by the steady omnibus of the Prayer Book. But now the moment of truth. Something must be said, lest the contrast between the high language of faith and the blasphemous white coffin become overpowering.

It's best to tread carefully; to begin amidst the despair and horror. He looks once more into the hollow eyes of the mother, by way of preparation.

The silence before he speaks is a great chasm reaching all the way down into unquenchable darkness. It's an ugly scar which separates his Christianity from the hostile glare of the mourners. He comes as their enemy; the angel of death. There is no sympathy or call for explanations, and disgust for any who would attempt them. The priest stands on the other side of the coffin—the representative of the God made hateful by death. In the face of such antagonism, it is necessary to employ a pre-emptive strike.

'Occasionally in the course of a career in ministry,' begins Alex, 'one encounters events which render one mute. Nothing which I can say or do or proclaim today can for one moment assail the terrible eloquence of the tragedy which confronts us. I do not feel that it is my task to offer a defence of the goodness of God. My task, on behalf of you all, is to extend our comfort and strength to those bearing the loss, and to offer up prayers for them and for Tessa.'

He notices the mother recoil under the lash of her daughter's name.

'The readings and prayers we have shared together thus far have included words such as hope and peace. In the presence of a young girl's life so horribly cut short, those words may seem unhelpful and even somewhat mocking. That is not their intention. At times like these, we confess ourselves empty and helpless, and we reach out for whatever may be familiar in order to sustain us. It is an acknowledgement that these events are not the truth about human life, but a damnable lie. Even while we are reduced to silence in our state of shock, we remind ourselves that this encounter with darkness cannot extinguish the light.

'The life of Tessa represented for us all that which is good and pure and innocent in our existence. When we are tempted to become cynical, we look to our children to remind ourselves of the simple beauty of human life. But now, this child has been taken from us in an act of unspeakable evil. Let us not pretend that such an event does not plunge a dagger into the very heart of any basis for hope or peace. It does. If the fate of Tessa represents for us normality, then we are all doomed. We have no reason to fear because earthly life has already become hell.

'But in the name of Tessa and for the sake of her life, we cannot accept this as normality. We cannot sit back and accept it in numbed silence, with no reaction. We must allow the anger to arise within us. We must feel the protest swelling in our hearts. We must recoil against all that violates the goodness of life and name it for what it is. That name is evil. In Tessa's death we are face to face with evil. We look into its appalling depth and find ourselves confounded.'

Alex appears to be gazing into those depths himself. He falls silent, and his eyes begin to glaze. In the quietness there is the sound of sobbing from several quarters. It might have been a powerful rhetorical device, had it been shorter. As it is, the pause lingers and lengthens, with no sign that the vicar is aware of the gradually gathering discomfort.

Detective Inspector Thompson's eyes narrow. He turns to follow the priest's stare, hoping to find some answer to it. But his eyes seem focussed on a spot somewhere above the rear pews. Eventually the organist coughs loudly and pointedly, and Alex is jolted to consciousness. He appears startled by his surroundings. Scanning the notes on the pulpit, he quickly finds his place again.

'How are we to respond? Not through vengeance, though our anger tempts us in that direction. Not through withdrawal, though our pain, and certainly that of Mark and Elizabeth, tempts us to do so. Not through denial of the facts, though our confusion tempts us to hide from them. No, we respond, when and as we are able, by affirming such distant concepts as love, forgiveness and hope. We refuse to be cowed by evil. We will not be defeated. We reach out our hands to one another for strength, and against all the evidence, we proclaim that life is good. We read the scriptures, we pray, we believe—God help us our unbelief.

'We cannot allow the life of Tessa to be further desecrated. And so we say together that this is not the end; that this is not all that there is to Tessa. That through some process unknown to us, Tessa continues to live. That, whether in this world or the next, justice will be done. That love is stronger than hatred; that good is stronger than evil; and that life is stronger than death. We may not feel hope, and indeed it may be many years until it returns to us. But we declare it. We declare it.

'Please join me as we stand and pray together.

> 'God our Creator and Redeemer,
>   all things proceed from you and return to you
>   and nothing is lost in your love.
> We uphold before you Mark and Elizabeth,
>   who are crushed by the weight of their grief.
> Grant them your peace and mercy
>   that they may continue to believe,
>   and, together with Tessa,
>   who is held in the mystery of your eternal grace,
>   that they might find consolation in their sufferings
>   and hope for the age to come;
>   through Jesus Christ our Saviour
> Amen.'

Mark is vaguely aware of the words washing over him. Now and again one stands out and hammers him sideways. His daughter's name arises in the midst of these ceremonies as if she had some connection with it all. As if that coffin could be linked to Tessa. Hah!

Sooner or later, he feels, I'll need to pull myself together. I'll need to find a way into whatever is going on here, instead of being a bit-part actor in a drama of somebody else's making. But it's not true, of course. None of it is true. This white box, that broken little body; they have nothing to do with Tessa. Any minute now she'll come skipping down the aisle, grinning and screwing up her eyes in that cheeky way she does . . .

I'll not accept it. She can't just stop like that, just disappear out of our lives and never come back. Tessa was too strong, too young, too full of joy and fun and . . .

He's aware of a noise in the vicinity of his lap. Mark looks down to see splatters on the order sheet. His face is wet. He notices his nails are chewed. That used to be a problem when he was young, but not for so many years now.

There must be something I can do; some way of taking control, of sorting things out. Tessa always wanted me to make things better for her. And Elizabeth too, in a strange sort of way, would always assume I could fix whatever problem she brought to me. And I could. Until now.

Now there was this huge wall of indifference. Now there was the damning stare of accusation which had caught Mark by surprise. He'd never seen his wife's face distorted by hatred before. What defence did he have? What can anyone offer against this?

She sits beside him as a stranger. Perhaps he's never known her. And never will again. You can fit a lot in a small wooden box. A whole life.

this morning on the way to school i found a treasure. it wasn't much of a treasure i don't suppose, but i was very excited to find it just the same. it was a necklace thingy with a little gold coin on it. the chain had broken so it must have fallen off some-one's neck. the coin had a picture of a person on it. all my friends at school thought it was probably worth an awful lot of money and i'd be rich.

but when i got it home my dad said it was only a cheap one. he said it was a saint christopher. he said that people wear them to protect them when they're travelling, because this christopher man looks after them. i asked him if he was an angel, but it seems not. he said it was all a load of nonsense anyway. but i don't know—i like it and i found it so i think i might keep it in my pocket just in case. it's all very well for daddy not to believe in it, but someone must have mustn't they? otherwise they wouldn't have had it in the first place.

Chapter Six

He shouldn't be doing it really. Nobody's told him to, and he could get bollocked for trampling all over the inquiry. But Harry feels this one personally. It's on his patch. And he can't get that first picture of the little girl out of his head. It comes back to him at odd times; sitting at a traffic light, or last night while watching the news on television. He's long since forgotten why he joined the police force. There must have been a reason, presumably. But while he's there, if there's one thing he'd like to do it's to get the evil bastard who did this.

He still fancies the choirmaster, even though they can't get anything on him. There's something there, some connection; he can smell it. The sad old meat-beater mentioned something during questioning that came back to Harry during an ad break. He'd met with his vicar, he said, and told him a little of what he called his 'troubles'. What if he'd told him more? You never know what might come out in the act of confession.

And so here he is knocking on the door of the vicar's study. Without authority.

There's surprise on the clergyman's face as he opens the door, and perhaps a little annoyance, but nothing more. Harry notes the man's firm handshake and confident manner. He's used to authority, to telling people what to do. The office is lined with bookshelves, and the desk supports the inevitable computer screen. Behind the vicar on the wall there is a crucifix, and a framed certificate for some sort of theological degree. A man who values his achievements, decides Harry.

'It's about the Tessa Bromley case,' he announces, too tired for pleasantries. 'Obviously you're familiar with it.'

'A terrible business. Let's hope for all our sakes you get the man who did it.'

'We don't need any encouragement, Reverend.'

'Alex, please. I'm not sure how I can help you, Constable . . .?'

'Peters. And it's Sergeant, actually, but let's not stand on ceremony.'

'As I say, I don't know that I can be of any great assistance. I can't say I knew the family well, you understand. They were nominal, really—Easter and Christmas sort of people. Anglican by culture rather than conviction, I'm afraid. Though the little girl, Tessa, had begun coming to Sunday school for about a month before this all happened.'

'You knew her, then?'

'Hardly at all. We'd exchanged a few sentences. I asked her about her parents. She was a bright little thing, charming really. I've come to learn more about her through my part in the funeral arrangements.'

Harry finds himself seduced by the power of that voice; a very persuasive man. He also notices the slightest of tremors at one corner of the minister's mouth. It's nothing really—a slight nervous tic. It wouldn't make any impression at all normally, were it not for the immaculately composed face which it disturbs. Like a tiny flaw in a gemstone. Harry vaguely remembers someone else who had it, but can't recall the details.

'Your choirmaster, Donald Evans, came to see you a few weeks back?'

'Well yes, he did. But you'll appreciate that I can't give you any information about that—the sanctity of the confessional presides, I'm afraid.'

'Yes, I respect your position. Were you aware that we've arrested Mr Evans for indecent exposure? He's been charged with a number of incidents which are alleged to have taken place in the Stoke Newington area over recent months.'

'Good grief. I can hardly . . . Well perhaps I can imagine it. Silly man.'

102

'You might also understand that we have a particular interest in Mr Evans following Tessa's murder. We'd be grateful for any help you'd be able to give us.'

'Help?' asks Alex, staring out of the window. He falls silent for a few moments before continuing. 'I can't really see any connection between Donald and this terrible event. He might be a silly old duffer, but he's not a murderer, for goodness' sake.'

'It can be hard to tell, Reverend. Sometimes the most unlikely people are guilty of crimes. We like to think criminals all have their eyes too close together or a shifty look about them. But in my experience that's not necessarily the case. It doesn't always show on the outside, especially when it comes to these sorts of crimes. I was involved in a case once where a very respected businessman was drugging young boys and sodomising them.'

'I know all that. But give me some credit for evaluating human nature. It's part of what I do for a living. We're both involved in the tracking down of human failure, sergeant, though for different reasons. Nothing which Donald and I talked about would lead me to suspect that he had any involvement in the crime you're investigating.'

Of course, that's where I saw that facial tremor before, Harry recalls.

'He never visited Abney Park Cemetery as far as you know?' he asks.

'We've never discussed it. It's rather ironic, isn't it, this murder taking place in a cemetery? Such terrible events in such a beautiful setting.'

'You know it?'

'Yes, I go there regularly. I find it's a good place to relax and think. As it happens, I suspect I was there on the day of the murder.'

'And you've never come forward to talk to us about it?'

'I would have, of course, if I had had anything to contribute. But I go there for solitude, you understand. I keep out of people's way. I don't remember seeing anyone or anything significant that day.'

'We've interviewed everyone we can find about who was in the cemetery that day. Not one of them has mentioned seeing a vicar.'

'I don't wear clerical clothes—I want to be unobtrusive. I'm afraid I don't even use the front gate, so it's easy for me to slip in and out again without seeing anyone.'

Harry stares at the man. There's not a sign of duplicity or fear. He wouldn't be telling me this if he had anything to hide. Still and all, you have to go where you're taken.

'There might be some details which would help our inquiry, Reverend; some small observation which you've forgotten. The mind plays tricks sometimes, keeps things tucked away in recesses which only emerge after a bit of prying. I'd like you to come into the station and have an interview with some detectives from the Homicide team. Would you be willing to do that?'

'Of course. Whatever I can do to help. But I honestly think it'll be a waste of time.'

'Even so, we'd appreciate it.'

'In that case, I'd be glad to.' Alex smiles.

'Just one other thing,' adds Harry, as if it has just occurred to him. 'We're doing routine blood tests on anyone we can find who had any connection with Tessa. With their permission, of course. It's just a way of eliminating people, really. I imagine you'd have no objection to giving a sample when you come down?'

'Whatever's necessary, sergeant. I've nothing to hide.'

i love having so much space to run and run. this must be the best park ever. the trees whispering with a thousand messages in their leaves. what a lovely big piece of sky—big enough to hold a million clouds, though there arent many today.

my rabbits are the luckiest rabbits in the world, living here. of course they deserve the very best. i wish everyone could see how beautiful they are, with their shiny big eyes. i wish everyone could be as happy as i am right now. i don't know why so many people walk so slow with glum looks on their faces. it

must be awfully boring to have to grow up. i hope i never do.
who's that man over there? i think i know him.

'I hear Blade has a broken finger,' says Kevin. He looks across at the man opposite him, who appears an urbane and settled character. There's not a hint of viciousness about him.

'That so?' replies Joe, with sleepy eyes.

'I've heard some people mention your name in relation to it.'

'You know better than that, padre. What I hear is that he caught it in the cell door. Always was a bit clumsy, was Blade.'

Kevin sighs. He half contemplates raising the subject of revenge, before rejecting it. Prison morality has a logic and completeness of its own. You might as well argue against gravity.

'You knew Hughie McCann, didn't you?' he asks instead.

'Oh yes. I was on the same block with him in my third lag. I had a lot of time for old Hughie. Hard man, he was.' Joe's eyes brighten at the memory.

'He came to see me once when he'd found out his sister was dying of cancer. It took him a good twenty minutes to get round to asking, but what he wanted was for me to pray for her. He looked a bit jumpy, which was unusual for Hughie. So I chatted to him for a while about this sister. It turned out that she'd brought him up for the most part, after his mother died. Anyway, she married later in life and had a few children—he'd been proud of her. She didn't like what he was doing, but she was good to him. One night, he told me, he cut his hand doing a job. Seeing he couldn't go into hospital, he turned up at his sister's house in the early hours of the morning, dripping blood all over the doorstep. She was fairly resourceful, and she stitched him up as best she could.

'But then she got stuck into him. Told him he'd screwed up his life and needed to get a decent job and so on. Well you know how long Hughie's fuse was. Before long they're cursing each other up hill and down dale. The husband wakes up and hears this commotion and calls the police. So before you know it there are sirens outside and they've got Hughie in bracelets. He thinks it's his sister who's turned him in, and he can't believe that the last person he ever trusted has betrayed him. So as he's being led out of the door, he turns and looks over his shoulder and calls out to her, "I hope you die a long death." It's just one of those things you might say when you're angry. But a couple of years later, when he hears she's got cancer, he's sitting there telling me he's scared he's put a curse on her.

'I said to him that there was no connection at all; that it was just one of those things that happens. But I said it might help his peace of mind if he was to send a note to his sister and tell her he forgave her. You'd think I'd suggested he nark on his best mate. His face locked up tight as can be, and I thought for a minute he was going to hit me. There was no way he could let go of it, you see. It was a matter of honour for him. Well his sister got better eventually. She had a breast removed, and went through chemotherapy, and it seemed to do the trick. But Hughie, he died himself when his ulcer burst. He never did let go of his anger at his sister, and never wrote to her either. I met her at his funeral; lovely woman, she was.'

Kevin doodles on the desk with a finger, as if he were just passing the time.

Joe looks at the chaplain, pondering. It's a challenge, and Joe finds it hard to resist a challenge. He can play the game as well.

'Where I grew up was a tough place. You had to be watching your back all the time. I had this friend I used to knock around with—Jamie. Jamie was a bit of a brainbox—knew all the answers to all the questions. Not very good with his fists though, so he was a sitting duck. I used to look out for him. We'd do shoplifting together, occasionally a house, but mostly small stuff. He didn't need to, really, but he liked hanging out with me, and that was the stuff I did. One time we were just walking down the street together, and this geezer we knew is coming the other way. As he's going past Jamie, he puts his shoulder into him and knocks him over. Then he tells him to watch where he's walking.

'I shape up to have a go at this guy, see? I know I can take him. But Jamie jumps up and grabs me by the shoulder. "Leave it out," he says, "let it go." So I think all right then, no skin off my nose. If Jamie wants to let him get away with it, then that's his lookout. About a week later I can't find him around, and then his mum tells me he's up in the hospital. I go up to see him, and there he is, smashed to a pulp with limbs hanging off hooks all over the place. It was the guy who'd put the shoulder in—him and a couple of mates had found Jamie on his own and stepped him. The worst thing about it was he ended up with brain damage. He could talk all right, but he was never any good at school after that.'

Joe pulls at his nose and stares at the chaplain.

'They picked up the signals off him, you see. He'd shown weakness, so they had to take him down. I knew it in my gut and I didn't do anything about it. Jamie didn't know the way things were. He probably thought life would be easier because he hadn't hit back. Nowadays I trust my instincts pretty much all the time.'

Kevin has a rueful smile on his face. A good return.

'What happened to the guys who did it?' he asks, guessing the answer.

'They had an accident. Must have beaten each other up— they were in a mess when the cops found them. Couldn't remember anything. And the leader, the one that had put the shoulder in, he seemed to have spiked himself with a big dose of H right after. He was dead before they could get him to hospital. A shame, but these things happen.'

'Did you ever want to do anything else?' Kevin probes.

'Weren't a lot of choices open to me, padre. People like you, see, you've got all these possibilities. You have to think will I do this or will I do that? You plan your life like it was a trip in the countryside or something. But people like me, we don't think that way. We wake up in the morning and wonder if we'll still be alive at the end of the day. What happens happens. It's like trying to stand upright in a storm—you don't give a toss where you end up, so long as you get through it.'

'That new chap—your cellmate—what d'you think of him?' asks Kevin, changing course.

'He's one of yours,' says Joe. 'He don't know his arse from his elbow. They should've kept him in Classification. I don't like his chances—these animals'll have him for breakfast.'

Kevin can't help glancing down at the file on his desk. If they knew what was in there, he wouldn't make it to tea-time, he's thinking.

Elizabeth slits open another envelope and extracts the card. She reads this new one, again trying to understand the message written on it. None of it makes sense. It's like trying to read a French newspaper, understanding just enough to make it frustrating that you don't know what it's saying. Certain words and the odd phrase are there often enough to register. 'Loss', 'bereavement' (what a strange word it is), 'deepest sympathy', 'condolences'. The jargon of death; as empty and meaningless as what's left of her life.

It shouldn't be possible to keep drawing breaths one after the other. The continued beating of her heart betrays her, pumping blood that can no longer flow in Tessa's veins. Ordinary human conversation seems an unforgivable obscenity—a blatant and deliberate trivialising of her mountain of pain. These friends with their gestures and flowers and cakes—what the fuck am I supposed to do with cake? She would have eaten it, she . . .

Tessa is still there in everything but flesh. Elizabeth can smell her in the bathroom; can hear the door banging open as she rushes in; can feel her hot sweet breath on the back of her neck while piggybacking her up to bed. Every memory has its own unique variation on pain.

She begins tearing the cards up. Slowly at first, and casually. Separating them along their spines. Then with increasing tenacity and frenzy, until there are small bits of cards going in all directions, and she can't see them properly to grip them.

'Fuck you all, fuck you, fuck you, fuck you . . .'

She fades into silence, and the cold chill of unrequited fury.

There is no relief anywhere.

From the doorway, Mark watches as if looking at some other woman. The back of his head aches, but his mouth will not open.

Thompson is smiling, which could be a good sign. Still, Harry's been around long enough not to presume that a smile represents anything, particularly on the face of a superior.

'I should be giving you a ticking off, Peters. You're interfering in my chaps' work.'

'Sir.'

'But you're lucky that it's worked out well for you. He's co-operating, and we've placed him in the cemetery at around the timeframe the pathologist has given us. Nothing significant so far, but we're just walking through it all a second time. He claims he climbed in over the wall where we found the blood.'

'You like him as a suspect, sir?'

'No, I don't think so. He seems straight enough, and he didn't have to come in in the first place. But I'm sure he's going to get us closer; I can feel it in my bones.'

There must be something primitive about territory and tribe. Joe owes Tom nothing. Who is he? A stranger who's landed on the doorstep. There's no history, no common ground; nothing. So why is it Joe feels even the slightest responsibility for him? Because anything happening to someone living on Joe's patch is a slight against Joe. And something is going to happen, there's nothing surer. Joe can smell it in the breeze. Tom is fresh meat, and the pack is circling.

'You need to watch your back, Tom,' he says to him at last.

'What?' Tom looks up from the exercise book that he's been scrawling in for the last twenty minutes.

'Your number's up. Someone's going to have a go at you. You need to keep your eyes open.'

'How do you know? What do you know?' Tom's eyes are clouded with fear. Joe can smell the sourness of it rising from the bunk.

'I know how this place works, that's what I know. You think this is a boarding school? This is the shit-heap of society; that's what it is. And the biggest shits rise to the top. You don't belong here, see. I don't know how you got here, and I don't want to know; but I look at your hands and I can tell that nothing you've ever learned in your life is of any use here. There's only one thing you need to think about here—survival. And right now your prospects don't look too good.'

Joe hoicks back a ball of phlegm to accentuate the risk.

'Why is that? I've tried to keep my head down and not upset anyone.'

'Think of it like a table-tennis ladder,' Joe explains. 'You're the new boy. No one knows where you fit on the tree. So what happens? You have to play a grading game to find out. They're all watching you, see? Trying to pick you. If they go up against you and lose, they go down a rung. But if they beat you, they climb up one. The way I see it, there's a lot of them figuring they can take you one-handed. It's just a matter of who gets in first.'

'So why hasn't it happened yet?'

'Because of me, that's why. They're trying to work out if I'm running shotgun for you. They don't want to pick you and end up with me on their case.'

'And are you? Running shotgun?'

'Nothing in it for me, is there? Why would I look out for your scrawny arse? I've got enough troubles of my own to see me through.'

'What would it take to get you on my side as a sort of protector?'

Joe looks at him, considering.

'You'd have to have something to trade. And right now, the way I see it, you've got nothing I want. You're on your own, Tom.'

Alex declines the offer of a ride home in a police car. He walks instead, taking the chance to clear his head. The questioning has exhausted him. They kept going back over and over the same details. He would have liked to be able to help them. But what was there to tell? A couple of hours sitting alone on his favourite bench, praying and dreaming. There may have been people walking past—there almost certainly were—but he screened them out. He recalls a few vague shapes, and the sound of feet on the gravel, but that's all.

And Tessa; he knew so very little about her. He'd seen her those few times in church, and once perhaps in the park. She was an engaging child, with her dark hair and serious look. How could anyone bring themselves to harm an innocent like that one? Yet they most certainly had.

There had been a moment in the interrogation when a ridiculous thought had suggested itself. He'd wondered fleetingly if they suspected him. They seemed to have lost interest in Donald. It's a strange thing, the way that you begin to feel guilty when questioned about a crime, even though you've had nothing to do with it. Universal guilt, looking for an event to attach itself to.

But this event is too repugnant to even contemplate. Alex wishes there was something else he could offer the police. Some fragment of memory which he could prise loose and contribute as a clue. But there was nothing; nothing at all.

There's a faint light which creeps under the door and washes the old garage in ethereal tones. Mark remembers how happy he was to find the lock-up, with so much demand for them. Tessa wanted to make a playhouse there, but it was too far from home and they worried she might not be safe...

He can smell the mustiness of it now. A mixture of stale grease and slightly damp timber. It reminds him of his father's workshop, where he was allowed to play as long as he put the tools back on their allotted hooks. Perhaps it was there that he learned to enjoy fixing things.

The car seat is comfortable. He leans back into it and allows his head to press against the headrest. Bright-green digital numbers declare the time. The spill of light reflects on the polished walnut dashboard. Through the open windows of the car he

111

can hear the rumble of the outside world. Everybody going about their business.

He feels tired in a way that he has never felt before. Weary to the bone. It's easier to go with it than to fight it; to welcome the narcosis and the womb-like comfort it promises. No choices are needed—just co-operation, the absence of resistance.

It's so easy now. Just one more quarter-turn of the key, and relaxing back into the arms of the one stroking his neck. Why is death pictured as male? She's a seductress—anyone who has got this far knows that. His fingers grip the key and begin to turn. He feels the cold metal under his fingers.

And then an image floats in front of him, unbidden. It's Elizabeth, staring at him in flat white horror. Every micron of pressure he applies to the key is increasing her pain a thousand-fold. She watches mutely.

He releases the key and cries out. Only now, after all this time, does the dam begin to crumble and the massive headwaters push out into consciousness. There, in the gloom, the flood begins its devastation.

Most people don't pay attention to details. I've always considered the small things to be important. It wouldn't be unfair to describe me as fastidious. I like order. Even when I was growing up, I liked to keep everything in its proper compartment. If a book ended up going on the wrong shelf, it upset me greatly. I couldn't get to sleep at night without having everything in its right place.

I could have done other things with my life; I'm sure I could. I had other talents that never found a chance for expression. I imagine I might even have been artistic, given different circumstances. My eye for detail might have been an asset in something like painting.

But then you wonder if you really have as much choice in life as you think you do. Maybe freedom is ultimately an illusion to make us feel as if we have some contribution to make. It's possible that we're simply carried along by the tide of events which surround us. The paths we end up on, couldn't it be that they were inevitable?

In which case it seems inappropriate to talk of guilt and responsibility. We do what we do. We are fated to be the people we are, and to live out the roles that someone else has given us. And not everyone gets the good parts. Some of us have to provide the counterpoint.

if i put my fingers on my wrist i can feel my heart beating. i like the way it does it all by itself without my ever having to stop and think about it. it's weird that your body should do all this stuff on its own. sometimes i try to see how long i can stop breathing for. the funny thing is that even if you wanted to stop breathing, your body won't let you. it just goes ahead and sucks in more air anyway.

yesterday at the park i tried to see if the trees were breathing. i put my ear up against one but i couldn't hear anything. so then i climbed up one, only a little way, and lay back in the branches and closed my eyes. and then i could feel it. its not breathing like we think of it—more of a sighing into the wind. but i felt the life there, just as if i had my fingers on my wrist. i don't think mummy believed me when i told her, but i don't care. there are some things that adults are too old to understand.

afterwards i made up a poem on the way home. i had to hold it in my head all the way until i got home and could write it down. i'll copy it out here.

> people have hearts
> and trees have leaves
> if you listen hard
> you can hear them breathe
>
> the sky has clouds
> and birds have wings
> if you listen hard
> you can hear them sing
>
> gardens have flowers
> and snails have shells
> if you listen hard
> you can hear them tell

god has angels
and rabbits have paws
if you listen hard
you can hear their applause

i think there's a lot more going on in the world than most people notice. one day i hope i'll be able to tell them.

'Control to 426.'

'426 here. Go ahead.'

'Harry, DI Thompson has a message for you that he says will cheer you up.'

'Well I could do with one, love. What is it?'

'He says to tell you they've got a blood match with the vicar. Does that mean something to you?'

'Darling, it means everything to me. Tell him thanks for letting me know, and I'll catch up with him when I come in.'

'Okay Harry. Control out.'

The sudden shudder causes a small cry to emerge from Mary. Alex looks up from his book.

'It's all right, she explains. 'Someone must be walking on my grave.'

Alex lays the book aside and frowns at the noise of the television bouncing through the wall from the next room.

'It's Ross,' she says. She sits for a few moments observing her husband. His face has changed since they first met, though not as much as hers. His hair has begun to grey at the sides, which only helps to make him look suave. The steady brown eyes are as embracing and commanding as ever. The hint of lines around the corners, but less than you might expect from the passage of years. He's more confident now—more sure of himself. But more distant as well. You'd think you would get to know someone pretty much exhaustively after living with him so long. But with the passage of years, she's less certain she knows him at all. Then again, she's growing less certain that she knows herself.

'What are you thinking about?' asks Alex. It's a question with a long history in their relationship, and he smiles at getting first-serve advantage.

She screws up her face in response.

'I was thinking of how little we knew each other when we first got married,' she says. It's almost true.

'No less than any other couple, I imagine. Though looking back, it's frightening. What a huge commitment it is to take on. But it's easier when you're young—you never consider what might go wrong.'

'Do you think about that now? What might go wrong?'

'Very little. We've been together long enough now to feel reasonably safe.'

'Not just with us, though Alex. I mean with anything. Sometimes I wake up at night with a terrible sense of dread—that's something that never happened when I was younger. I sometimes think that it's having children which has made me nervous. You're just so aware of the dangers that are out there. And then there are horrible things like the Tessa Bromley murder which just seem to make the whole universe threatening.'

'I don't want to sound pious, but doesn't your faith come into it somewhere?'

Mary looks down at the carpet before answering. The intervening silence adds poignance to her response.

'It used to, I think. It seemed all very simple at one stage. I did what I could for God, and God took care of the rest, including keeping us all safe. But when we came so close to losing Nancy, it shook me to the core. I realised that things could still fall apart, and there were no guarantees that I'd be protected from disaster. Ever since then it's been as if I've been waiting for the other shoe to drop. I still feel scared when Nancy's out late at night, or Ross forgets to ring and tell us where he is. Even this interview you had with the police; that has me disturbed.'

'You worry about so many things, Martha,' Alex quotes from the gospels. He walks over to where Mary is sitting, and, standing behind her chair, begins to massage her shoulders.

'I'm a hopeless case, Alex. I don't know what's going on with me at the moment. I feel awful; I cry at the slightest provocation; I have trouble sleeping at night. I'm all over the place like a teenager. If only I knew what it was that was unsettling me, I could do something about it.'

'Do you want to talk about it?'

'No more than I am now. I'm sorry Alex. I know I've been acting like a cow lately, and you've been very patient with me. I suspect it'll all blow over and I'll find my feet again. Just give me a little time.'

'All shall be well,' quotes the man with his hands caressing her neck, 'and all manner of things shall be well.'

'All right,' continues Thompson. 'Let's not get too excited yet. We still haven't got enough. We have the blood match, we have existing knowledge of the girl, we have time and place. But we've got no motive, no previous history and no other evidence.'

The assembled police officers are tensed and keen. They have the scent of closure in their nostrils. This is the vulnerable stage, when a case can be ruined by over-enthusiasm on the part of investigators. Thompson doesn't want this one blown.

'We're going to turn him over, obviously. We'll go in at dawn to do the house, and bring the whole family in for questioning. Delta squad will handle that end of things, with Ernie's boys doing the search. The rest of you I want on the vicar's background and movements. I know you're all wound up by this and want it cleared. But let me remind you again, it's careful, basic police work we want from you. Keep it slow, keep it steady, keep it professional. We might have our man, we might not. Our job is to prove it one way or the other.

'One more thing. I want wraps kept on this as best we can. It's going to be tricky, but do your best to be discreet. On the chance that the man's innocent, we don't want to destroy his life unnecessarily.'

There's an angry red sky over Stoke Newington as dawn breaks. The city is awake, though only just. A few early-shift workers gather at bus stops. The air is sweetened with a yeasty fragrance as bakeries exhale. It's the quietness you notice at that hour of the morning. A reverent pause before the action.

Cars are sliding quietly into position. Their closing doors thud along the echoing street as if in warning. Somewhere a dog begins barking.

Alex shifts in his sleep.

The door resounds to a gloved knock.

Mary sits on the hard chair, weeping. There's a policewoman in uniform sitting opposite her.

'Where are my children?' demands Mary between sobs.

'They're just answering a few questions. You'll see them soon enough,' promises the young constable.

'What's it all about? Is it the Tessa Bromley case?'

'I'm afraid I don't know, Mrs Hanson. There'll be a detective along to ask you a few questions shortly. There's nothing to be frightened of. Would you like another cup of tea?'

She's been trained to be civil.

'So you skinned your knuckles climbing over the wall? Any sign of that now?'

'No, well there wouldn't be, would there? It's healed up. It wasn't much of a scrape, but it bled a lot. You know how it is.'

'And was there a reason you didn't mention this to us the first time we questioned you?'

'I didn't think it was important. I scraped my hand, for goodness' sake. How's that supposed to contribute anything to your investigation? I didn't even notice I'd done it at the time. It wasn't till I was sitting on the bench inside that I looked down and noticed what had happened.'

'Do you think you might have dropped blood anywhere else, Reverend?'

'No—I don't think so. On my clothes, perhaps. I don't know. Look, what is this, for goodness sake? You can't seriously be treating me as a suspect? I'm an Anglican vicar. You've got my wife and children through there. Do I look like a rapist?'

117

Thompson is entirely unmoved.

'I don't care if you're the Queen Mother. And no, you don't look like a rapist any more than anyone else does. They don't come in particular packages, you understand. Just answer the questions we put to you, please. Now, did you wash the clothes you were wearing that day shortly afterwards?'

Nancy is more scared than she's ever been in her life. She keeps waiting for her father to come through the door and clear it all up, but he hasn't emerged. Such dumb questions. How would she know what her father does on his day off? She's tried to tell them who he is, but they don't seem to understand.

They asked her if he'd ever touched her. She didn't know what they meant. Of course he touched her. How was a father supposed to bring up his children without touching them? But then they used the word 'intimately', and she saw what they were asking and recoiled from it. How could they? What a foul, disgusting suggestion to be making. She got angry with them and started shouting, and then she was crying and crying.

But still her father doesn't come.

There's a knock on the door of the interview room, and DI Thompson is summoned out. It's Johnson on the phone, in charge of the search team.

'I think I might have some good news for you.'

'Go on.'

'It's a bit early to say as yet, but we've found a roll of masking tape in a kitchen drawer. The brand and width match what we're looking for. I've got it bagged up and on its way to Mullins, and told him we want it tested yesterday. With any luck we'll get something indicative before you've finished questioning him.'

Thompson takes a deep breath before replying. It could just be that things are beginning to turn his way.

Chapter Seven

The night before there is a dream.

Alex wakes with his face frozen rigid in fear. He's scared to breathe lest it all starts again. The dream fills the room; more present than consciousness.

He's walking in the park on a sunny afternoon. There are people all around, enjoying the warmth of the day. They nod to him and smile as he passes by. He's wearing his clerical collar. He can feel it against his neck, and it seems to be shining like a beacon.

Off in the distance he can see Mary and the children. They're sitting on the grass. They see him and call out, beckoning him closer. How happy they look, smiling and waving. He begins to walk in their direction.

Something makes him look down. The path he's on has a ragged diagonal crack running across it. He deliberately steps right on it, laughing in the face of childhood superstition. But as his foot touches it, the crack opens into a chasm, and the slabs of concrete fall away from under his feet.

He's tumbling into the darkness, into the great void which lies under the crust of the world. It's cold and black, and there is a terrible empty silence. He falls and falls, and he's aware that what he's falling toward is terribly dangerous.

The fear is enough to wake him, and leave him here now trying to regain his breath and composure. The spectres of the night.

*

nightmare ('naɪt,mɛə) *n* **1** a terrifying or deeply distressing dream. **2** an event or condition resembling a terrifying dream. **3** a thing that is feared. **4** (formerly) an evil spirit supposed to harass or suffocate sleeping people.

Tom has taken to hiding out in the cell much more since Joe's warning. He's nervous and watchful. He spends most of his time reading, occasionally writing in the exercise book.

He's not bad as a cellmate, reflects Joe. Leaves you your space; not in your face all the time. Poor broken-arsed bastard, still claiming innocence. About to lose it any day by the looks of things. Almost cause to feel sorry for him, if pity existed in a prison.

Tom looks up now from his book, and sees Joe watching him. He's at something of a loss. None of the old rules apply. All of the subtle learnings about human interaction are useless here; worse than useless. They lead you into trouble. He feels like a child in an adult's world, watching but not included.

'What d'you write in that book?' Joe asks him.

'Thoughts, reflections, whatever—it's a sort of journal. I started doing it years ago and it's become a habit.'

'So what d'you do with the stuff you write there?'

'Nothing much. Sometimes I might read back through old journals to see what I was thinking about. But mostly it's just a way of processing what goes on in life. A bit like a diary. Haven't you ever done that?'

'Me? Nah. I don't write much at all if I can help it. No point in leaving clues about with the filth breathing down your neck. I keep track of things all right, but I do it where no one can get at it—in my head.'

'You're a solitary sort of character, aren't you?'

'Leave off the psychoanalysing, all right? If I need a mind-fucker, I'll use the bird from Prison Services—she's a sight better looking than you. I keep myself to myself is all. I once did a lag with a Palestinian lad. He told me this Arab proverb: "Buy, don't sell." Not bad, as a rule of thumb.'

'I'm not sure I understand you,' admits Tom.

'Too many people are sellers, you know? They want every-

120

one to buy what they've got, so they put it all out there on display for the customers. But every item you put on the counter gives some bastard a potential handle on you to screw you over. Give them nothing, I say. Play your cards close to your chest. Buy, whenever you can. Keep your eyes and ears open, watch and listen. Observe. Take it all in, and keep it there. Maybe there'll be a time when it'll be useful. Give nothing away you don't need to.'

'Why is it you look out for George, then?'

'Ah, for Chrissake, why is the moon yellow? Don't pull my tit, Tom, or I might smack you over myself. George is an old-timer, a decent lagger who knows the way things are. He's done his time, see, and he's looked after me when I was too young to know shit from clay. That was the way things were, in the old days. Honour among crims. All gone now, of course. The place is full of these viscious little mothers who only care about themselves. You can't count on the code any more, so you end up having to play them at their own game. But they're stupid, see? No brains. It's all aggro with no style.'

Tom stares blankly for a few moments. He blinks three times before opening his mouth.

'I know you said I had nothing to trade with you for protection, and you're right. But I'm terrified of what's going to happen to me. I won't survive on my own...'

'Stop right there. I don't care if you're so scared you're pissing your pants—you don't ever admit it, you understand? Don't even admit it to yourself. Squash it down, deny it. And especially don't let anyone else know. They can smell it, see? Like vicious dogs, you know? They catch the scent of your fear, and they home in on it. This is a different place, see. I don't know what planet you come from, Tom, but in here the rules have all changed. The place is populated by bastards, and your only hope's to become a bastard like them.

'In the nice civilised society you come from, you learn to be polite and generous and decent, right? In here, all of those are liabilities. They're weak spots, and you can't afford to have weak spots. What you have to do is reach down inside yourself and find all of the stuff that's been suppressed over the years. Get hold of your dark side—your hatred, your rage, your bitterness—and dredge it to the surface. Find the mongrel in you, Tom, or you're going to be living in hell for a long time. You've got to be hard on the outside, see? Like wearing a suit of armour; like a crab or something. No gaps, no weakness, no point of entry. Once you learn that, then you can do what you like on the inside. That's your private space, but only as long as the security fences are strong enough to keep out the animals.

'You have to become an evil bastard, Tom. Have you got that in you?'

Tom is staring into the distance, with no sign that he's understood any of it.

The old man turns it all over once again. He's seen what he has seen. He's done what he has done. He didn't ask for it, didn't seek it out. But now it's on the inside of him, part of him. Like a cancer. It lies in wait for him, until he's almost forgotten and begun to enjoy life. And then it rises to the surface, swift and silent and reptilian.

What can he do? What could he have done? Nothing. What's happened has happened. Sleeping dogs and all that. I don't want to know, I don't want to know.

A woman walking a small dog turns to look at him, and he realises he's muttering.

'I don't want to know,' he says again.

'Mullins here.'

'Well?' asks Thompson. So much of the case rides on this one answer. He closes his eyes and tries not to anticipate.

'Exact match,' is the reply.

'Absolutely sure?'

'It's the roll, no doubt about it. Not only the same brand, but we've got a match on the fresh end. One hundred per cent. It doesn't get any better than that.'

Thompson at last lets his breath release in a slow sigh.

'Good work, George. Thanks.'

122

He pauses for a minute to collect his thoughts. We must be there by now. Better run it past the prosecutor's office, just the same. I think we've got you, you evil bastard.

Elizabeth narrows her eyes at the sight. He looks like a derelict. Dark circles under his eyes, hair unkempt, snot and tears running into each other on his face.

'Mark?' she asks.

He stands motionless in the doorway, a suffering statue. She reaches to embrace him, reluctantly and stiffly. For a moment they stand there like embarrassed strangers. She leads him silently inside and shuts the door. He's mute in grief.

Elizabeth once more puts her arms round him, this time leaning into his chest, her own tears flowing again. And then she reaches up and kisses him. It begins as a brush of the lips, but quickly becomes a painful, crushing, biting act of aggression.

There's a kind of madness which ensues. They're at each other like animals. Clothes are torn and buttons spun across the floor. Mark is conscious of an erection bigger than anything he's known before.

They lunge at each other, striking and flailing and wrestling their way to the carpet.

'Fuck me,' implores Elizabeth in a foreign tongue.

There's a violence to their lovemaking. A desperate, driving rush to the climax. When it comes they are bucking and groaning and writhing on the floor. For a few sweet seconds the wave of pleasure purges the pain from their souls.

A few brief seconds.

what happens when people die? i know they get put in boxes and planted in the ground like seeds, but is that the end of it? i like wandering around the gravestones at the church. it feels safe there somehow. mummy says i shouldn't play there because it's creepy, but i don't find it creepy at all. i've never seen a ghost so i don't know if there really are any or not. more likely it's just a story that boys make up to frighten themselves.

i remember when snowy died. he was there one day, and then i didn't see him for a long time. it wasn't till i asked the man at the park where he was that i found out that he was dead. and when i asked where he was now, the man just smiled at me and went away. daddy said he was eating grass in the green fields of the sky. i don't know. all i know is that he's not there any more, and the rabbits and i all miss him. it seems strange that he should just stop being alive.

i don't think i want to stop being alive.

Alex is calm, despite all this fuss. He has nothing to fear, nor cause to be concerned. The chair is uncomfortable, and the bare room cold. He's happy to assist the police in any way he can, but they've overstepped the limits of enthusiasm with this disruption of his family. It's time the whole thing was over, so that they can all go home and get on with the day.

The uniformed policeman sitting near the door is silent and unsympathetic.

Approaching footsteps bring hope and distraction. The door opens to reveal the man who's been asking all the questions—Thompson, wasn't that his name? He stands there staring at Alex, saying nothing.

'Well,' says Alex in perfectly modulated tones, as if concluding a pastoral visit. 'I expect you've cleared up all the loose ends and we can get on with things? I've a busy day, and I imagine you have too.'

'A few more questions, I'm afraid, Reverend Hanson. Tell me again about the roll of tape we found in your drawer.'

'There's not very much I can help you with. As I said, I'm not sure where it came from. I was surprised to find it. I expect Ross picked it up from somewhere—he's a bit of a magpie, always on the lookout for treasures. Why don't you ask him about it?'

'It appears to have your fingerprints on it.'

'Yes, well it would, I imagine. I picked it up when I discovered it and asked Mary where it had come from.'

'Did you rape and murder Tessa Bromley?'

Alex looks at the inspector in sheer incredulity. For a few moments he can't even formulate a reply. There's not much that surprises him, but this has him stunned into silence. How strange that such a gap can open up, as if your own world has broken free like an ice floe and is drifting away from the mainland. The policeman studies Alex's face as he waits.

'Don't be ridiculous,' he manages at last. 'I absolutely did no harm to that little child whatsoever, and I'll swear to that effect on the Bible if you wish me to. I find it incredible that you could make such a preposterous suggestion. You must be desperate if you're drawing me into your net of suspicion.'

'Let me spell it out for you, Mr Hanson. We have you at the crime scene at the time of the murder. We have your blood on the cemetery wall where we suspect the girl was taken in there. And now we have the roll of tape with which young Tessa was bound, discovered in the drawer of your home with your fingerprints all over it! Would you like to give me any good reason why I shouldn't arrest you for the crime?'

Alex is reeling backwards, clutching for the arms of the chair. The corner of his mouth is twitching furiously. He seems to be having trouble catching his breath. His face is distinctly pale. At last he draws a large draft of air, shakes his shoulders like a dog refreshing itself, and replies.

'Because I didn't do it, inspector. I'm a minister of the gospel, an evangelical, a representative of God. I find your suggestion absolutely repugnant. I don't know how that tape has come into my house, and I've given you an explanation of what I was doing in Abney Park on that day. I can understand why it looks to you as if I've been involved, but you're quite mistaken. And all the time you're wasting interviewing me and my family is time which could be spent pursuing the person responsible.'

Thompson has the flint in his eye of twenty-seven years' police work; half a lifetime of sniffing for the truth. For the present his instincts are clouded.

'I'll tell you what I'm going to do, Hanson. I'm going to leave you to think for half an hour. And then I'm going to come back and talk to you again. Perhaps you may have re-membered something else to help us, so that we don't need to end up charging you with murder.'

'The truth will still be the truth in thirty minutes. Perhaps it's you who should take the time to think,' replies Alex evenly.

i need to find the doorway. i have to get across to the other side, where everything will be the same. i don't know what to do, i don't know what to do.

> **violate** (ˈvaɪəˌleɪt) *vb (tr)* **1** to break, disregard, or infringe (a law, agreement, etc.). **2** to rape or otherwise sexually assault. **3** to disturb rudely or improperly; break in upon. **4** to treat irreverently or disrespectfully.

'Give us a fag, will you Harry? I feel the need for some nico-tine.'

The canteen at the station is cramped and dirty. There's been talk of refurbishment for the last five years, but somehow the budget never runs to it. Cockroaches scuttle under the cup-boards if you switch on the lights suddenly. Thompson has often thought of it as some sort of symbol for the work they do. He prods at the grey coffee with a stained plastic spoon which might have been white once. Harry slides the packet across the table.

'I hear you've got him with the tape,' he prompts. Though Thompson hardly looks like he's riding a wave of exhilaration.

'I don't know, Harry, I just don't know. We've got a strong case which points right to him. But there's something I don't like. He's a clergyman, for God's sake. And not a bent one, either. No sign of deviation anywhere. Married with a couple of kids, respected in his parish. He's cooperative, confident, even arrogant. It doesn't fit. Something's not right.'

'I can't see why anyone would set him up. He doesn't move in those sort of circles.'

'I know that. But I'm running out of options that make sense.'

Harry looks at his superior across the table. They joined the

126

force about the same time, though have only worked the same station for the last ten years. Both of them are old school cops, working by gut feelings more than computer profiles. They respect each other.

'You're going to let him walk?'

'I'm not sure. I want to wait for the legal beagles. But I don't want to bang up the wrong man, and have the offender still prowling the streets. We need something else, Harry. We need him to crack if he's the one.'

'I don't think that's very likely. I can't see that at all.'

They lie there on the floor afterwards, drained. It takes them some time to break the silence. They both recognise the sex for what it was; an act of angry escapism, a furious stabbing rejection of the present. But it has somehow managed to shift things, to tear the membrane of silence which has cocooned them in private pain.

'I don't know if I can bear it,' says Elizabeth to the ceiling. Mark parades a variety of responses in his imagination, before dismissing them. It's like trying to drain the ocean with a tumbler. He guiltily recalls his own temptation to end the pain for ever.

'I'm not sure there's much of a choice,' he says at last.

'Do you think she's all right, Mark?' Elizabeth asks after another long pause. Her voice is that of a child at bedtime.

'I don't know what you mean,' he struggles to answer, reeling under the weight of memory.

'Do you think she . . . that there's some place for children after death, that there's someone to look after her? I can't stand the thought that she might be alone.'

'Oh God, I don't know. I don't know what to believe. You were always more religious than me. But for the first time in my life, I want to believe in something more. I want her to be safe and loved and cherished. But what I don't know is if that's just another way for me to avoid reality or not. I'd like to say she's fine, but she's not fine, she's . . .'

'Tessa!' says Elizabeth angrily. 'Why can't we say her name?

127

Tessa, Tessa, Tessa, Tessa. She never hurt anyone, Mark. She didn't have a bad bone in her body. My little Tessa. Why would anyone do that to her? How could they do it? What sort of human being is it that could take a little girl like that, and . . .'

'I've never told you, but when I first saw her, when I saw her in the mortuary . . . I felt disconnected from her. As if it was someone else's child. I knew it was Tessa, but I couldn't make the connection between that broken little body and our Tessa, with all the life she had. It was as if someone had made a dummy of her, but she was still out the back playing. I still don't always believe that she's dead, you know . . .'

'You know how horrible it's got? I look at children in the street, and I think 'Why not them?' Why did it have to be Tessa? There are so many children around, some of them dull nasty little brats—why Tessa? I think if I could take one of these others and swap them for my little girl so that it was them that got murdered and not her . . .'

'The worst part is that it never changes. Every day you wake up, and before you can even think what's causing it, there's that crushing weight sitting on your chest. And then it all comes sneaking back, and it's even worse than you can imagine it to be. Whatever you do, whatever little mind games you play, you can't change it. You can't wind it back and replay it. It just goes on and on . . .'

'All those years of trying for a baby and not being able to. All that waiting and praying and trying everything under the sun. And now sometimes I think, God save me sometimes I think . . .'

'No! Don't ever think that. Don't ever take away what she gave us. However much we suffer now, it has to have been worth it, Elizabeth. That's what we've got now; those years that she gave us. That's all we've got.'

'I'm sorry,' she sobs, 'I'm so sorry.'

I've always wanted people to like me. I suppose a psychiatrist might say I'm hungry for affection, but I think the truth is that all of us like to be popular. Some people have an arrogance that puts them beyond caring, but I've never had that luxury.

I may have presented the better parts of my personality, and concealed that which wasn't so attractive, but I'm sure I'm not unique in that. I don't regard that as deception; in fact, it could be regarded as a commitment to virtue.

There was a story I heard somewhere so long ago that I've forgotten the circumstances. It concerned the daughter of a Chinese emperor. She was exquisitely beautiful. When it came time for her to be married, her father was determined to find the best possible groom for her. So he made a public declaration that there would be a search for potential husbands, and that aspiring contenders should present themselves at the royal palace for inspection.

Off in a corner of the kingdom lived a man who was a petty thief and villain. When he heard of the emperor's search, he began to dream of the fabulous wealth that would come with marriage into the royal family. But his face betrayed him—it was distorted by his dishonourable life. What could he do?

He went to the best mask-maker in all of China. There he paid to have a mask made which would transform his face into that of a handsome and well-bred noble. The mask-maker took great care, and the result was the finest mask he had ever created. When the impostor put it on, he was entirely transformed. He looked into the mirror and smiled.

Such was the craft of the mask-maker that the man, when he presented himself at the palace, was selected to be the husband of the emperor's daughter. She was delighted with him, and spent much time simply gazing at his face. Their marriage was a great occasion for the whole of the kingdom.

In order to maintain his pretence, the man began to act in accordance with his looks. Because his face showed generosity and kindness, he acted kindly and generously. Because people expected wisdom and insight, he considered his words before uttering them. Because he radiated goodness in his visage, he began to live as he imagined a good man would live.

One day a jealous villager from the man's hometown travelled to the emperor and revealed the deception. The emperor was furious, and ordered the trickster beheaded. While he awaited execution, the *man was visited in prison by his beautiful wife. She was curious, she said. Just once, before he died, she wanted to look at his true face.*

In great trepidation, the man began to remove the mask which he had worn since the day it had been made for him. Finally it was stripped away, and in shame he turned to face the woman he'd betrayed. She was furious with him.

Why have you played this trick on me, she asked him. Why have you pretended to have fooled me? Bewildered, the man asked for a mirror. When one was produced, he was shocked to discover a face identical to the one which the mask-maker had so carefully fabricated. By living according to his mask, the man had become what he had acted. And so his life was spared.

That story shaped my life. I think it may help you to understand me, and how things went wrong.

Perkins has been a Crown prosecutor for as long as anyone can remember. He seems mild and inoffensive, with round spectacles and a small moustache. A paunchy, balding man with a dark mole on his chin. It all makes for a useful disguise for the snake-like mind lying in concealment. Many a witness has woken too late to the latent danger.

Thompson is glad to have him on his side. They've worked together on a number of successful cases, and the inspector prefers him to some of the new ones who carry laptop computers and business cards. He listens now while Perkins makes his usual masterly summary of the case thus far. Remarkable, considering the brief survey he's had of the evidence.

'Until a few minutes ago,' says Perkins, removing his glasses and peering through them at arms length, 'I would have said your case was borderline but worthy of pursuit. I would have advised you to arrest the man, and trusted in your usual competent work to gather the extra detail necessary for conviction. That's what I would have said.'

The weary detective is not so tired as to miss the implication that the tide has somehow turned.

'And what exactly is it that leads you to revise your opinion?'

'I had a phone call from the chief prosecutor. It seems he plays bridge with the bishop. They went to the same school, and their wives are on a committee together—something to do with multiple sclerosis, I understand. Anyway, the bishop's had a word in his ear. Frightfully upset that one of his best vicars has been dragged into the station like a common criminal. Obviously some sort of mistake, the man couldn't possibly have anything to do with that sort of case.

'The chief prosecutor is of course cautious. He doesn't want to interfere in the case, naturally. He just wants to make sure that we give due weight to any reservations we might have. He'll leave it completely in our hands, and knows that any decision we make will be based on the clear evidence to hand.'

'I see,' Thompson responds. 'And so you'll be advising us to make our case a little stronger before arrest?'

'I'm sorry. I think for both our sakes we need to tread carefully in this sort of territory. Both of us know there's room for ambiguity anyway. We'll simply be erring on the side of caution. A bit more legwork before we can spring the trap, I'm afraid. Of course it's your decision ultimately.'

And that, both of them know perfectly well, is an outright lie.

He's begun to look forward to the shower. It's an echoing concrete bunker, and he showers in full view of several other prisoners. But the water is hot, and Tom luxuriates in the sensation of a purging cleanliness. It's not much different from the shower shed at the ground where he played rugby, if you bend your imagination a little. And those were some of the happiest days of his life. He was good at rugby, a fast winger with a beguiling step.

Amid the sluicing water and banks of steam he finds it easy to drift a little, to find some continuity with other showers in other places at other times. It's an escape not found in many other places in the prison.

He leans his head back and allows the torrent to massage his face, with its hot cleansing pressure. There's a sensation something like contentment. He allows himself to drift with it, relaxing.

The sudden piercing of his retreat comes as a psychic as well as physical assault. His senses flail like a fish flapping as they respond to unexpected intrusion.

There's a calloused hand which has gripped his scrotum, squeezing. And at the same time an erect penis is thrusting hard up against his anus. An arm wrapped across his chest prevents him from turning.

'Fancy a bit of this, do you darling?' The voice rasping in his ear is full of menace. Tom recognises it as that of Hammer, a Scotsman with a piece missing from one ear. He's been looking at Tom strangely over the last few days.

Afterwards Tom thinks of a whole range of responses. Anything would have been better than the stunned silence which passes for acquiescence. He knows he has failed to learn anything of what Joe has been teaching.

The worst thing of all is the shame. The unbearable knowledge that in those few seconds of sexual assault, his own penis began to swell in response. And Hammer felt it; could not have failed to.

The showers will never again be a place of refuge.

she looks like me, that little girl lying in a white box. but she can't be, because i'm up here. it's so good to be able to fly like this. I like looking down on people from above. it's a dreary old song they're singing, and they do all seem rather glum. she's very still, that pretty little girl.

mummy and daddy are there! i can see them in the front, but they're not singing. i think mummy's been crying. i wonder how i can make her happy? there's no need to cry, mummy; i'm up here. can't you see me? i'm just having some fun flying. i'll come back soon, i promise. i hope i haven't upset you, going away like this. sometimes i just get caught up in what i'm doing and forget the time, and then before i know it, i'm already late for getting back. don't be sad—i do love you.

i know i shouldn't have gone with the man after all you said to me. but i thought it would be all right just this once. i thought i'd still get home in time. and now i'm enjoying this flying so much that i've quite forgotten where i'm supposed to be. i'm on my way home, mummy and daddy. i'm on my way home.

'I'm going to release you, Reverend,' Thompson confesses. 'I wouldn't want you to think that we have no interest in you, however. As I've already outlined, there's some strong evidence which links you with the crime. We're taking you at your word, in the circumstances, that you're the victim of a false trail. But in the meantime we'll be pursuing a number of possibilities, one of which is that you're the man we're looking for. I want to formally caution you not to move outside of London in the next week or two without informing me first of the nature of your journey. And we may wish to question you further at some later date. Understood?'

'You have your job to do, Inspector Thompson, as I have mine. I bear you no malice in the pursuit of truth. I'm just pleased that you've seen reason and decided not to pursue ridiculous charges which would only bring embarrassment both to my position and to yours. I'm happy to co-operate in any way I can. I just hope that next time you wish to talk to me or members of my family, you call at a more convenient time.'

This with a vicar's reassuring smile, by way of reconciliation. Thompson has the unmistakable impression that he's being patronised.

'Show Mr Hanson the way out,' is his only response. When the interview room is empty, Thompson sits alone and stares at the table. As a younger man he might have felt angry and frustrated. Now he simply feels very old.

It's something she has avoided until now. She remembers back to dental treatment when she was a schoolgirl. Sometimes, when the Novocain was wearing off and sensation beginning to return, she would worry at the freshly drilled tooth with a finger. It increased the pain, but in a curiously satisfying way.

Elizabeth extracts the album from the bookcase where it

133

has been waiting all this time, and places it closed upon the table. She toys with the corner of the cover for a few moments. Then she rises, and hunts amid the bottles in the corner cabinet. It's mostly Mark who buys the spirits, and even he rarely touches them in the absence of guests. She settles on whisky as the most familiar and trustworthy.

The taste is bitter and unwelcome to her palate, but the spreading warmth in her stomach provides the comfort she's looking for. Another few gulps and she's ready to open the album.

It begins in pregnancy, with profiles hoping to accentuate the small bulge in her belly. There's one a few months on in just bra and knickers. Elizabeth remembers feeling ashamed to pick the photos up from the chemist. But as Mark had predicted, no one was in the slightest bit interested. She notices that she's smiling in all of the pictures, with the slightly arrogant air of accomplishment. She recalls feeling radiantly superior to women who carried nothing in their womb.

She never got that big at all, when you look at it now. It felt huge at the time. The last month would have been unpleasant if it hadn't been for the overwhelming anticipation.

And then with a turn of the page, they start. The photos of this new person who has arrived in their lives. Mark had wanted to take a camera into the delivery suite, but she absolutely forbade it, and suspected it wasn't allowed anyway. So the first picture is about an hour after the birth, when the baby has been cleaned and prodded and returned.

Elizabeth is in it, with the lopsided grin produced by a combination of motherhood and Pethidine. But the centre is of course Tessa. Her eyes open, a shock of black hair, newly red skin and a kind of clothes peg clamping the blackened umbilical cord. It could be any child at birth, thinks Elizabeth now. There's no way that the camera can recall the magic, the blessedness, the overwhelming astonishing awe of the moment which enveloped the pair of them. Only memory can supply that.

Surprising herself, Elizabeth smiles again now.

The photos go on. How many different ways can there

be of capturing the same tiny human being? Mark had bought a box-load of films on special at the supermarket, she remembers.

The images begin to change. Elizabeth can see it there even in the first pictures of course, but gradually with age the features shift and rearrange themselves into the first intimations of personality. The eyes remain the same: cheeky, curious, insightful, devilish.

Tessa eating. Tessa at toilet. Tessa playing with toys. Tessa sleeping. Tessa banging a piano. Tessa laughing. Tessa blowing out candles. Tessa doing dress-ups. Tessa swimming. Tessa in school-clothes. Tessa with grandparents. Tessa holding a huge white rabbit.

The large album is incomplete. The last lot of photos have been jammed in, still in their packet, awaiting mounting. Elizabeth opens the envelope. The first of them is Tessa at Hampstead Heath, on a perfect afternoon.

She fills the tumbler half full with whisky this time, and drains most of it in one draught. As she smiles again at her beautiful daughter, the rolling tears collect at the corners of her mouth.

He could have asked them to drop him further up the street, and walked a hundred yards or so to the house. But he doesn't mind. He has nothing to hide. In fact he makes a point of thanking the uniformed policemen for their courtesy. The older one in the passenger seat is the sergeant who first interviewed him. Who watches him now as he breezes up to the front door. Who sighs in resignation.

Mary and the children have been returned sometime earlier. He calls out as he closes the door, to let them know he's back. There's no response. Alex wanders through to the kitchen, where he finds his wife clutching an empty cup and staring at him.

'All finished,' he reports, as if returning from morning eucharist. But already he can see in her eyes that this is not to be so easily dismissed.

'Where're the children?' he asks, hoping to delay the inevitable.

'Nancy's gone off with Daniel, terribly upset. Ross is in his room wearing headphones and banging his head against the wall.'

'Any chance of a cup of tea?'

'For God's sake sit down, Alex. And don't say a word about taking the Lord's name in vain or I'll hit you, I swear I will. This is not some pastoral visit we've all been on. We've just been subjected to a dawn raid by the police; held and questioned for hours. I'm shattered, and the children are ashamed and frightened. So don't come in here with your false jollity in the hopes of cheering us all up. You're a suspect in the rape and murder of a child, Alex. Have you understood that? I thought they'd arrested you. For a while there I thought . . . I can't stand it, do you hear? I want to know what's going on.'

Alex walks behind his wife and begins to massage her shoulders. She bridles and pulls away. He finally sits at the table and looks her in the eye.

'For goodness sake, Mary. Have we been married all this time and you still don't know me? I can't believe that even you . . . It's simply a case of misleading evidence. I happened to be in the wrong place at the wrong time, and the police have added up two and two and come up with five. I know it's distressing for all of you, and I wish I could have prevented it. But once these things get under way, it's impossible to stop them. It hasn't exactly been easy for me, you know. But it's over now. They've cleared it up and it's all finished.'

'What about the tape, Alex? They kept asking me about that blasted tape. It's got something to do with Tessa's murder, hasn't it?'

Alex stares at the back of his hand for a moment.

'They seem to think it's the tape she was bound up with. I don't know for the life of me how it came to be in our drawer. You remember me asking when I found it there the first time? Have you asked Ross about it?'

'He just says he knows nothing about it. He's gone sullen

136

on me. This is horrible, this is worse than I could have imagined. There is a link to us, isn't there? If they found that tape in our house . . . And you were there, Alex, in the cemetery.'

'I'll not dignify this turn of conversation, Mary,' rules Alex with full Anglican pomposity. 'I'll not have you questioning my integrity, however upset you are. Now this is an unfortunate incident, and I don't understand quite how the confusion has arisen, but it's behind us now. I have explained my movements to the police; I don't expect to have to explain them to my wife.'

'Oh, grow up Alex!' cries Mary, hurling the cup across the room.

Harry's just called in at the newsagent's for a packet of mints and to say hello to Rajeeb, who runs it. It's on his way out that he spots the old man on the bench seat. They've had him in once or twice for drunk and disorderly, but he's a harmless enough chap.

Can't remember his name, thinks Harry. But he smiles at him in greeting just the same.

As he settles back into the car and connects the seat belt, he ponders for a moment the look in the old vagrant's eyes. Fear, was it? What's that old boy got to be feeling anxious about?

Chapter Eight

ou know how it is when you try to build a house out of playing cards. You spend a long time getting the base good and solid. And then you begin building upward. Each card is placed so delicately and carefully. You find yourself holding your breath and clamping your lips together at each new addition to the construction. Card by card, layer by layer, the tower climbs impossibly into the air. It becomes higher than you've ever built before, and you begin to think that this time you're going to complete it without mishap.

It's often difficult to know what causes it. A small movement of the air; a transgression of some engineering principle of load bearing; an imperceptible tremor of the hand. It takes just one card to slip or fail, one component of the fragile structure to shift, and the whole lot comes tumbling down. Once it begins to tumble, there's nothing you can do to stop it. It all goes—the whole edifice—and you're left with what you started with. A flat surface covered in playing cards.

They make beautiful structures. But they fall. They do fall.

they've got her dressed in my clothes, that little girl. that's my best blouse that daddy brought me back from a trip to Paris. and my toy rabbit, tucked under her arm. i don't know what she's doing with him. i should be jolly angry with her for taking my things, but she looks so happy and peaceful asleep like that. my goodness, why do all those people look so sad?

down the back there are some of my schoolfriends. polly

138

and deborah and mani. at least they don't look as sad as the adults. mani's giggling at timothy in the next row because he's pretending to write things on the back of the person in front of him. what a funny collection of people. i wonder what they're all doing here. it seems like church, but they don't usually have someone lying in a box in a church service.

i think she may be dead. she's certainly lying very still. perhaps she's like snow white, and some handsome prince will come along soon and kiss her, and she'll wake up. one of my favourite stories is about the awfully nice giant. he lives in a big castle in outer suburbia, where he has lots of kitchen appliances and is terribly nice to all his servants. but he has a horrible secret. if ever he drinks tea with sugar in it, he turns into a nasty ogre, and goes off causing mayhem around the place.

most of the time he keeps it under control, and everyone says what an awfully nice giant he is, and how lucky they are to live near him. but one day the maid gets two teacups mixed up, and the giant ends up drinking tea with sugar in it. he flies into a terrible rage and roars off into the city, banging into chip shops and turning over buses.

when he finally comes to his senses, he finds that he's accidentally trodden on his cat, tigger, and squashed it. the awfully nice giant is so sad that he cries and cries and cries until there are great floods of tears and everyone in outer suburbia is getting wet feet. the little girl next door named anna calms him down and tells him how awfully nice he really is. she tells him that he'll just have to give up drinking tea to avoid the danger of it having sugar in. so they sit down and have a ginger beer together, and everything is awfully nice again.

but the cat stays dead.

Harry can't get to sleep. In the end he gets up and goes through to the lounge. No point in lying sleepless in bed. There's only one thing on his mind, and he can't let it go. He picks up a pen and paper, ready from long experience for anything which might come to mind.

Various images come and go. Always they return to that

first disturbing glimpse of the body in the cemetery. It shouldn't happen to young girls. And certainly not on his patch. It eats at him, that picture, as if it's a symbol of everything he endures the job for. The desecration of innocence; the creeping incursion of evil. It has to be stopped; removed; excised.

It doesn't add up. There's something not right, not clear. He can't bring it into focus, no matter how he tries. He stops straining and relaxes. Sometimes it works.

For a long time there is nothing but tiredness. And then he sees something surprising. That old man sitting on the bench, and the fleeting look of fear which crossed his eyes. Why?

I need to find that out, Harry tells himself.

'So you did nothing?' asks Joe incredulously.

'No.'

'Said nothing?'

'I couldn't think of anything. It took me by surprise.'

'You're fucked, Tom. You're absolutely fucked. I don't know why I bother telling you anything. Maybe you have to learn the hard way.'

'Can't I just tell someone? Talk to the wardens?'

'Talk to the screws and I'll take you out myself. This is it, man. This is our territory, our world, our jungle. We rule it ourselves. Let that go and we've got nothing left, see? We sort out our own problems. You talk to the screws, you step over the line and there's no way back. No one's ever going to forget that. You'll turn up dead or you'll wish you were dead, one or the other. No, Tom. This is your world now. You have to learn to survive here.'

'I don't know if I can.'

'I don't know if you can either. But I've got a feeling we're going to find out fairly soon.'

He may have been daydreaming, lost in the sort of numb stupor which seems to distract him. It may have been some sort of Monday reluctance to return to work in a job which has become meaningless.

140

However it happened, Mark has hesitated long enough for the compact BMW to nip in front of him and take the parking space that he had claimed for himself. For a moment he simply stares in astonishment. Then there's something cold and hard in his stomach and a buzzing in his ears.

The BMW man climbs out of his car, feigning ignorance. He's wearing a sharply tailored suit and carrying a briefcase. He looks Pakistani.

Mark wrenches his door open and strides over to the stranger, who has armed the locking system.

'You just took my parking space,' he growls.

'You talking to me?' It bothers Mark that the man with the brown face has a slight East End accent and wears a gold ring on his finger.

'You just drove right in front of me as I was parking here. I'd like you to move your car so that I can occupy my space.'

'What the fuck are you talking about, guv? I just took an empty space. You was stopped out in the middle of the lane like you was lost. I gotta go, but there's a few more parks up a bit, look.'

'This is my park, and I'll ask you once more to move your car.' Mark's voice has become low and measured.

'Ah grow up will you? It's a tough life out there, but we all have to get by. Now leave it out and find yourself a park. I'm sorry if I took *your park*, but I can't stand around talking about it.'

With that the man turns his back on Mark and walks off. He's almost a hundred yards away when he hears the sound which turns his stomach.

'Oh fuck. Oh you crazy fucker,' he mutters in disbelief.

The back end of his BMW has been stoved in under the impact. The boot has popped, and the alarm is already adding to the attention which the initial collision engendered. Mark's car is damaged too, with the right fender buckled.

Mark feels no satisfaction. The rage is still burning, threatening to get out of control. It's only English reserve in the face of a gathering crowd which prevents him from attacking the man who is hurling abuse at him now.

He no longer cares for consequences.

They found him at last down the High Street, where he was catching the early-morning sun on the steps of a bank. An inconspicuous old man soaking up any warmth he could find.

Harry knew it wouldn't be a difficult task. He'd checked back on the old man's name. Wal Redman. Not a lot in the file on him—a widower who'd hit the bottle a bit after his wife had died. Just the drunk and disorderlies.

They brought him into the canteen rather than an interview room, and Harry fetched him a Chelsea bun and a cup of tea. No point in getting the old boy agitated.

'It's good of you to come in, Wal.'

There's no doubt that he's worried, observes Harry, noting the way the yellowed fingers tremble as they tear open the little sachets of sugar.

'I haven't done anything wrong, have I? The cops in the car said I wasn't being arrested or anything.'

'That's right, Wal. If you've done something wrong, we don't know about it. I just wanted a bit of a chat with you, that's all.'

'What about?'

'It concerns the death of a little girl by the name of Tessa. We found her body down in Abney Park a few weeks back. We're asking all sorts of people all sorts of questions. It occurred to me that you might have seen something, being out and about the way you are.'

Wal is busy now with his bun, feeding it into his mouth with one hand and using the other to catch the crumbs which fall.

'Would you like to see a photo of her, just to help you remember?' asks Harry.

A rise of the eyebrows seems to indicate agreement. Harry pulls out the picture provided by her parents and slides it across the table. He watches intently for the reaction.

Wal stares at the photo while his jaws chew mechanically on the slightly stale bun. His mouth is still full when the tears

142

form in those ancient eyes, and begin to trickle silently into the white stubble of his face.

Harry draws a very slow breath.

There's a storage room off the gym, where mats and other bits of gear are held. Normally there's a screw sitting on a chair near the open door. There was always supposed to be a camera in the room, but the budget didn't stretch. So an eye has to be kept on it.

This morning it's Chromefang's job. Except that he's been called over to a minor scuffle on the other side of the hall. Nothing serious, but you can't be too sure.

Tom is doing crunches near the door when he hears a whistle. It's Billy, one of the younger and slightly slow inmates.

'Could you ever just give me a lift with one of these mats, Tom?' he calls.

It's a chance to help out; maybe develop a new friendship. Tom hoists himself up and wanders across to the store.

As soon he enters he's hit from behind and stumbles against the far wall, sinking to his knees. Then there's the toe of a gym shoe which catches him in the temple and knocks him sideways.

As he turns to try and defend himself, Tom raises his legs in a semi-foetal position. It's more luck than management that his assailant is leaning towards him at the same time. Tom snaps his right leg straight and catches the corner of the man's mouth, sending him staggering backwards. In that instant he recognises that the attacker is Hammer, and fear curdles in his belly.

Then someone has gripped his wrists from behind and is dragging them down to the ground. Hammer comes at him again, evading the flailing feet and pressing a knee into Tom's chest. He strikes him a sharp blow across the face with his forearm.

Up until this point no one has spoken. Tom lashes with his feet and writhes in a desperate attempt to free himself.

'Turn him over,' Hammer hisses to whoever has Tom's wrists pinned. Together they roll him onto his stomach. Hammer kneels with a knee on each of the prone man's thighs. He tears the gym shorts away, and then does the same to the underpants.

Tom emits a quiet high-pitched squeal and shuts his eyes. He feels his bladder collapse and a warm pool of urine spreads underneath him.

Hammer leans down and whispers in his ear.

'I'm going to fuck you up the arse, my beauty. And when I've finished, my friend here will take over. Doesn't that get you excited?'

The world seems to go cloudy and indistinct, and all Tom is aware of is the pain and heat and hardness. He can taste the vomit rising in his throat. And then there is a grunt and a shift of weight and the pain has gone. At the same time his wrists are released.

'Jesus,' whispers the man who's been holding them, who turns out to be Rollo. Tom turns his head to see what has happened.

Joe holds a handful of Hammer's hair, and has pulled his head upward and back. With his other hand he reaches down and inserts two fingers into his victim's nostrils. Hammer's eyes are popping, both with pain and surprise.

'If you want to talk to Tom, you'll need to come through me,' is all Joe says. 'Understand?'

Hammer grunts his assent. Rollo is already backing out the door, clearly frightened.

'Well don't forget it,' suggests Joe, stabbing a vicious kick into Hammer's kidneys and leaving him writhing on the floor.

'You all right?' he asks Tom, smelling the ammoniac staleness of the piss.

But Tom cannot yet bring himself to speak. There seems to be liquid seeping from each of his bodily orifices. He feels pathetically grateful to the stocky man brooding over him.

> **guardian** (ˈgɑːdɪən) *n* **1** one who looks after, protects, or defends: *the guardian of public morals*.   *adj* **2** protecting or safeguarding.

*

Elizabeth feels like a schoolgirl. It's ridiculous. She sits outside in her car for five minutes beforehand, checking the people coming and going. It's unlikely she'll see someone she knows, but you can never tell. When the pavement is relatively quiet, she summons enough courage to get out of the car and walk the short distance to the shop door.

It's perfectly legal, she tells herself. It's just that she's never shopped for alcohol on her own before.

It's not like she doesn't know what she's doing.

There's no one home but Ross, and he's watching MTV in the lounge. Nancy strolls in, picks up the remote and turns it off.

'Hey!' shouts Ross, lunging for the remote.

'We have to talk,' says Nancy.

'We can talk with the music on,' he sulks.

'No we can't,' she insists. 'We have to talk about the police and Alex, and what happened to that little girl.'

Nancy has begun to call her father Alex as a sign of her sophistication, though certainly not in his hearing.

'Why?' demands Ross.

'Because we have to know what's going on, that's why. Everything is just so weird about this whole thing. I'm frightened, Ross, I'm really frightened. I know he can't possibly be involved, but what if they think he is?'

'Don't be stupid,' dismisses Ross. 'You can't imagine that pious prat killing anyone, can you? Let alone raping a little girl. So if you can't imagine it, I expect nobody else will either. It's the dumbest theory out. His biggest crime is likely to be dropping the communion wafer or something. It takes a bit of style to be a criminal, and our father's not in danger of showing any of that.'

'But what about the tape? Mary seems to think it's the tape that was used to tie the girl up.'

Ross scowls at her. It was only a month ago that she was still saying Mummy. Must be the new boy, with his fancy psychiatrist father.

'I wish everyone would give over about that tape. The pigs

145

kept on at me about the bloody tape. Was it mine? Did I bring it into the house? Had I touched it? Did I know what it might have been used for?'

'And was it yours, Ross? You're always bringing home that sort of stuff.'

'No! At least I don't think so. I don't remember it. Anyway, I told them I hadn't seen it before.'

'But don't you see that makes things worse for Alex?'

'You want me to lie about it, is that it? To say I bought it and put it there? I suppose you'd like me to confess to the rape as well, would you? Anyway, like I said, no one's going to suspect him, are they? They let him go, didn't they?'

'Yes, but . . . Mary's still worried that it's not over.'

'If she didn't have something to worry about, she'd feel lost. And stop calling her Mary, it drives me nuts. Now give me the remote back!'

'DI Thompson.'

'It's Harry Peters here, inspector. I'm in the canteen. I think you better come down.'

'What is it you're up to now, Harry?'

'I've got someone in here who's telling me a little story, and I think you might want to hear it.'

'Right you are. I'll be down in a few minutes.'

He sounds unnaturally cheerful, thinks Thompson as he hangs up the phone. I wish I had his optimism.

Joe can't stand it any more. Tom's pacing up and down in the cell. His hands are trembling.

'Look, do us a favour, will you Tom?' he pleads. 'Go and sit on the stool. That's right. Now clasp your hands together and hold them in your lap. All right. Close your eyes. Feel your weight settling down onto the stool. Concentrate on your breathing. Slow it down. Deep breaths in, long slow breaths out. Every time you breathe in, you're centring yourself. Every time you breath out, you're letting go of all the stress. Nice and slow, that's it. You're nothing but a breath breathing. Travelling down

146

into that centre. Where everything is calm. Steady breathing, in and out. Okay. Now keep doing that for a few minutes.'

Joe returns to his book, and is at last able to concentrate without distraction. Eventually Tom opens his eyes. They look clearer than before; less cloudy with fear.

'Better?' asks Joe.

'Thanks,' says Tom, looking Joe in the eye. 'I owe you an awful lot for today.'

'Don't worry, I'll find a way for you to pay it back.'

'Do you mind me asking why you did it? You didn't need to look out for me—in fact you said you weren't going to.'

'Ah, fucked if I know. People like me don't analyse things. We just do them and let them speak for themselves. It's your sort that spend whole lifetimes sitting on their arse wondering why. It's a product of luxury, that is.'

'What do you mean by my type?'

'Educated, middle-class, soft white professionals. The people who run the world.'

'I wasn't always that, you know.'

'Here we go. Working-class roots, was it? Proud of them now you've left them behind? Pull the other tit, Tom. The difference between you and me is that you can look back on your roots and pretend you still feel some connection. You can cross over and have a guided tour and then go home to where you belong. But for us, we're stuck here. We don't have anywhere else to go. No horizons to reach for. No ambitions to pursue. It's a life sentence, see?

'The only problem for you is that you've got stuck on the wrong side of the bridge. For however long, you're here in our world. Not quite as romantic as you might have thought, is it? Ugly as fuck, to tell the truth. The whole universe has been turned upside down on you. We're the ones who know what's going on and you don't know your arse from a hole in the wall. Though let's face it,' Joe chuckles, 'you nearly found out to-day.'

'So why d'you step in for me?' insists Tom.

'You don't let go, do you? I felt sorry for you, I suppose.

Lambs to the slaughter. I couldn't stand sharing my cell with the consequences. Let's not set too much by it, all right? I followed my instincts and it worked out in your favour. Let's just leave it at that.'

'There was a time when I used to be able to help people myself,' says Tom with a blank stare.

'All right, I'll play your little game. What were you then? A teacher? An accountant? Curator of an art gallery?'

Tom looks at Joe, and then down at the floor. There's a hint of colour come to his cheeks, Joe notices.

'I'd rather not say,' he decides. 'I'll tell you sometime, but I'm not ready to yet. Let's just say that I used to work with people, before all this started. I still can't believe that all that has gone so quickly.'

'Not the past nor the future, only the present,' reminds Joe. 'You still think you shouldn't be here, don't you?'

'I know it. I know I shouldn't be here. Sometimes I think I'm living in a dream, and I'm going to wake up and it'll all be over.'

'There's what you want, and then there's what you get. It doesn't help to get the two confused.' Joe runs his hand over his head, hoicks back the phlegm in his throat, and then continues.

'Let me tell you a story. I met this woman in a pub, right? Flash clothes, not the usual clientele. Older than me. She's not a bad looker, just the same. Got bedroom eyes, but I'm wondering if she might be a bit of a cocktease. I buy her a few drinks, and we have a good time. By the end of the night, she's getting pissed, you know? Not falling down drunk, but slurring her words and getting all emotional. I'm half-tempted to take her home and shag the arse off her, but the better part of me is sending out warning signals.

'So I order a taxi for her, and ease her into the back. I lean over to give her a last kiss, and she grabs me by the balls and whispers in my ear to come home with her. I'm not long out of the joint, and my balls start doing the thinking at that point. On the way home, she's all over me, and the taxi driver's looking in the mirror for a bit of free entertainment. We get up to her place, which is a bit of a mission seeing it's on the third floor. As soon as I get inside I start feeling nervous. She's got money. Lots of art on the wall, and originals too. She pours us both more drinks—Johnny Walker Black Label.

'I ask if she's all right, you know? She just laughs and starts unzipping my jeans. We go through to her bedroom and she sort of falls across the bed. By this stage she's gone slightly mental on me. She's wild as hell, and we're not at it for long before she comes. I have to clamp a hand across her mouth to stop her screaming, and she's scratching the shit out of my back. Anyway, I still haven't got there, so we get under way again, a little bit slower this time. Must have been too slow, because before we've finished she goes out like a light, dead asleep. I just keep going and finish off. Took me a few minutes on account of the alcohol and her being like a dead fish.

'I yell out as I come, and it must have startled her into waking up. She opens her eyes, calls me a bastard, and goes back to sleep. I think nothing of it. When she wakes up in the morning, she can't remember anything except that one image burned on her brain—waking up with me on top of her. She sees the tattoo on my hand and orders me out of the place. I've got this sick feeling that there's trouble brewing. A day later the filth are onto me and charging me with rape.

'They've got her story, they've got my skin and blood under her fingernails, my semen inside her. They've got a statement from a next-door neighbour who heard screaming coming from the apartment. They've got me with a record and her as a respectable woman with a good income. My word against hers. Open and shut. Seven years. I could say I'm innocent as well. I could feel all bitter and twisted about it. But there's no future in it, see? Doesn't change anything. And I'm not innocent anyway. I fucked someone above my station. That's the real crime. That's always been a crime, only it's not on the books. She got pissed and wanted some rough trade, but then she woke up and remembered who she was and who I was. In her mind it had to have been rape. Otherwise what would it mean?

'And there's other things I've done I never got caught for. Terrible things that I wouldn't tell anyone about. It's all swings and roundabouts.

'Events are just events, Tom. You have to accept them. This is a schoolhouse of the soul, if you want it to be. Years ago people used to go into cells voluntarily to follow the spiritual life. And here you are getting it all laid on for you. It's a crucible, prison is. You'll learn a lot about yourself here.'

I think I know when it started.

I kept a Playboy *magazine under my mattress. I hadn't bought it—I found it in a box of rubbish which was outside the doorway of a shop in Rotterdam. I put it down the back of my trousers and pulled my jersey down over it. I felt guilty and excited at the same time. It was like some other person doing it. I knew it was wrong, but I wanted it at the same time.*

The very first time I was in my room on my own, I ferreted under the mattress to get that magazine out. My heart was beating and my skin felt kind of itchy. All my senses were heightened because I was listening in case anyone came along. I flipped over the stories and advertisements to the pictures. The pleasures of the flesh. Those perfectly formed American girls with tanned breasts and big lips. With hands lingering near their pubic mound and eyes smouldering.

I imagined them talking to me. I could hear the words they were saying as they got more and more excited. They turned out to be dirty little whores, all of them, whispering filthy words in my ear. I would be kneeling on the floor with the magazine open on the bed in front of me, with one hand doing the business and the other ready with a wad of toilet paper to prevent any spill. They reached out from the page, those girls, and I could feel their tongues and their breath and their juices. I fucked them into silence with my hand. I made them stop.

And then there was always the aftermath. A thick hot head; a hand holding a sticky clump of tissue; a pungent sweet smell and a knot in my stomach. The sickening awareness which inevitably followed. A sense of dirtiness and dishonour; a feeling of betrayal. I hated myself and that magazine and those girls. They'd played on my weakness, tricked me. I would be stronger next time. I would throw away that Playboy, *just as soon as I had the opportunity. I would put it all behind me, and stop that disgusting habit.*

Thompson sits behind his desk with a smile on his face. He rearranges a couple of files so that they sit more neatly on the desktop. For perhaps thirty seconds he closes his eyes and savours a sense of satisfaction. Another man might gloat or go out for a drink. But he finds his half-minute sufficient.

He punches in Perkins' extension number.

It's a small supper party organised by Beryl, a long-serving member of the parish council. There are savouries and a variety of good wines. She says she feels it's time they enjoyed a social function together rather than another meeting. Nobody mentions the police or the recent dark events. Alex is grateful.

He moves among them, spreading charm and expressing unfailing pastoral concern in the movement of his eyebrows. At times he lowers his voice and lures his listeners closer. And then he is laughing, and the sound of his wonderful voice fills the room with glad relief.

Mary is not there. She was invited, but declined. I don't go to your meetings, she said. And I'm not up to seeing people just yet. Alex didn't push. There was talk at times about Mary, and the neglect of her role as a vicar's wife. Alex resisted it, and would tackle critics head-on if they spoke out.

He likes being here. He enjoys the way they defer to him. He revels in being the centre of gravity for this community of people. This is his vocation; what he is gifted to be and do.

Ah yes, he sighs, draining the entirely satisfactory glass of chardonnay. God is in his heaven once again, and all's right with the world.

'I'm afraid there's a telephone call for you, Alex,' apologises Beryl. 'You can take it in the kitchen if you like.'

On the tube ride home, a woman jams an umbrella into the small of his back without apology, and a crazy man mutters about radiation in a torrent of nonsense. Mark hates public transport, but only has himself to blame.

By the time he's changed to a 73 bus and stood the whole way, his frustration levels are climbing. He's an hour late getting home.

An unusual smell greets him as he opens the door.

'Elizabeth?' he calls.

A snorting laugh comes from the lounge. He finds her there with the bottle, reduced to one-third of its original contents. She's slumped back into the sofa, and is struggling to focus on the man who's entered the room.

'What's going on?' he asks, with a coldness in his voice. 'I take it you haven't been to work.'

'You can take it anywhere you like. Only I won't take it any more,' she mumbles, and then begins chuckling at her little joke.

Mark grabs her by the shoulders and pulls her forward.

'For God's sake Elizabeth, look at you!'

'Sorry? For who's sake did you say? You might be right. Only I feel sick right now, Mark.'

He escorts her through to the bathroom, but she's already started retching.

mani and i tell each other secrets. i told her about the time i couldn't find a toilet anywhere and so i went down the alley and did it there. i even showed her where it had been. i told her about when peter wrote me a note telling me he loved me, and we laughed and laughed about it. she told me about her granny, who sometimes farts when she coughs.

mani has a big secret which she says she's not allowed to tell anyone. it's a secret between her and her father. i think she might tell me one day, but i don't ask her to anymore because it made her cry last time. i can't think what it might be. perhaps her father is a famous prince or something.

i've only seen him twice and he seemed quite nice, but he looked at me funny. i thought perhaps he didn't like me, but after that he went and got me an ice lolly from the freezer, so it can't be that. he said i had lovely hair and kept wanting to stroke it. mani said we should go outside and play, so we did. i said i thought her father was nice, but she didn't answer.

Harry finishes typing up his report. He attaches it to the statement with a paper clip. Perkins wants it urgently. Which is only to be expected.

He should be feeling happier than he is. He sits for a few minutes, trying to discern the source of disquiet. And then he remembers. That twitching at the corner of the vicar's mouth which stirred memories.

It goes back six years. There was a bag snatcher at work on the High Street. A couple of the assaults were quite vicious, with elderly women needing hospital treatment. Harry worked the case for a month and still couldn't find the villain.

Then they brought someone in on a shoplifting charge. A little bloke with a leather jacket and weaselly face. He was close to the description of the snatcher, and so Harry did the questioning. He denied any knowledge of it for close to two hours. And then the corner of his mouth started twitching. Harry recognised it as the telltale crack. He may have belted the little fellow a few times. Nothing serious; just some inspiration to come clean. It worked, and the thief signed a full statement admitting to all of it.

Harry was pleased. Cleared the whole lot up, and gave him the satisfaction of getting another crook behind bars. Took his wife out for a meal on the strength of it. Gratifying it was, to get success.

Until a few weeks later, when there was another snatch. With a description not much different from the earlier ones. It was another three weeks and four victims before they caught the perpetrator, and only then because a member of the public chased him and tackled him.

Harry had sent the wrong man down. Not that he wasn't a villain anyway. But he wasn't the right villain for the crime. There was nothing to be done except to learn from it.

Have I, wonders Harry?

*

The television is on with the volume muted. Mark sits staring at the flickering screen without comprehension. From the bedroom comes the sound of Elizabeth's genteel snoring. He's finished the rest of the whisky himself.

And now he sits there. Alone with his fury. A rage roaring in his belly, and nothing to do with it. Nowhere to take it; no one to bear it. He can feel the pulse surging in his temples. I'm going to do something, he tells himself.

But what is there to do? Where is the enemy? Who can I punish? It's all been taken from me now—my daughter, my wife, my sanity. I can't even fucking kill myself.

I want an enemy. I want to meet the devil. I want to see, face to face. I want vengeance, and I want to wreak it.

Mary replaces the telephone receiver in its cradle on the wall. She reaches out one hand to steady herself, and slowly slides to the floor. She sits there for some time in silence, without expression.

Nancy comes into the room sideways, still yelling at Ross even as she retreats. It's a moment before she sees her mother slumped beneath the kitchen bench. It gives her a fright.

'Mum! What's wrong? Are you all right?'

Mary says nothing, but turns her head to look at her daughter. Nancy kneels beside her stricken mother.

'What is it? Are you sick? Do you want me to call a doctor?'

'That was the police,' says Mary. 'They've just arrested your father for the murder of Tessa Bromley.'

t takes so long to build. And so little time to tumble.

Chapter Nine

The drive up is a welcome chance to be alone. Not that she does much thinking. These days her mind is in a constant swirl, so that it's a matter of riding whichever currents happen to be flowing. By the time she arrives in Leicester, Mary is a little calmer. The mindless motion of motorway travel is soothing rather than demanding. She learned how to disconnect when the children were young.

She makes her way along the familiar route across town. In earlier years they came twice or even three times a year, mainly for the children's sake. Now it's not even an annual event. Alex has to be persuaded against his will to make the journey. She finds it hard to understand how anyone could be so distant from their parents, but he refuses to talk about it. This is the first time ever she's come on her own. But now everything has changed.

Brian, Alex's father, has always been terrifying to her. Sullen, moody, capricious. Prone to long periods of silence punctuated by angry or sarcastic interventions. The toad, she used to call him behind his back; enthroned in silence with his tongue always coiled to lash out.

The stroke has only made him more frightening, with the threats now issued in guttural but indistinct words. He sits in front of the television as he's always done, except now he has no other choice. Maureen continues to tiptoe around him, fawning and subservient; incapable of pleasing him. With the stroke, the beatings have stopped. He simply stares at her with such a blaze of anger that she almost prefers the way things were.

Mary bends to kiss him dutifully, but his only response is a frustrated grunt as she blocks his line of sight to the screen. He smells of some medication or other. Maureen hurries her through to the kitchen where the tea is waiting. She busies herself with the ritual of it all, but when she turns back from the bench, Mary can see that there are tears forming in her eyes.

'I'm sorry,' she says from long habit. 'I've been a bit of a mess since I heard. How is he?'

'Alex? He's better than you might imagine. Indignant that this should have happened to him. Supremely confident that he's going to get off. I think he's already considering what legal action he has against the police for false arrest. You know how he is, Maureen; it takes a lot to dent his bravado.'

Alex's mother smiles briefly at some fleeting memory of her son.

'But he will get off, won't he dear? I mean this is all so stupid. Alex could never do anything like that. Of all the children, he could never do that. There's been some terrible mistake, hasn't there? I can't believe that the police could have got themselves in such a mess as to charge an Anglican priest with, with . . . such horrible things.'

'They have a lot of evidence that points to him. They wouldn't have arrested him otherwise.'

'Oh goodness, Mary. You don't doubt him, do you? You don't actually think that Alex is capable of vile deeds? He's your husband, the father of your children. You mustn't let him down, dear. He needs you most of all at the moment.'

'I don't know what to think anymore. I'm all over the place. I want to believe in Alex, and underneath it all I do. But every now and then I find myself wondering, "What if?" And then I start looking at him, and trying to imagine if it's possible. It's awful, Maureen. I've started treating him like a stranger, like someone I don't know. That's partly why I've come up here to talk to you. I want to know what you think—whether you can remember anything or tell me something helpful about him, something I might have missed. I want to trust him, you see, but I've just lost my confidence all of a sudden, and I hardly know how to talk to him any more.'

'Oh no,' says Maureen, shaking her head. 'Our Alex, he's always been special. Never a nasty bone in him. His father used to knock him around a bit when he was young, like he did with all the children. Only I think Alex got more than the others because he was brighter. His father never liked "smart" people—he always thought they were trying to show him up. But where Peter would start yelling and punching, which only made things worse, Alex would just take it, quietly. Never a hint of retaliation or answering back. He just took it like a man and got on with things.'

'He was never in trouble for anything, at school or anywhere?'

'I'm sure you know most of it, dear, having been married to him for so long. But no, the others were always in trouble, and we'd be called in to talk to the teachers. With Alex, it was completely different. The teachers kept telling us that he was a bright boy, and that we should make sure he was given the opportunity for a good education. His father took no notice of it, not that he came to the meetings anyway. He seemed to think that anyone who got good grades at school must be a bit of a pansy. He'd take Alex out with him bricklaying in the holidays, and the boy would come back with huge blisters on his hands. I suspect Brian tried to find ways to humiliate him on the site, because sometimes Alex looked very sullen when he came in. But he'd never tell me about it. That's the way he was, you see—uncomplaining, even then.

'We only had one incident in the whole time he was growing up. He played rugby at the weekends, and I believe he was pretty good at it. I never used to take much interest, because I'm not a sporting sort of person. But one Saturday he came home with a black eye, and there was a bit of a to-do afterwards. It seemed he had been involved in a fight on the field—apparently they happen quite often in rugby. Anyway, the coach said that Alex completely lost his temper, and wouldn't

157

stop even when the referee was trying to pull him off. He did something to the other boy's eye so that he ended up with impaired sight. Alex was terribly remorseful. He went round to the parents and apologised. It was so out of character for him, that violence, and for a while I thought it was the beginning of him going off the rails. But no, he was back to normal straightaway, and there were never any other problems.'

'I can't imagine him even knowing how to fight,' muses Mary. 'Was there anything else that made you worry about him ever?'

'No, Mary, nothing. He had a strong faith from quite a young age, you know, and that really influenced the whole of his life. Alex was always a genuinely good boy. I haven't had an easy life in some respects, but Alex is one of the bright spots. He's always wanted to help people, and Lord knows he's been a comfort to me at many stages. I just wish we saw more of him than we do. And now… This whole performance is ludicrous, Mary, really it is. A mother knows her children, and I know that Alex could never do the things they're accusing him of. Never.'

'You're right, and I'm being silly. But I just want to put my mind at rest. I've been back over everything I can think of since I met him, but I can't find any cause for concern. There's only one incident which stands out as being slightly mysterious. We were at a conference of some sort, and ran into an old friend of Alex's from the days when he did that three-month tour on the mission ship. They had a grand old time swapping stories. But Alex was decidedly edgy, and a couple of times changed the topic of conversation rather clumsily. I asked him about it afterward, but he said it was my imagination. Do you know anything about that?'

'Only that he came back from that trip a little subdued. He'd been having a fabulous time—kept sending us postcards from all over the place. At one stage he half wondered if he might stay on for the whole year. But the next thing we knew he turned up at Heathrow a fortnight earlier than we'd expected him. Where was it he'd come from now? The Philippines,

I think. He said he'd been feeling a bit claustrophobic in the cabin, and he did look a little off colour. He perked up again shortly after, and got on with his studies. It wasn't too long after that he met you, was it dear?'

'Ahhh, yes, I think you're right. Oh God, Maureen. How could this have happened to us? I don't want to be doubting Alex. I know he can't be guilty. I just wish I could find some way to turn the clock back, that's all.'

They meet in the chapel, as arranged. There's been an attempt to make the place look vaguely ecclesiastical, but the bars preclude much sense of grandeur. It looks like what it is; a large cell with a cross in it.

'I've been wondering when you might want to talk to me,' observes Kevin.

'I'm not sure that I do want to talk to you as yet,' responds Tom.

'Did you know that prison chaplains have access to inmates' files? I've had a look through yours.'

Tom spends some time considering this while pretending to pick pieces of lint off his prison trousers.

'What's that supposed to mean? Are you trying to intimidate me?'

'No, I just want us to start off on a clear understanding. I try not to make judgements about people, but it helps me to understand what sort of pressures you might be under. And gives me a little sympathy you might not get in other quarters.'

'I'm not looking for sympathy.'

'What is it you're looking for, then?'

'I'd like to confess my sins.'

'Very well. I'd be happy to help with that.'

Tom stares at the chaplain, and runs the tip of his tongue over his lips. He appears to be about to speak, but eventually lets out a long sigh. Then he's standing.

'It's no good. I'm sorry to have wasted your time. I can't do it.'

159

Kevin remains silent as the prisoner leaves. He knows better than to try to hurry the process of unburdening.

Elizabeth can't bring herself to attend the trial. She's begun to let things go. More and more days off work. Mark notices that sometimes she doesn't bother putting on make-up when she does go out. And he's begun to count the empty bottles.

He can't resist turning up for the hearings. He has to know, to see, to understand, if it's in any way possible. And he wants a target for that hatred; that fierce hunger for retribution. From time to time the cold clenching in his gut feels almost like lust in its intensity.

Unfortunately the man sitting in the dock is an unlikely recipient of it. Mark stares at him, trying to penetrate the sophisticated exterior. But there's nothing there. Not a clue either way. Not that he knows what to look for. Some sign of deviance, perhaps? Of inhumanity?

Instead there is the clergyman who acted so professionally at the time of Tessa's death. They've reached an agreement that he dispense with his collar in court in order that it not sway the jury. But everything about him—his thick hair, the way he carries himself, the sound of his voice when he pleads—all of it marks him out as a respectable citizen. He lacks the demeanour of a child rapist. You expect something at least; bad breath, acne.

The police are convinced; Mark not yet. God knows he wants the man to be guilty, wants to despise him and anchor this burden of vengeance. But try as he might, he cannot find any connection between Alex Hanson and the awful image of his broken daughter.

It's a lot less exciting than Mark had imagined a murder trial to be. Very slow and ponderous, with the barristers droning in such a way as to send you off on day-dreams. Though during the description of the scene of the crime, he had to get up and leave the court.

It started to change the way I saw things. Every time I looked at a girl,

160

I'd be imagining what lay under her blouse. Standing close to a woman on the bus, I'd start to get short of breath. I began to get the faces mixed up. I'd picture some of the girls I worked with as the ones in the magazine. And now and again, I pretended that one of the whores who beckoned me from the shiny pages was Linda or Jenny, my workmates. That's when the problems started. I became confused. It seemed to me that many of the women around me were sending me secret signals in the way they stood, or looked at me, or accidentally brushed up against me. And then later I'd build on it in my imagination.

It was like a force that came on me from the outside. I tried to resist it in every way I could. I avoided people, I worked out, I took cold showers. It was hopeless. The whole world seemed to be charged with sexuality, and I was a hungry man. All of this was going on inside my head. I never touched anyone, I swear it. I never let my guard down. None of them ever suspected, though some of the girls became nervous if left alone with me.

I wanted to talk to someone about it, but I didn't know where to start. I was thoroughly miserable, apart from those grubby little waves of pleasure which would make my eyes glaze and leave me with a damp hand. It was as if something had attached itself to my soul; a parasite which demanded satisfaction. I don't know where it came from.

i have a special place in the park. no one else knows about it. i found it quite by accident when i was chasing a ball one day. it's round the back of one of the old sheds. it's just a bit of a clearing, really, but it's cut off so that no one can see you when you're in there. it's my magic place. i sneak away there whenever i can, and no one knows where i am. sometimes i read books there. other times i lie on my back and look at the clouds and try and work out what shapes they are. the trouble is i always see rabbits.

i think everyone should have a secret place they can go to. you need to get on your own every now and again so that you can feel really safe. i haven't even told mummy or daddy or my friends or anyone about mine. though one day when i went there, i found an old plastic bag with half a sandwich in it, and i knew that someone had been there. it made me scared for a while, but there was never anything else that turned up. i felt awfully sad at the thought that someone might have spoiled my hidey-hole for me.

'So what happened today?' Elizabeth wants to know.

'You could always come down and find out for yourself.'

'I don't bloody want to go, I've told you that.' She slams the glass down for emphasis, and refills it. 'Now are you going to tell me or do I have to go and buy a newspaper?'

Mark sniffs and tries to keep the disdain off his face. Somewhere in the depths he feels sorry for her, but the feeling's lost in the press of his own disorder.

'It was prosecution evidence again,' he relents. 'There was a long time going through DNA tests from the blood found on the wall, and matching it with Hanson's. Which they did, give or take some ridiculous margin of error.'

'Is that significant?'

'It's all part of building the case. Though he's admitted skinning his knuckles while climbing over the fence, anyway.'

'What else?'

'They had some little forensics guy, Mullins, reporting the results of tests on a roll of masking tape found in the kitchen drawer at Hanson's place. The most damning part was that the ragged end was an exact match for a piece that was used on Tessa. And it had his fingerprints all over it.'

Elizabeth is crying again, sparked by the mention of her daughter's name.

'The cross-examination made a lot of the fact that there were no fingerprints on the tape found at the cemetery. Why would someone go to that much trouble to conceal their identity on the one hand, and then leave incriminating evidence in their home, was the implication of it.'

She wipes her face with the back of her hand and takes another swig from the glass.

'You don't think you've had enough of that, do you?' asks Mark quietly.

'Fuck you! Don't you start giving me any of your little lectures, you bastard. I'll drink if I fucking well want to and when I want to, you understand?'

Mark reaches out a hand to touch her shoulder, but she slaps it aside.

'Leave me alone, you hear? Leave me alone. I don't want lectures and I don't want sympathy and I don't want you with your bloody sanity. I want my daughter. I want Tessa, I want Tessa.'

Now she is wailing and sobbing, and spilling the drink over her jeans. Mark gets up and walks away. He has learned the hard way that there is nothing to be said.

'Is that James Greenaway?'

'Speaking.'

'Listen, you won't remember me at all, but I'm Mary Hanson, the wife of Alex Hanson.'

'Ah, Mary, of course I remember you. We met at the Anglicans for Renewal conference in Bath. Sorry to hear about Alex—terrible business. How can I help?'

'You and Alex travelled together on that ship, didn't you?'

'The *Evangel*, that's right. Spent nearly three months trundling around Asia. That's where I first got to know Alex.'

'Would you mind terribly if I came in and had a chat about all that?'

'Only too happy to, Mary. Hang about a bit, I'll just find my diary.'

Alex discovers the loneliness of the accused. There's nothing said. It's all in the way that people look at him, turning their eyes away whenever he discovers them staring. He feels the opening rift with his wife, who alternates between comfort and suspicion. Worst of all is Nancy, his beloved daughter. Ross has always been distant anyway. But Nancy… She suspects it could be true. He's sensed the way she's withdrawn from their embraces; duty fighting against recoil.

He knows there's nothing to be done about it. The bishop has relieved him of duties, which saves embarrassment but makes the days interminably long. At least he's not in custody. It was an unusual decision, probably aided by the bishop's intervention. It involved surrendering his passport, and there are strict reporting conditions. But he's saved from the horror of the remand cells.

No, the trial must take its course, and he must bear the burden of suspicion until his name has been cleared. The initial anger has turned to a mix of fear and acceptance. Even Christ was accused, he recalls on more than one occasion. If this is my cross, then I must carry it.

He's taken to sleeping in the narrow single bed in the spare room. He volunteered, and Mary didn't offer a word of protest. The isolation is the cruellest part of it all. Bad enough to have those you love suspect you of evil, but to discover that they are prepared to abandon you in your hour of need is a revelation he could have done without.

The question which rakes him from time to time is whether there's any way back from here. Even after it's all over and his name has been cleared; after he's been found innocent and welcomed back to the parish—will there be any hope of forgetting the eyes? They might forgive, but can I?

Mullins steps down from the stand with the satisfaction of having done well. He has weathered the assault from the defence and reiterated the facts. Thompson, seated in the gallery, nods to him in approval.

The jury is tired. There's been a lot of factual evidence to concentrate on.

'Who's your next witness?' the judge inquires of the prosecution.

'Wal Redman, your honour.'

'And will he have extensive evidence to give?'

'Half an hour, perhaps. But I suspect my learned friend may want extensive cross-examination.'

'I certainly will, your honour,' confirms the defence lawyer.

'Very well, then. We'll adjourn until morning.'

*

There's never silence in a prison at night. Even beyond the snoring and rustling, there are strange noises which echo down the corridors. Joe lies listening to them in the darkness. Footsteps somewhere, and a closing door. A sound part-way between a hysterical laugh and a ululating cry.

He has woken with an erection, closely followed by a creeping shame as he recalls the dream. A beautiful Irish woman with black hair, dancing in front of him. She's removing her clothes as she dances. He can't hear the music, but he knows it must be there. She's naked apart from a pair of black knickers. And then she begins to undress him, continuing the dance all the while. After she has his trousers off, she kneels in front of him and begins to move toward him with her tongue.

Only when she looks up does he recognise the face as his mother's. She cackles at him with her bad teeth. It jolts him out of sleep, and into the mild cacophony of the night.

This dream holds no surprises for him. It travels with him like a long-familiar passenger. Once again he turns it all over in his mind.

He was twelve years old at the time. The first thing he was aware of when he woke was the fog of whisky fumes. She was drunk, there was nothing unusual in that. She leant over him, stroking his hair, and smiled at him as he opened his eyes.

'I can't get to sleep,' she says.

He squints at her and screws up his face against consciousness.

'Come on through and sleep in my bed,' his mother insists.

He's slept there from time to time, when she's been sick or sad. You do what you can for your mum when she's all you've got. He stumbles through to her double bed and climbs into the luxurious space of it. Almost immediately he falls into a light slumber again.

There's a warm and not unpleasant sensation which summons him back to the surface. The first reaction is one of incomprehension. He's not sure if he's awake or asleep.

It all gets confused from there on. He genuinely doesn't know what's happening. The part of him that recognises it wants

165

to recoil, to run away. But the spreading warmth and the sensation of her flesh has him in thrall. Afterwards, she falls asleep. He sneaks back to his bed and cries and cries.

Neither of them talk about it in the morning. He keeps his head down over his plate, though he knows she's watching him. It's the one and only time it happens, and sometimes he wonders if he imagined it. But he remembers the sticky mess in his loin, and the way he had to clean it up in the bathroom.

A week later he stole his first car.

> **damage** ('dæmɪdʒ) *n* **1** injury or harm impairing the function or condition of a person or thing. **2** loss of something desirable. *vb* **3** (*tr*) to cause damage to.

i'm lying on my tummy looking at a daisy when a shadow passes over the sun. everything goes dull and cool. i roll over onto my back and see that it's a cloud which has got in the way. it won't be there for ever, and anyway, it's still sunny up above the clouds. when mummy and daddy and i flew across to ireland in a plane, we were in beautiful sunshine until we went below the clouds again. if i was a bird i'd want to be able to fly high enough to be above all the clouds. i'd want to feel the sun on my back and the air on my wings.

daddy says the dark is just because there's no light around. he tried to explain it to me with a stick and the shadow it had in the sun. i'm not sure if i agree with him, even though he's probably right. i think dark is something like light—that it can fall on us just like light can, except that it makes things dark instead of light. i believe there are rays of darkness in the same way there are rays of light. i tried to explain it to daddy, but he just laughed and said that was my funny way of looking at the world. i think it's him that sees the world funny. the night is not just a gap between days—it's the night. anyone would know that.

it could be that light is just a gap in the darkness, couldn't it? that would make just as much sense. oh, that's better. i can feel the sun again, though now i have to shade my eyes. if you wait long enough, even the biggest clouds pass.

*

It's Saturday morning. Mark is sitting at the table, reading the newspaper. Elizabeth has the television on. There's a documentary on sea lions showing. She hates documentaries, but she watches with her eyes unfocused.

Mark finds the remote and turns the television off. She closes her eyes in weariness.

'What?' she asks.

'We have to talk,' he tells her.

'Oh, how original. You should be writing scripts for the soaps.'

'I don't want to argue. I want to talk—we need to talk.'

'Do we? I don't need to talk. I'm perfectly happy keeping silence, which seems the best possible thing to do. So it must be you who *needs* to talk. Go right ahead, feel free. You won't mind if I watch this programme while you're doing it?'

'For god's sake, Elizabeth! Snap out of it! You don't have a mortgage on pain, you know. It's not just you who's suffering. I know you're hurting and you want to withdraw, but it's killing us. We're living in the same house but we might as well be on different planets. We've lost Tessa, let's not lose each other as well.'

She sits impassively, except that the skin around her lips has become white.

'I can't bear to see you shutting down like this. You won't talk to me, you won't touch me, and I don't know how to reach you any more. I'm scared, Elizabeth. I'm scared of losing you altogether.'

'What the fuck do you want from me, Mark? Comfort? Is that want you want? Normality? Conversation? "Pass the salt will you darling. What do you think the weather's going to do? I do like the new comedy on Channel Four." Well, I can't do it any more. I can't *be* normal any more. I can see myself as I used to be, but I can't get back there again. I don't even breathe without thinking about Tessa. I smell her in the bathroom. I feel her in the sheets. I can't get rid of her and I don't want to get rid of her. She's my baby and she's gone. Whoever did it, this bastard, he ripped my womb out. There's just an empty space in there. That's all I've got left for you, Mark; emptiness. You can share it if you want to, or you can leave. I don't care any more. Nothing touches me. It's all gone. It all went with Tessa. There's nothing left, and I don't even feel sorry about it.'

Elizabeth walks across to the television and turns it on again.

Wal takes the stand. His skin is still red from the unaccustomed scrubbing. The copper, Harry, has paid for the suit from the Oxfam store. He feels decidedly uncomfortable.

Counsel for the prosecution is a big-boned man with thick white hair. He could probably function without the reading glasses, but they make a useful prop.

'Mr Redman, you stated your occupation as unemployed. Would you please tell the court how you spend your days.'

'I'm out and about most of the time. I wander round Stoke Newington; keep an eye on what's happening. In the library a lot during the winter, but out on the streets when the warm weather comes. I like to try and catch the sun wherever I can.'

'Quite. And on the afternoon of the twelfth of June, do you recall where you were?'

'I'll never forget it. I was out doing my rounds, see? I'd been up early seeing the sun was shining, and I spent the morning on the High Street, chatting to a few people. I had a sandwich at the pub for lunch. It was dole day, so I usually treat myself while I've got the money. After that, I headed up to Clissold Park.'

'What time of the day would this have been?'

'It would have been not long after one o'clock, I reckon, because the chemist shop on Church Street was just closing up for their half-day when I went past.'

'And what did you do when you arrived in the park?'

'I sat on a bench in the sun. Right near where the animals are. I might have dozed off for a few moments, seeing how warm it was.'

'Was there anything in particular which caught your attention while you were seated there?'

'There was a little girl over against the rabbit cage. She was kneeling down talking to the rabbits. She might have been feeding them as well, I couldn't see properly.'

'I have here a photograph, which has been admitted into evidence as exhibit 27, Mr Redman. Would you look at it and tell me if you recognise the person in it?'

'That's her; that's the girl.'

'Let it be recorded that the witness identifies Tessa Bromley as the child concerned. Now, can you tell the court what might have happened after you observed this girl?'

'I went for a walk around the park. I have a little round that I usually do. Some people leave things about, and I keep an eye out for them. You'd be surprised what I find there from time to time.'

The prosecutor adjusts the glasses on his nose in mild impatience.

'I didn't find much that afternoon, as I recall. A couple of cigarettes and a 50p piece. There's this clearing where I go for a smoke sometimes. It's just a little space in the middle of some bushes really, but you can't see it from the outside. Gives you peace and privacy. So I was headed off there, but when I got close I could hear the sound of people moving about in there.'

'Could you see what was happening?'

'No, I just heard sort of rustling sounds. I thought it was probably a couple going at it. It's happened before.'

'What did you do next?'

'Well I didn't want to disturb them, did I? I'm not a pevert. I wandered off to another spot I know, not far away, where there's an old tree stump. I sat down there and rolled myself a smoke.'

'And did you subsequently observe any activity?'

'Not for a while. I thought I heard a cry coming from the clearing at one time, but that's only to be expected, isn't it? I didn't think anything of it. I finished my smoke, and was just sitting there having a think when I heard someone coming my way. I thought it was probably the couple, so I crouched down behind a bush. I didn't want to embarrass them, see?'

169

'What did you see?'

'I saw a man dressed in casual clothes carrying a little girl in his arms.'

The prosecutor removes his glasses in an indication to the jury to pay attention.

'Did you recognise that little girl?'

'It was the girl I'd seen over with the rabbits.'

'The girl you previously identified as Tessa Bromley? You're quite sure about that?'

In the gallery Mark lowers his head into his hands.

'That's who it was, that girl with the black hair. She had a pair of bright-yellow leggings on that you could hardly miss.'

'What condition would you say this girl was in when you saw her being carried?'

'At first I thought she was asleep. She was really pale, and her arms and legs were just hanging down. And then I wondered... I didn't know what to think.'

'What did you wonder, Mr Redman?'

'I wondered if she was dead.'

'And the man who was carrying her, did you recognise him?'

'I thought I might have seen him around at times, but I didn't know him, no.'

'Have you seen that man subsequently?'

'It's him, over there.'

'Let the record indicate that the witness identifies the defendant, Alex Hanson.'

There's a scraping sound in the momentary silence as Alex shifts his weight in the chair. His mouth has dropped open, and the colour has drained from his face.

He feels paralysed; unable to speak or act. He stares at the old man in the witness box, trying to understand. For the first time in the whole drama, a deep misgiving corrodes his stomach.

Alex looks desperately round the courtroom, but there are no friendly eyes to give him comfort.

*

'Tell me, Mr Redman, how long were you in the pub at lunch-time?'

The counsel for the defence has a sharp face, and a habit of clinging to the hems of his robe as if they held him upright. His thick eyebrows are lowered as he questions the witness.

'About an hour, I'd say.'

'About an hour. And how much would you have had to drink in that time?'

'Two pints, that's all.'

'Two pints. Enough to cause you to fall asleep in the park.'

'I might have dozed for a while, like I said.'

'What's your eyesight like, Mr Redman?'

'Pretty good.'

'I'd like you to read this for the court, if you will.'

The barrister hands him a sheet of paper with typescript on it. Wal holds it at arm's length and peers intently before giving up.

'I can't read it,' he admits.

'Because you can't see it properly?'

'I'm not too good with reading. But I can see in the distance all right.'

'A short time ago you identified the girl you saw as Tessa Bromley by looking at a photograph. But now you admit you can't see properly close up.'

'It's different, isn't it? A photo from writing.'

'Is it, Mr Redman? Is it, indeed? Let's move on to the clearing which you found to be occupied. You stated that you moved to a place nearby and had a cigarette?'

'That's right.'

'Why didn't you move right away from the area? Why stay close by at all?'

'I don't know. I wanted a smoke, that's all.'

'Were you watching and listening, Mr Redman? Were you getting sexual satisfaction from the noises coming from that clearing?'

Wal colours immediately. He scratches the side of his face furiously before answering.

'I was just having a cigarette. I couldn't see anything or hear anything.'

'And yet you testified that you heard a cry.'

'Well, yes.'

'So you must have been able to hear something, mustn't you?'

'I suppose so.'

'You'd been drinking, your eyesight is not too good, and now you're not sure whether your earlier testimony is correct or not. Do you think your evidence is reliable enough to bring serious accusations against the defendant?'

'I know what I saw. I saw that man over there carrying the girl in his arms. There's no getting away from that, whatever you say.'

Chapter Ten

At the end of his testimony, Wal is drained. He's glad to get back to Stoke Newington for a drink.

Wal has a secret. He was worried it might come out in court.

For many years after the merchant navy, he and his wife used to live in Nottingham. When the children left home, the house seemed empty. Margaret had never enjoyed sex anyway, and now she seemed determined to avoid it at all costs. Wal began to drink quite heavily.

She came home unexpectedly and found him with his twelve-year-old niece. They were playing a game, the girl explained. She was naked from the waist down.

After the row they decided the best thing was to keep quiet. The girl was bribed to keep 'their secret'. He lived in fear that she would tell her parents and the police would get involved, but nothing ever happened. Shortly afterwards, Wal and his wife moved to London. When she died, there was only the niece and Wal who knew. She'd gone off the rails for a while, but was now married with a child of her own.

For the most part he'd curbed his behaviour. Sometimes he'd masturbate with magazines; occasionally in the park while secretly watching couples. That was how all this trouble started.

lie[1] (laɪ) *vb* **1** (*intr*) to speak untruthfully with intent to mislead or deceive. **2** to convey a false impression or practise deception. ® *n* **3** an untrue or deceptive statement deliberately used to mislead. **4** something that is deliberately intended to deceive.

*

The jury's job is straightforward, the judge informs them, but he wouldn't want them to underestimate the care with which they need to pursue it. The evidence is largely circumstantial, apart from the roll of masking tape, which is a direct link between the victim and the defendant. As the prosecution has explained, the case is based on a web of indications which provide a weight of probability that the accused was involved. Chief among them has to be the testimony of Mr Redman, which you will need to consider carefully.

The defence case, on the other hand, argues that sufficient reasonable doubt exists in regard to Mr Hanson's connection to the crime. They have argued the absence of motive or any prior criminal inclinations. They have brought testimony as to the character and reputation of the defendant. No implication should be drawn from the fact that Mr Hanson has not taken the stand himself. That is his right, and should form no part of your deliberations. And finally, the defence has cast doubt on the evidence of the aforesaid Mr Redman, questioning its veracity and accuracy.

The task of the jury is to consider whether the weight of evidence is sufficient to overcome any hesitation you might have about the likelihood of the accused committing a crime of this nature. Such doubt would only be natural and reasonable, given the defendant's station in life. You must decide whether the evidence presented by the crown is sufficient to move you past the threshold of reasonable doubt. If so, you must find the defendant guilty as charged. If not, you must find him not guilty.

He then instructs them once more on the procedure to be followed, before sending them off to the jury room.

The waiting begins.

Alex sits in the cell trying to find some reference point from which to understand it all. There seems a relentless inevitability about the whole process. He's being carried along without any chance to stop and draw a breath. It should have stopped some time ago; it should have all been cleared up by now. But it goes on and on.

The evidence presented against him astounds him. Especially that of the old man. What possible reason could he have for it? For the first time, Alex considers the possibility that he might be convicted.

He observes the confines of the cell, with its drab concrete and odour of urine.

My God, my God, why have you forsaken me?

I went out on my own into the city. It was wonderful, with all the strange sights and smells. I found a market, and spent a long time just taking in the excitement of it. A wonderful mix of people and products.

I'd heard about the sex trade, of course. It was difficult to ignore it in a place like that. But I swear I never set out to find it. I'm not even sure to this day whether I stumbled across a special district where the trade was plied, or whether that was just normal street life. But suddenly I was being propositioned. I ignored it at first, feeling slightly sickened by girls selling themselves like that. I didn't even look at them at first.

But then the craving began, like a hunger for something more than food. I found myself picking them out as they stood at the side of the street. I started looking them over, imagining how they would be without clothes. There was a war going on inside my head. I was disgusted by the whole thing; the sordid sad predicament. Everything within me recoiled from it.

Almost everything. Alongside it there was a longing for what they had to offer. I could already feel the fresh moist flesh enveloping me, the thrusting and clawing. Just like the magazine. My mouth was dry and my head was pounding. I kept forcing myself to look straight ahead and keep on walking. I needed discipline. I could get through it, I knew I could.

I stopped at a stall to look at some second-hand books. One of the girls came up beside me. She slipped her hand down the inside of my thigh and began rubbing it. It was the touch which ruined me. I could have resisted without that, I'm certain of it. But I began trembling, and there was a sort of red haze at the back of my eyes.

She didn't even speak to me. She took me by the hand and led me through narrow alleyways. I was worried about all the people around, but no one seemed particularly interested. She brought me to a small shack. There was an old woman there who said something to her and took money from me, then went out.

We were in a back room with a sort of mattress on the floor. It was a dirt floor, but everything was tidy. She had her clothes off in a couple of deft movements. I stood there staring at the tiny breasts, and the black pubic hair. There was such a heat and pressure in my loins that I thought I was going to spoil it all before time. I couldn't speak. I could barely breathe.

She took my hand and placed it very gently between her legs, while she began to remove my clothes. A sort of madness took over after that. I honestly can't remember much about it except for me crying out at the end and the girl smiling politely. That was the point at which I woke up, as it were.

They play checkers, sitting on Joe's cot. It's a fairly even match, with Tom having more plan to his game and Joe more cunning. Joe wins the fifth and deciding game.

'I haven't seen George around lately,' notes Tom. 'He all right?'

'Better than that,' smiles Joe, savouring the victory. 'He's out of here. Paroled out last week. Left me his baccy.'

'How's his wife doing, then?'

'So-so. They've finished the treatment for the meantime, so it's just a waiting game. She'll be happier having George at home, at least for a while.'

'You ever been married, then?'

'Me? You have to be joking. I've shacked up a few times, but never longer than a month or two. Soon as they slow down passing jewellers' shops, I'm out of there. I prefer this prison to that one.'

'It's not as bad as all that,' muses Tom.

Joe looks at him long and hard.

'I see. I never picked you as married. Probably seeing you don't get visits or anything. She ditched you, then?'

'I'm not sure. We agreed that she'd stay away for six months anyway, until I got this sorted out.'

'You're ever hopeful, aren't you Tom? You'll still be here in six months, or six years for all I know. The only thing likely to be sorted out is you. You think she'll wait?'

'No, I shouldn't think so.'

There's a period of silence as Joe packs the checkers and board back into the box.

'All that meditating you do,' Tom asks, 'do you think of yourself as a religious sort of person?'

'Nah. Don't think anyone else does either. Not too much honest religion here in the cells. Sometimes a guy will work it up for the parole hearings—spend time with the chaplain and start going to services and so on. And then you get the odd nutter who thinks if they pray hard enough the doors will spring open. Mostly a way of avoiding reality. I've got my own code, but it's got nothing to with religion.'

'What about God, then?'

'Fuck me, you're a nosy bastard. Why don't you ask a big question for a change? I believe in something. God'll do for a name if you like. But if there's a God, we mostly leave each other alone. I don't blame him and he doesn't blame me. And neither of us expect anything of each other. That good enough?'

'I'm not sure any more,' mutters Tom, away in his own thoughts. 'I used to believe. It all seemed fairly simple to me. There was good and bad, God and the devil, sin and righteousness. I knew which side of the fence I was on, and I was glad to be there. But now it seems as if it's all been mixed up. I find myself looking from the other side, and it all looks quite strange. It sounds pathetic, I know, but I've never seen it that way before. Now I still believe there's a God, but I just don't know whether he's good or evil any more.'

'God from God, light from light, true God from true God,' recites Joe.

'Where d'you learn that?'

'Sunday school I guess. Not that it did me much good in the long run.'

'If God does bad things in order to bring good, doesn't that make God bad?'

'Ease up, Tom. How the fuck would I know? Go and talk to the padre if you want to discuss that sort of stuff.'

'No, come on. Don't pretend you're dumb on me. I've seen the sort of books you read. There's all those Jewish people going through the concentration camps, and coming out for the most part still believing in God. But if there's a God in the midst of those gas chambers, doesn't that make him an evil bastard? It doesn't matter what excuses you come up with in the end—if God sits on his hands while that's going on, then God's responsible for it.'

'I don't know why I'm getting into this. But I'm not sure what you're saying now's much better than when you saw everything as black and white. You're still wanting all or nothing. You don't leave any middle ground. If I hold my hand up against the light, it makes a shadow, see? So maybe you can say the light caused the shadow. But does that mean the light is shadow? I don't know about that one, Tom. You want to know how I see God? I knew a kid at school who got hit by a car. Went into a coma, and lived for three weeks afterwards. I used to go up and visit him in the hospital. He was alive, breathing, but he couldn't speak or anything. I don't know if he could hear or not. I used to talk to him anyway, just in case. That's how I picture God, see? Deaf and dumb and helpless like that kid, smashed unconscious. But still there. And maybe I'll still talk to him if I feel like it.'

'God's a victim?'

'If you like, yeah. So maybe we're the evil bastards, Tom. Maybe we're the ones who've knocked him around.'

in the church they kept talking about eternal life. i didn't know what it meant so i asked my sunday school teacher. she said it was life that had no end to it. i thought everyone died, i said to her. everyone dies, she said, but some people live beyond death because of what they believe. she talked about jesus dying so that we could live, but i couldn't see what the connection was. why can't we just keep on living? i don't want anyone to have to die because of me. she said it didn't matter because jesus

178

came back to life again. it might have been easier if he'd never died in the first place.

i think of all this now because that girl in the box is me. i'm sure of it now, though i couldn't see it at first. but how can i be looking at myself? and why would i be dead anyway, if mummy and daddy and all my friends are still alive? i don't know what any of this means. i'd just like to go home now.

The gallery is packed for the return of the jury. The trial has generated a huge amount of public interest. Everyone has an opinion.

Harry is there among them, waiting. He senses the tension of anticipation, sparking round the courtroom like a firestorm.

This is it. After all the hours of work. The fruits of their labour. Their offering on behalf of the small girl with her limbs protruding from the bushes. In a few short words the matter will be decided. Harry doesn't know what he's hoping for. And he certainly can't predict the outcome. Even the legal teams are edgy, despite their respective attempts at confidence.

Finally the judge returns and the jury is ushered in. Harry can hardly bear it now. He leans back and begins to count the holes in the fibreboard ceiling as the formalities are carried through.

At the judge's question, he closes his eyes tightly.

'Guilty,' says the man in the corduroy jacket.

In the midst of the ensuing murmur, Harry sighs to the depths of his soul. It's over.

He sits there quietly, waiting for something to happen. There's the man who is guilty of raping and murdering his only daughter. But the hatred refuses to be dislodged. He can feel it there as a hard knot in his stomach.

There should be some emotion, Mark thinks. People are watching him amidst the uproar. There's nothing to see. He exists in the limbo of the lost; the glorious detachment of misery.

This is the final cut of his tragedy; to discover vengeance to be impotent. What else is there to hope for?

Nancy hears it on the radio. Her heart flips in her chest like a wounded bird. With the dextrous ease of adolescence, the life-long love for her father turns to revulsion.

She's branded. Marked for life as the daughter of a murderer. And not only a murderer, a pervert. She wants to get away, to go into hiding. Anything to avoid facing people who know her.

This is the end of her life. There will be nothing beyond it but living out her days in shame. Unaccountably, she feels dirty. Blackened on the inside as well as the out.

And angry. So unbelievably angry.

There's an image which comes back to haunt her. That clergyman, coming into my house and holding me. With the same hands that . . .

The television continues to drone. There's a picture of Tessa, a school photo in which she's not sure whether to smile or not. Various people are talking about the case. Elizabeth has not registered much since she heard the guilty verdict.

The whisky doesn't seem to be working. The soothing fog has rolled off her coast into the distance. The foreground of crushing pain stands out, starkly clear.

He touched me. That filthy filthy bastard put his arms round me. I was that close to him. Oh fuck. Oh Jesus.

Her skin is crawling as though there are vermin all over it. She scratches at it and grimaces in loathing. She needs to have a shower. But there's something she has to do first.

It takes her a while to find the Bible on the bookshelf. Mark picked it up in a sale, saying he thought every home should have one. No one's looked at it since she tucked it into the bottom corner.

She carries it at arm's length, as if it was dangerous. On the kitchen bench she begins to tear at the pages. They won't rip at first, and she has to take just a few at a time. Her attack becomes frenzied, and she bruises her arms several times as her fingers slip. Eventually a pile of torn pages fill the sink.

She sets fire to them, and watches as the flames lick and consume and the thick black smoke rises to the ceiling.

'Burn, you fucking loser, burn!' she calls into the tempest. And then the sobs are uncontrollable, as ferocious as the fire.

The staff canteen is no more human than any other part of the prison. What was once government-green linoleum is speck-led by the brown smudges of stubbed out cigarettes. The red-flecked Formica of the table tops is chipped and peeling, with gaps round the edges where bored guards have aided the process.

Kevin comes there because the food is cheap, and it's better than eating alone in his office. It gives him a chance to talk to staff out of sight of the inmates. But as he contemplates the plate of beans topped by a greasy sliding egg, he doubts whether the benefits outweigh the indignities.

His reverie is broken by someone arriving at his table. Chromefang, the inmates call him—and most of the staff, out of his hearing.

'Mind if I sit here?' he asks.

'Glad of the company,' says Kevin, smiling politely. 'How's the shift going?'

'Not too badly. Everything's calm, which is the way we like it. A quiet block is a chance to play cards, I always say. You busy saving these villains' souls, padre? God knows they could do with saving.'

'I do what I can, which isn't much I'm afraid. The only advantage is I don't have to worry about my flock dwindling.'

'True enough. I see you had that new boy who's bunked up with Joe come to see you the other day. Read his file have you?'

'Mmmm. I have actually.'

'You want to watch yourself round him. When word gets out, you wouldn't want to be seen to be chummy with him, would you?'

'I have to be available for anyone who wants to talk. It's not

181

always easy,' replies Kevin. Available even to staff, he thinks.

'Suit yourself. We already had a couple of the thugs have a go at him the day before yesterday. And they don't know the half of it.'

'I wouldn't expect they would.'

'These things have a way of getting out,' says the man in the serge uniform, with bright-yellow egg yolk at the corner of his mouth. And there's a glint of silver in the midst of his smile.

In the cavern of his bedroom, Ross has the amplifier wound up with maximum distortion. He chops at the strings with his fist in a pounding rhythm. One of his fingers has begun to bleed and is making a spray of blood on the white strike-plate of the guitar.

He can't believe that it's gone this far. I only wanted to take the smart prick down a peg or two, that's all. Sick of his little lectures and sermons, his high-and-mighty rules about what's right and wrong.

It seemed a small way to get back when he started. It wasn't much of a lie. To tell the truth, he couldn't remember where he got the tape from. Picked it up somewhere or other. And then once he'd told them he didn't know anything about it, he couldn't change his story. It would have got him into trouble. He just kept quiet that's all. Not a huge crime, is it?

I didn't know it would come to this.

> **revenge** (rɪ'vɛndʒ) *n* **1** the act of retaliating for wrongs or injury received; vengeance. **2** something done as a means of vengeance. **3** the desire to take vengeance or retaliate.

They meet in a coffee shop not far from his office. Mary is worried she won't recognise him, but he rises to greet her as soon as she enters the door. James insists on buying the coffee, and they face each other across the stainless-steel table top.

He is a balding man with what Mary secretly calls a 'Christian beard': a neatly trimmed growth which excludes a moustache. He has a sharp nose and eager eyes. At the conference she had initially disliked him, but warmed to his seemingly genuine enthusiasm.

'Thanks for agreeing to meet me,' she murmurs, toying with her coffee.

'I'm happy to help in any way I can. Especially with things as they are at the moment. I'm so sorry the way that this has worked out, Mary. You must be devastated. Let me know if there's anything I can do to help.'

She's lost count of the number of people who have said something similar. It's meant well, but there are some things that can't be helped. Certainly there's nothing she can think of to ask for, short of a change of identity.

'You must be wondering what this is about,' she says. 'I'm just trying to understand Alex, that's all. I mean I thought I knew him, of course I did. And to all intents and purposes I still do. But since all this began, I've questioned whether there's something about him I've missed, some terrible secret. It's probably just my paranoia, but I have to ask.'

'I certainly don't know any terrible secrets about Alex, if that's what you're looking for. I've always admired him deeply, to tell the truth. He's always had a way with people that I would love to have, and his preaching leaves mine for dead. I'm not aware of any skeletons in his closet. He had a hard childhood that he doesn't like to talk about much, but I'm sure you're aware of all that.'

'His mother said something to me in passing the other day, about him coming back early from his trip on the ship. She thought he'd returned from the Philippines, instead of waiting for the end of the journey in Hawaii.'

James sips at his coffee and reflects.

'Yes, by Jove, I think you're right. It was all rather sudden, now that I recall it. I was in a cabin just along from Alex, and we used to spend a lot of time together doing Bible studies and so on. He was very zealous in those days, you know.' James smiles.

'I was off on a team doing some street theatre inland a bit. Alex stayed behind on ship duty. When I got back after a couple of days, he'd gone. I thought it was very strange, because up until then he'd been talking about staying on for another tour. Everyone was a bit tight-lipped about it. The story was that a family member had taken ill and he had to get back sharpish. But when I saw Alex back in England, he said they must have got it wrong. He went back because he'd had a revelation that he should go into ministry, and he'd found out the interviews were being held. If he'd stayed on he would have had to wait another year. I remember thinking that was a little odd, because I had another friend who had his interview delayed and got in on provisional entry, and I wondered why Alex couldn't have done the same.

'So there you. A bit of a mystery, but nothing sinister in it as far as I know. I don't think there's much that's sinister to be found, to tell the truth.'

The smoke alarm is squealing as he rushes to get the door unlocked. There's a faint pall of smoke hugging the ceiling of the kitchen, but no fire to be seen. Nothing but a pile of ashes in the sink, and the mutilated remains of the Bible lying on the floor.

He finds her in the bedroom, naked and drying herself after a shower. Her eyes and cheeks are red, her lips swollen. She looks for all the world like his private image of a whore.

'You heard, then,' he observes.

Elizabeth staggers sideways while drying her back, and lurches drunkenly into the side of the bed. She reaches out a hand to steady herself, and then claims the safety of the bed by sitting on it.

'I heard, I saw, I believed. Have you killed him yet?'

'Are you all right?'

'Listen to yourself, Marky-Warky. Am I all right? Oh yes. Yes. I'm English so I must be fine. God, stop that fucking noise, will you?' She clamps her hands over her ears.

Mark finds a chair, reaches up to the alarm and removes the battery. When he comes back to the bedroom, he finds her stretched out on the bed, still with no clothes on. Several centuries ago, he might have felt something other than despair.

'You let her go,' she says, tightening her lips.

'What?'

'You let her go to the park on her own, you bastard! You said she'd be fine, that I shouldn't worry so much. You told me it would be all right, and I believed you. Look what happened, just look what happened!'

Mark sinks to his knees at the end of the bed and emits a low wail. It's part-way between a growl and a whine, a terrible inhuman keening.

'What is it about men?' she carries on relentlessly. 'Where does it come from, this sickness you have? Why can't you ever get enough? Why does it go on and on? It's not just sex. Oh no, it can't be two people just giving and taking, loving each other. It's darker than that, isn't it? It's all fucking and screwing and shafting. Anger and power and something else I don't even begin to understand. You hate us, don't you? You want to destroy us, to torture us, and you make us love you because you know it'll hurt all the more. You're a part of this, Mark. Even with your educated fucking liberal ideas. You're a part of what killed Tessa, what destroyed my beautiful girl.

'You want to fuck me? Come on, here I am, Mark. Get it over with. Look, I'll open my legs for you and you can stab as much as you like. I want it Mark. I want to die. I want to be raped, not her. Not my baby.'

But Mark is crouching on the floor like a frightened animal.

There I was, still inside her, when I felt this overpowering sense of loathing. I was sick to the pit of my stomach, so much so that I thought I was going to vomit. My head was aching and all my limbs had turned to lead. As if the life had been sucked out of me.

She'd tricked me. I'd been doing well. And then the dirty little whore had touched me, and got me excited. All very well for her to be looking innocent now, but she'd corrupted me; dragged me down to her tawdry level. I knew it had all gone wrong, and that it was all her fault. It made me angry.

I only slapped her the once at first. I didn't think about it. It just happened. But then when she cried out I hit her again to keep her

185

quiet, punched her with a closed fist. The next thing I knew, her face was a bloody mess, and I was still on top of her. There were people there, holding me by the shoulders and dragging me backwards, and voices shouting all around me.

I remember her body, so smooth and child-like. I hated myself, but I was pleased that I'd made up for it, that I'd atoned in some way. I'd fought back against her evil, even if it was too late. Perhaps there was still some hope.

They play crash-tackle in the gym. It's not a game for the faint hearted. There are no rules, only an object. The object is to get the ball past the opposition players to the other end of the hall. There's always blood and there are often injuries, with the wooden floors unforgiving in impact. Periodically it gets banned by the screws, but eventually it re-emerges. In truth they're happy to see inmates battering each other.

Joe is a sought-after player and has the highest number of points scored. Today he shoulder-charges the last opponent into the wall and scoots to the far end, touching the ball against the climbing bars once again. He turns and throws his right arm up in a victory salute.

No one is watching. Their attention is taken by a fight at the other end of the gymnasium. The inmates are standing in a circle round the action, preventing the guards from getting near. Someone has already hit the alarm bell.

He can't see Tom among the spectators. He drops the ball and sprints to the small arena where there is the unmistakable sound of bone meeting flesh.

It's Hammer on Tom. Joe unleashes a deadly elbow into the cheekbone of an unlucky bystander to gain entrance to the circle. Hammer is delivering a series of forearm jolts to the skull of the man beneath him. In his left hand he holds a prison knife, ready to strike.

Joe simply kicks Hammer from behind, striking him cleanly between the legs and driving him forward onto the floor. The knife skitters across the polished wood.

'I thought I told you to lay off him,' growls Joe, placing a foot across Hammer's windpipe and beginning to push down.

'He's a fucking spider, Joe,' rasps Hammer. 'A rock spider. He's in for doing a little girl.'

'Bullshit,' Joe challenges.

'Straight up,' says Blade from over Joe's shoulder. 'Ask the screws if you don't believe us. He's been using a fake name to keep it under wraps.'

Tom is cowering in terror. But also there is a feeling of something unexpected. Relief? Yes, the inevitable has come. And now the consequences.

A few days after the verdict, she goes to see him. Just the process is humiliating enough, without all that has brought it about. Walking through a metal detector, and having men with large bunches of keys usher her through steel grates.

Mary is entirely out of her element, light years away from anything her previous experience has prepared her for. She tries to stop herself trembling, without success.

She's taken to a desk with a large metal grille across the middle of it. She sits in the hard wooden chair. Shortly there is the clanging echo of steel doors opening and closing, and Alex is guided to the chair opposite her.

He's wearing prison issue: an orange T-shirt and blue jeans. He appears to have aged, but perhaps it is just the strange setting and apparel. The slumping posture is completely uncharacteristic.

All of a sudden Mary feels the accumulated tiredness of the last months descend upon her. There is a short silence, as if they were strangers who didn't know how to begin. She can hardly bear to meet his eyes.

'Thanks for coming,' he says at last.

'I'm your wife,' is all she can think of to say.

'Yes. But I could understand it if you wanted to keep away. You must be confused about all this . . .'

'Confused? That's one part of it Alex. Crushed, bewildered, embarrassed, angry, lonely: there's a lot of things I feel. I can't imagine how this has happened. But it has, and I'm here.'

'You know I didn't do it, don't you Mary? You can't possibly believe that I'd be involved in any way? I don't think I could bear it if I thought you suspected there was any truth to these charges.'

'Convictions, I think they are now. I don't know. I'm terribly mixed up. To be honest, no, I can't believe that you could have done it. But here you are behind bars, so I have to try and adjust to it. If I thought you were guilty, I don't imagine I would have come, wife or no wife.'

'I understand. Or at least I think I do.'

'What happens now?'

'I'm to be transferred on Monday to the maximum-security prison. All the lifers go there as a matter of course, apparently. I want to clear this up, naturally. I've already talked to the lawyer about an appeal, and we should be able to proceed. He says it might take as much as a year to work through to that.'

'Oh,' she says. There's the hint of tears as Mary digests the news.

'There's something I'd like to ask you. Just hear me out before you answer. I don't want you to visit me any more. Not until I've got this all cleared up. This is not me, sitting here in prison clothes, and I don't want you to see me like this. And I don't want the children to come either, though I don't suppose they want to anyway.'

Mary's silence is sufficient confirmation. His shoulders sag a little in response.

'It's a terrible place, the prison I'm going to. Some of the wardens here have taken great delight in telling me about it, and what's likely to happen to me there. I'm going to try to disguise my identity, Mary. I've decided to take my middle name, Tom. My mother always wanted me to be Tom anyway, but my father insisted on Alex. Nobody knows me in there, and I'm hoping they don't find out. It'll make things easier for me.

'I'm sorry for all this, more sorry than I can say. But the most I can do for you, and you for me, is that we stay apart until it's all cleared up. Will you do that for me?'

'All right Alex,' she sighs, trying not to let the relief show.

It's only on the way out that she remembers. She had meant to ask him about that trip to the Philippines.

The wound to the face required seven stitches. And his jaw is broken in two places. The rest is mostly just deep bruising. They're the sort of injuries that are bread and butter in the hospital block.

Alex welcomes the physical pain. It's a distraction from the deep anxiety welling from within. Now that his identity is known, there's nowhere to hide.

And Joe—what will Joe think of him? There's been no chance to explain.

sometimes i watch mummy and feel terribly sad for her. i don't even know why. she seems happy enough and daddy loves her as much as i do. yesterday i saw her staring out of the window in the kitchen. there's nothing really to see out there, but she seemed to be looking at something in the distance. and then i felt it again, that sadness.

i went up to her and cuddled her without saying anything. she just looked down and smiled, and ran her fingers through my hair. what is it about adults that makes their lives so hard? i hope it doesn't happen to me when i grow up, whatever it is. i think people have too much work to do, so that there's not enough time for them to play any more. if everyone had a rabbit to look after, maybe they would have more fun. i'd do anything to take the sadness out of mummy's eyes.

Chapter Eleven

'Thanks for coming in, Harry. Shift those files and have a seat.'

Thompson smiles at the uniformed man and leans back in his chair, placing his hands behind his head.

'In trouble, am I?' jokes Harry.

'No, quite the opposite. I know I've already thanked you for what you did on the Bromley case, but there are a couple of loose ends to be tied up.'

Harry's brow creases and his jaw sags.

'New evidence?' he ventures.

'No, nothing like that. You did a lot of good work for us, you know. I've got a team of detectives working on it for me, and it's a uniformed man who comes up with the goods. We may have got there ourselves, eventually, or we may not. But I suspect it was mainly down to you that we put this chap away.'

'Happy to help out. Sometimes you get a few lucky breaks, you know how it is.'

'What I've got you in for, Harry, is to tell you some good news and to ask you a question. First up, I put in a recommendation for a special commendation for you to the super, and it's been approved. There'll be a small ceremony on the nineteenth—you'll get official confirmation shortly, I should think. That's by the by; what I really want to discuss with you is the possibility of a change.'

'I'd not be keen on a transfer, inspector. I've got quite attached to this patch.'

'You've got the nose of a detective, Harry. I'd like to have you on my team. I wondered if you'd consider jumping ships, as it were, and coming across to the non-uniformed branch. There'd be no loss of seniority, and a pay rise of sorts. What do you think?'

Harry shuffles his feet and looks down at the carpet. There've been plenty of times when he's considered it. Wanted it, even. But since this girl and the vicar, he hasn't been able to sleep at night. He lives with the doubt, and under it a creeping fear. What if they were wrong? What if there's still someone out there, laughing?

'I'd like some time to think about it. I appreciate the offer, don't get me wrong. But I don't know, I just don't know,' says Harry.

'No hurry,' Thompson allows. 'Give it a week or two and get back to me. I'd like to have you on board, Harry.'

He does the hospital block every couple of days anyway. Often they get reflective while they're on their backs for a while and out of the vortex of cell life. Sometimes the odd one will ask for prayer. More often they want him to contact their families. Kevin's happy to help out in any way he can.

But this morning he comes with a more specific mission. The story was all round the canteen. How they'd uncovered the child rapist's identity and already had a go at him. Chromefang had laughed loudest, and winked at Kevin in response to the accusing stare.

'Hello Tom,' he begins, pulling up the plastic chair.

'It's Alex, as everyone seems to be aware now,' the prone man announces painfully from his bruised face.

'Yes. I'm sorry that it's come to this, Alex.'

'Are you? You're sure you don't think it's what I had coming? That seems to be the common wisdom, even among the nursing staff.'

'You of all people should understand my role here. I'm a neutral—I have to be. I try to stand outside the various camps. I've read your file, as I said, and I'd be less than honest if I didn't admit it shocked me. But I'm here as one human being to be with another human being. I'm not here to make judgements.'

'That's right, we're both clergy, aren't we? Servants of God, ministers of the gospel, ambassadors of reconciliation. Only I've fallen from grace, you understand. It's made me think about the devil; strange, isn't it? But he fell too, or so the story goes. Fell from a high place to become the scourge of all. So I may be on the other side from you now. I may have been judged and rejected.'

'There's no rejection beyond the reach of forgiveness. You came to me, the other day, wanting to confess your sins. I wondered if you were any more ready now?'

'Now? Because I've had a beating? No, there's a reason why I couldn't confess to you, and it hasn't changed. Tell me what I'm in for, chaplain.'

'You know why you've been convicted; I don't need to tell you.'

'Say it, just the same.'

'You've been convicted for the rape and murder of a small girl,' sighs Kevin.

'Yes. The rape and murder of a little girl named Tessa Bromley. She used to come to my church, did you know that? A delightful girl. Did you think it strange, when you were reading my file, that a priest could do that to a member of his flock? That he could switch from being shepherd to wolf? Perhaps it didn't surprise you, being in this place. You might have begun to believe anything of anyone. But as God is my witness, I'm not guilty of this crime.

'I didn't do it, you see. How could I? How could anyone believe it of me? And yet here I am, just the same. That's why I didn't confess to you the other day. Confession requires repentance, doesn't it? And I don't feel repentant. I haven't done anything to deserve being here. I'm not a sinner, you see, or at least not any more than anyone else. But I've been sinned against. And you know who's sinned against me, don't you?'

Kevin remains silent, watching and listening.

'God. I've lived my whole life for God, given everything

I've got. And now I've been banished. Now I'm here in this shit-hole, with no hope. My family has gone, my reputation has gone, my vocation has gone. So lately I've been feeling a little sympathy for the devil. I know what it's like to be rejected and fall. And I have to tell you, the view looks very different from down here.

'So that's not quite the right attitude for confession, is it? I don't have contrition, you see. Just bitterness. Bitterness and pain.'

Kevin observes the way that Alex's face has compressed into a grimace of pure hatred as he speaks. It's almost frightening.

No matter how many times he goes over the figures, they don't look any better. The firm's been willing to cut him some slack, given the circumstances. But Mark knows it won't be indefinite. At some stage he has to start performing again. It would be easier if it weren't for the blank spots. Time and again he finds himself staring blankly, with no recollection of where he's been.

Christina interrupts with a memo. She frowns at his vague acknowledgement.

'I don't want to intrude, Mark, but you're looking terrible. Is there anything I can get you?'

Of all of them at work, she's been the one he's sometimes been able to talk to. The rest of them have been terrified, tip-toeing round him after the initial stunted expressions of sympathy. He feels as if he has some disease which they're scared of catching. Christina, the sales manager, has spent a couple of sessions listening while Mark talked endlessly about Tessa. Having a miscarriage in the days when she was still married has given her some insight into pain.

'Why don't you sit down. If you've got a minute,' Mark offers.

'Hard times again?' she prompts, taking a seat and smoothing her skirt.

'Yes. I keep thinking I should be getting over it by now, or at least learning how to live with it. My mother keeps ringing up and hinting that I'm dwelling on things. Insists on telling about how it was when she lost her fiancée in the war, as if that somehow helps. But I can't seem to get to the end of it, you know? I'm scared I'll never find a way out, that this is the way it's going to be for ever. And things are not too good on the home front.'

'Elizabeth?'

'I think she might be going under. She's been drinking too much for a long time. I thought it was just a phase, a temporary thing. But it seems to be getting worse. I'm scared for her and scared of her. She hates me you know. Blames me for what happened.'

'Oh Mark, I'm sure that's not true. She's just angry, and you're the one closest.'

'No, it's more than that. I've seen it in her eyes. She loathes me. I don't know that there's any way for us to get back from here now.'

'It got that way with Frank in the end. I woke up one morning and realised it was over, before either of us had made any decisions. After that it didn't need any deciding—whatever we'd had before had gone. I just looked at him and I knew it without him saying anything.'

'Yes,' is all that Mark can manage. Tears are easing their way down the side of his nose. So much slipping away, and no way of holding it.

Christina has moved behind him, and is massaging his shoulders. The comforting touch of a woman is so very, very welcome.

It shook me. I was forced to realise where all of this was taking me. I knew that I had to conquer it before the damage was too great. I'd come close to the edge of the cliff and had a look over the side. It was enough to frighten me and bring me to my senses. I burned the magazine. It surprised me how difficult it was to do. Even when it was well alight, I was tempted to reach my hand into the fire and rescue it.

But my will was resolute. I was determined to leave all of this behind me. And the sense of relief was immense. It was as if I had passed some elaborate test, and been strengthened because of it. My whole life lay before me, and I'd been given the opportunity to correct a mistake. I felt enormously grateful, and it gave me a new burst of enthusiasm and energy. I looked at it as one of those experiences which are difficult but ultimately beneficial to character.

For a time afterwards my head was clearer than it had been. The fog lifted, giving me a clearer perspective on my life and what it was about. Sometimes the image of the girl's battered face would come back to me in a dream, and I would wake rigid with fear. But it soon passed, and there would be a huge wave of relief when I registered that it was only a dream, and that all of that was behind me now.

From time to time other images would come to me. At odd times, often when I was relaxing or on my own. Images from the magazine. The sultry eyes, demanding satisfaction, calling me to return to them. Only their bodies had changed. They no longer had the huge tanned breasts or welcoming thighs. No, they had small child-like bodies, with smooth skin. Like fruit not fully ripened. They wanted me; they were luring me, trying to call me back.

I was strong, so very strong. Whenever they came, these pictures, I refused to linger on them. I pushed them down, squashed them, and renounced them entirely. I would not entertain them. I purged my imagination with my will. Sometimes it took enormous amounts of mental energy to keep the images exiled. But I was resolute. I was battle hardened, and now I knew how to achieve victory.

> **repress** (rɪ'prɛs) *vb (tr)* **1** to keep (feelings, etc.) under control; suppress or restrain. **2** to put into a state of subjugation. **3** *Psychoanal.* to banish (thoughts and impulses that conflict with conventional standards of conduct) from one's conscious mind.

there was a time when i was in the bookshop and a man came in who was dressed in old clothes. he looked quite old, and a bit untidy. he said hello to me and i smiled at him and went back to reading. he was looking at books, but out of the corner of my eye i could see that he was watching me as well. i felt funny about him, so i moved round to the other side of the shop, pretending to be looking for something.

he just worked his way round the stacks, scanning books

and moving slowly, but getting closer and closer to where i was. soon he was almost beside me, and i could smell something funny like the sherry which mummy sometimes uses in cooking. then he passed behind me, and sort of rubbed up against me as he was doing it. he said sorry, but he did it on purpose, i'm sure he did. i was frightened and disgusted, and i went out straightaway. he was watching me as i left. i never told anyone about it because there wasn't really anything to tell.

In every prison there are inmates who have privileges. They're assigned work which allows them wider access to the facility, in recognition of their behaviour. Often these prisoners operate as go-betweens: eyes and ears of both guards and inmates. Some of them do well from their trading of information. Occasionally they deliver messages one way or another.

The hospital cleaners are Bill, a big Scouse muscle man, and Reggie, a drug-dealer of Italian extraction. They work for two hours a day, mopping and cleaning. Reggie likes being around the pharmacy counter, from which he supplies a reasonable internal trade.

Alex is reading a book when Bill begins mopping under his bed. Normally they start at the other end, but there may have been some change of routine. He's surprised when Reggie turns up, smiling, and starts closing the curtains round the bed.

The medical staff are off at a seminar, and the only guard is the fat Welshman, who Alex hasn't seen for the last ten minutes. His attempt to call out is stifled as Bill holds his shoulders and Reggie applies surgical tape across his mouth.

It's all happening so quickly now as Bill turns the injured man effortlessly and Reggie obliges by taping his wrists behind him. Then they roll him onto his back once again. As Alex's eyes bulge, Reggie removes an object from the front of his trousers.

It's a sawn-off piece of broom-handle, perhaps a foot long.

Reggie speaks.

'We've got a little present for you, Tom. Or Alex it is really, isn't it? Had us all fooled you did, for a while. Anyway, we've all had a think about it, and we've decided on something special for you to remember us by. It'll be right up your alley, so to speak.'

Reggie removes Alex's pyjama bottoms. He does it slowly and carefully, as if it were a seduction.

Alex thinks about kicking out, but Bill's huge fists are either side of his broken jaw.

'Now that's right, just hold him still there for a minute, would you Bill? We've got a little something extra for you, Alex. We heard what you did to that little girl, see? Some of us have got little girls of our own, haven't we Bill? And we don't much like the thought of greasy fucking spiders like you sticking your big dick into them. It's not meant to be, see? So we're thinking we might give you a little taste of it for yourself.'

Reggie disappears through the curtains, eventually returning from the nurses' station carrying a glass vase.

'See this, Alex? Looks like water, doesn't it? Only it's not. It's some sort of acid. I don't know what sort—I was never very good at chemistry. We use it for cleaning the bedpans, and it works quite well. So what we're going to do, we're going to dip this little stick here in this acid—that's it—and Bill's going to hold you down while I find somewhere to put it. You just relax and lie back and think of that little girl. Oh dear, Bill, I do believe he's pissed himself.'

The other inmates in the ward know better than to interfere with what's happening behind the curtains. They will have seen nothing at all.

She's almost scared to admit she likes it. Even having the entire bed to herself is a small luxury. For the first time since she married, Mary's life doesn't revolve round the world of Alex. And so, in amongst the bewildered guilt, she finds moments of genuine enjoyment.

Such as this one. Sitting alone in the empty house with a cup of tea, and nothing but the silence. She's grateful to the bishop for pulling strings and organising for her to be able to stay on for at least a year.

197

And then what? That's the question, isn't it? How do I put the pieces together again when I can't even find the corner bits?

She likes to pretend that Alex is dead. It's preferable to the thought that he's alone and neglected in prison. Death is normal. It happens to other people, and so may be forgiven. And he is dead, anyway. In a sense. The man I married, my Alex. These things could never have happened to him. If it should be a betrayal, it's also my lifeline. Bereavement is something I can get through. The other is impossible.

In the substratum of her soul, a seed is cracking open. She has not yet begun to feel the exploration of its tendrils. There is no sign of what it might become. There is only the cracking and opening; the first fragile hint of life unfolding in the depths. It may come to nothing. But it is worthy of nurture.

> **nascent** ('næs²nt, ·neɪ) *adj* starting to grow or develop; being born.

In his cell, Joe plays solitaire to distract himself. It's not working.

They went into graphic detail in the telling; especially Reggie. Like schoolboys reporting on the torture of a kitten. Every element was relished in the recounting, a tribal saga of sadism. The laughter was a little forced. He finds himself recoiling at some residual level from the violation of humanity, even in the cause of justice.

Joe walked away in the end. No one noticed. They were spellbound in feeding at the troughs of vengeance. He walked away and returned to his cell. Even a tough man has his limits.

It's the code by which he lives. The rule of the jungle, in which he is a supreme predator. It's the way it has to be. He understands it. But he despises the world in which it is necessary. Despises himself for going along with the plan.

There is the one question which re-presents itself with every card he turns over. What if Alex really is innocent?

It's raining when she arrives, and she hasn't got an umbrella. By the time she finds her way to the headstone, Elizabeth's hair is flattened against her skin, and she's cold. It seems the right sort of weather to come visiting in.

She kneels down in front of the granite slab and traces the gold words with her finger. The stone is cold and wet and lifeless. There is nothing in it to give any clue to the magic of the name it bears. What other memorial could they have given her? She leans her head against it, and wraps her arms around its sharp edges.

'Tessa, can you hear me?' she whispers. 'I'm sorry, darling. So sorry we couldn't keep you safe. I would have swapped places with you if I could. You know that, don't you? You could have had my life. I wish I could give it to you now. Oh God, Tessa, I wish you were alive and I was dead.

'I should have come here before now; I know I should. But I haven't been able to, darling. I couldn't make myself. Where are you, Tessa? Are you all right? Are you safe now? Is everything better? I love you, sweetie. You can't know how much I love you. You were so beautiful, so beautiful. You still are, for me. Nothing's changed, you see. None of this happened, this ugliness. I see you laughing and playing and asking questions, and you'll always be alive like that for me. I won't get to see you grow up or get married or have children of your own, but you'll be my little girl, Tessa. My precious little girl.

'I'm going to give you what I can of my life now. I'm going to live for you and no one else. I won't betray you again, Tessa. I won't stop thinking about you or talking to you. I won't love anyone else. Not even Daddy. Not even him. You can count on me. I'll stay with you. I'll be here, Tessa.'

There is nothing but silence and cold, and the grey, slanting rain mingling with the tears. The stone is inside of her as much as in her arms. She no longer resists it.

It caught me in a moment of weakness. I was tired and lonely and feeling sorry for myself. Someone had left a magazine in the toilet. It was one of those fashion journals with the glossy photos. I was only flicking through it out of boredom. There was a picture of a young woman wearing a T-shirt and knickers. She had the hem of the shirt lifted up with one finger to just above her navel.

Her hair was lank and black. She had a child's body. I don't know how old she would have been, but looked no more than twelve. It started all over again. I wanted to turn the page. That's all I needed to do, to turn the page quickly and break the spell. But I couldn't do it. I was powerless. She was looking at me, willing me to linger and stare.

And my hand crept down with a will of its own, and I lost my control. I don't expect anyone else to understand it, but it took over. And the release was glorious.

I cried afterwards. Sitting there in the toilet with the tears running down my face, and feeling so empty. I ripped the page out and screwed it up and tried to flush it down the toilet. It wouldn't go at first—it kept bobbing around on the surface of the water, as if it were taunting me.

That was the start of it. At first I would go to libraries, and pretend to myself that I was there for some other reason. It was accidental that I found myself in the magazine section. Within a few weeks I was buying them from shops. I was lucky. It seemed that child-like models were very much in vogue. I didn't need to buy pornography, though in the end it came to that. Women's magazines were full of suitable material.

I despised those girls, you understand. I never loved them at all. They were foul and cheap, prostituting themselves for money. Without them, I might have been safe.

Alex flinches as the face of Joe appears through the curtain. The terror is worse than the pain. You can take medication for the pain.

Joe has special permission from the super to be there. He's not sure why he's come. It may be nothing more than curiosity. He finds Alex lying on his side. He says nothing, sliding into the chair next to the bed.

A thin film of sweat has broken out on Alex's brow. He doesn't know how Joe is going to react. He can't predict anything any more. Life has become a horror film in which random violence erupts without warning. Why should his cellmate come now? For a visit? To abuse him? To mete out further retribution? There's no way of knowing.

'I didn't do it, Joe,' he starts.

'What?'

'I didn't do it. I couldn't have harmed that little girl, you have to know that. I knew I'd never be able to convince anyone; that's why I used another name. But I didn't do it.'

Joe narrows his eyes and looks at this enigma of a man.

'I hear you're a vicar,' he says at length.

'I was, before all this started.'

'Bit of a joke, that. Me sharing my cell with a fucking vicar. I knew there was something funny about you—just couldn't figure it. We don't get a lot of priests in here, not on our side of the fence leastways. You had me sucked in, Tom. Or Alex, isn't it? I can't quite get used to it yet.'

'I'm sorry, Joe. But I didn't do what I'm accused of. I hope you believe that.'

'You all right?'

'I've been better. The colostomy's only temporary, until the burns heal. I don't sleep much.'

'What you're up for, raping a girl—that's the bottom end of the food chain in here. I shouldn't even be talking to you. Won't do me any good. I just wanted to come and look you in the eye and try to figure it out for myself.'

'And what do you see?'

'I dunno, to be honest. Usually I can pick 'em pretty well. But you're so far off the square that I don't have anything to compare it with. You might have done it; you might not. Only you and God know that, and God's not telling.'

There's a pause as Joe rubs the back of his shaven head and considers before continuing.

'I let them do it, Alex. They came to me, see, because I'd been protecting you. They needed my permission before they dealt to you. I could have said no—it would have been hard, but I could have if I'd wanted to. I didn't want to. So it's down to me, in some ways. I didn't know how they were going to do it, but I knew it wouldn't be pretty. I turned you over to them, see? Very easy, in the end. Just one word.'

'So you think I'm guilty,' groans Alex in abject defeat.

'No, like I said, I don't know. I couldn't take the chance though, see? Better that you should be innocent and done over than that we let some child-fucker break the code. That's what's important in the end—lose the code and we lose everything. So I had to put you to the sword to make sure.'

'Like God,' the prone man mutters.

'You what?'

'You were playing God, Joe. And doing a good job of it. Giving me up for the sake of preserving the game. That's what my faith is all about. I don't expect you to understand it, but that's the story of Christ, isn't it? Turned over to be punished for something he didn't do. Delivered up by God for sacrifice.'

'I would have thought that was down to Pilate,' responds Joe.

'No, God wanted it, you see. There was some reason for it to happen, and so God passes up his only son to achieve his purpose. The end justifies the means, Joe, even for God. I've never seen it before, until it got to this. Crucifixion, humiliation, rejection; it's all part of God getting what he wants in the world. We go on about the love of God, but only because none of us are honest enough to look into the dark side and talk about it. There's a shadow there; a great black chasm which swallows up people like me as if they never existed. No, you were right, Joe. You only did what you had to do; I understand that.'

'You ever think about the girl?'

'Of course I do. How could I not?'

'Only I hear you talking all along about yourself and how innocent you are and how you've been falsely accused. But what about the girl, then? What about her innocence? What about justice for her? Only she's dead now, so nothing can bring it back for her. She's gone. You want to put that down to God as well?'

'Yes,' replies Alex, staring at the wall.

'You're a sick fucker.'

'You want me to be, don't you Joe? You want me to be a miserable pervert, a despicable piece of humanity. You want to be able to despise me and persecute me and make me something other than you are. And you know why? Because you need someone to blame. It's as simple as that. Something like the girl's death is too much to face, and so you need someone to blame. Evil has to be somewhere else, doesn't it? In other people, crazy, twisted people. Or in the devil. You're just part of the game, but it's bigger than you. Scapegoating, it's called. Where you pour all your sins onto some innocent animal and destroy it. You know where it comes from, Joe? From the Bible, that's where. Because it's God's game to start with. I'm just a scapegoat, another victim along the way. Well, I've got beyond caring. I don't want sympathy. I don't need friendship. I just want an end. A way out.'

'They're moving you next week.'

'Where to?'

'No one knows. Another prison up-country somewhere. You'll be classified as protective custody. Very nice. Get a cell to yourself. Only you'll need to keep an eye out behind your back all the time, see? Word gets about, much as they try to keep it quiet.'

'You'll get a new cellmate?'

'I guess so. I've still got a long lag to do. I just keep my head down and get on with things. In some ways I'm sorry it had to come to this, Alex.'

'I should thank you for looking out for me.'

'Didn't save you in the end, did it?'

Joe rises and turns, pulling aside the curtain to leave. He pauses before facing Alex again.

'By the way,' he says.

'Yes?'

'I think you did it.'

There's no answer. Mark replaces the phone gently. She might be there, dead drunk. Or she might be out buying more. Probably there's something he could do to help, if he had the energy.

As it is, it seems easier to fold the remains of the marriage up like a news-sheet table-cloth that's served it's purpose and

203

dispose of it. Perhaps he has some residue of love for her. But the stew of emotions in his belly permits no clarity. Love is indistinguishable from nostalgia for the way things used to be, and both are subsumed in the omnipresent ache of grief. It may have been that they loved at one time. Or it may have been that they found a way of living that was comfortable, and love only began with the arrival of Tessa. And left with her departure.

And if she had lived? Impossible to say. Too painful to even contemplate. The past is fixed and cruelly indifferent.

He'll not do anything to precipitate matters. There's no need. They're already so isolated from each other that they might as well be living in separate houses. Eventually form will follow inclination. Separation may be the only path to healing that either of them has. Not that there can ever be healing as such. But a lessening of the agony would be something to hope for.

It will come, one way or another. Elizabeth may become alcoholic; might already be. He may summon the courage for suicide now that the consequences have changed. Or it might be different. There are other possibilities.

He raises his hand to his shoulders and recalls the feel of Christina's fingers caressing them. Not now, but some time in the future. Other things may happen.

i like to kneel beside the pond and put my head down low so that my eyes are close to the surface. the skin of the water is so still and smooth, and i like the way that you can see everything reflected in it. sometimes i take a stone and throw it into the centre, and then watch what happens. i love the sound of that little 'plop' before the movement starts. and then those circles, starting out so small at first, and spreading out all the way to the edge where i sit waiting.

everywhere the ripple spreads to, it changes the picture of what you see reflected. like someone taking a knife and cutting through it. and it touches everything—the whole surface of the pond. isn't that amazing? when you think that just one small stone can make all that difference.

right now i think my life is like that pond. clear and smooth, with nothing to trouble it. i'm so lucky to be as happy as i am. i hope no stones fall.

Dear Alex

I know you asked me not to write, but I need to keep you up with developments. This is perhaps the most difficult letter I have ever written, and I'm sure you will wish you never saw it.

The fact is that the space since the trial has given me the chance to see things more clearly than when we were both caught up in the midst of events outside our control. To this day I preserve a belief in your innocence, if for no other reason than that to contemplate the alternative would be more than I could bear. So I want you to know that the decisions I've made have no bearing on my opinion as to the convictions.

I went to see a lawyer yesterday, and asked her to begin proceedings for a divorce. It seems to me to be the best way forward. Try as I might, I'm unable to imagine any way in which we could recover from this, even if your appeal were to prove successful. The tragedy which has resulted in your imprisonment has done damage which is irreparable. We would be living our lives in the shadow of it always, and I'm not prepared to do that.

I realise that this is a terrible thing to inform you of by mail, especially at a time when you feel so low anyway. I do feel horribly guilty for doing it this way, if that's any consolation. I've rung the prison and spoken to the chaplain, and asked him to spend some time with you.

Nancy and Ross are well, though Nancy has broken up with her boyfriend and doesn't go out much in the meantime. Ross, surprisingly, has begun to do better at school. Neither of them is ready to come and see you as yet, nor to write. I continue to hope that this may change in the future, and you can be sure that I will not stand in the way of your continued relationship with them.

There's much which can't be said by mail, and I won't insult you be trying to express my continuing fondness for you. I do want to thank you for what have been happy years for the most part. Our marriage has been struck down by forces outside our control. I will hold many memories.

I'm not sure when I may come and see you. Certainly not in the next few months, and I will await your reply to learn whether you want to see me at all. I'll understand if not.

Yours in sorrow,
Mary

'I can't persuade you then?'

'No, I've thought it through,' says Harry. 'I appreciate being asked, just the same. But I think I'll keep my shiny buttons.'

'Can I ask what decided you against it?' inquires Thompson.

'Doubt, sir.'

'Doubt? In yourself?'

'No. In the system. I think I'll stay over here where the crooks are easier to spot. I suspect I'm more cut out for the sort of policing where you can spot the good 'uns from the bad 'uns.'

The inspector smiles. 'If you can find it, you better stick to it.'

Chapter Twelve

account (ə'kaʊnt) *n* **1** a verbal or written report, description, or narration of some occurrence, event, etc. **2** an explanation of conduct, esp. one made to someone in authority.

account for *vb* (*intr, prep*) **1** to give reasons for (an event, act, etc.). **2** to make or provide a reckoning of (expediture, payments, etc.). **3** to be responsible for destroying, killing or putting (people, aircraft, etc.) out of action.

i just wanted to see the rabbits. it was a sunny day, and i didn't think anyone would miss me if i spent a little time talking to them. the park was like home to me, so i felt quite safe there. i had my yellow pants on, and they shone brightly in the sun. it was the sort of day when the grass smells like summer, and everyone you pass seems to be smiling.

You think it's easy, don't you? You think it's just a matter of stopping, of deciding not to. But you reach a point when you're beyond that; when you're not responsible. After all, you can only be responsible for things you have some control over, can't you? I wanted to stop in the beginning, as I told you. But that was before it got too late. After that it was something happening in me rather than anything I initiated. It's something that's difficult for other people to understand; I know that. I can only tell it the way it happened.

queenie comes right over to see me as soon as i get there. i put my finger through the wire and try to scratch the side of her nose, but she backs away a little. she's been hoping for food, but i didn't bring any. oh yes i did! my sandwiches. i quite forgot about them. i get them out of my bag and unfold them from the greaseproof paper. they have lettuce and cheese in them. i break bits off and start feeding them to queenie. it's not long till they're all coming over to get some. back off bounder and let greyskin get some. oh, you're so greedy, nancy. there's plenty more here, look.

the sun's very bright in my eyes. i have to hold up a hand to shield them, and it makes my face all squinty.

I wanted more than the magazines. I still used them whenever I could, but I didn't get the same satisfaction after a while. I'd still be hungry for something more. I wasn't sure what it was that I wanted, or at least I didn't like to think about it. And then the old mind games started again. I would see the bodies of the girls in the magazines imposed on the faces of those around me. It wasn't something I did consciously, I swear. I would have preferred anything but that. I hated myself for it, just like I did the first time it happened with the Play-boy pictures.

Only this time it was worse. I tried to keep it out of my mind, but I couldn't. It was unbearable.

Because now the images were not attached to women. It was young girls; lovely young girls.

i hear a siren going past at the edge of the park behind me. i turn round to watch, and see that it's an ambulance. there's a man watching me. i've seen him before.

it's the old man who followed me in the bookshop. he's looked away now that i've seen him, pretending that he wasn't watching. but i know that he was. i don't much like him. he gives me the creeps.

i frown at him, and then turn back to the rabbits. greyskin gets the last piece of sandwich, and queenie hops away in a sulk. i don't know what you're worried about, i tell her. now i haven't got any lunch at all.

*

It all goes back to that damned whore who touched me in the markets. All of this started from there. If she hadn't got past my defences, I could have kept it all under control. But no, she had to spread her filthy contagion to me; make me share in her misery. I think I knew, even back then, that I'd been infected. That must be why I hit her, to try to put an end to it.

She had a child's body, you see. And once I'd joined with her, I was addicted. All these years later, she still held me between her legs and punished me.

after a while i stand up and stretch my legs. a butterfly goes past, and i run after it a little way. then i stop and close my eyes. i hold my arms either side of me and twirl round and round in the sun. when i stop and open my eyes, that old man is still watching me. i think it's best if i go somewhere else. mummy's always warning me about strange men, and i don't like him anyway. so i follow the path round by the trees. i look over my shoulder and there's no one there, so that's good.

i sit on the grass under a tree making a daisy chain. you have to concentrate really hard to get them all joined together properly. one time when we were on a picnic i made the biggest one you could imagine. it took me most of the afternoon, and daddy laughed at me, but it looked so pretty when i draped it round and round mummy's neck. perhaps i'll take this one home for mummy.

As soon as I see her I feel the hard ball grow at the base of my neck. I've seen her before of course, but not when I'm feeling the way I am now. I go strangely cold as I watch her. She has black hair, like the girl from the markets. And her face is so pure and innocent. I realise that I'm licking my lips, and I tell myself that it's because my throat is dry.

But it's not that at all. I know it. Now the madness starts. A part of me is standing off, observing, horrified at what's going on. But another part of me is on fire; insistent, urgent. There's never any question who's going to win. I've felt it before, and it's never turned out any differently.

*

209

out of the corner of my eye i see someone leaning against a tree in the distance. it's the dirty old man with the droopy eyes. he must have followed me. my heart starts going fast, and i'm frightened now. i look around but i can't see anyone else close by. i think i need to get away and hide somewhere until he goes away. the daisy chain's not finished, but i drape it round my neck and get up. i look back to where the man was and i can't see him. he may have seen that i spotted him.

i don't like to run, but i walk as quick as i can. i know where i'll go. my secret hidey-hole. no one can find me in there. it's my safe place.

It's already there in my heart, what I'm going to do. Like something perfectly formed and nurtured. It's been growing there for some time, an embryo turning in the dark waters of my imagination. But I can't let it come into my mind. Can you understand that? If I knew what I was about to do, I'd have to stop it, you see. I couldn't let it proceed. So I'm unaware. Even during the preparations. There have to be preparations. You can't just do something like this on the spur of the moment, unless you want to be caught. There are things to gather, like the tape and the condoms and the rubber gloves. They never knew about the rubber gloves—that's been my little secret.

So I have to tell myself I'm getting these bits and pieces for other purposes. I manufacture reasons for the collection which satisfy my mind. That's where conscience resides, I suspect—in the mind. There's some material you don't want to submit to it for consideration. Don't pretend you don't know what I'm talking about. There are things lurking within you, aren't there? Forces and instincts that you don't allow to the surface? Of course there are. That's why you don't want to be alone in the dark, in case you meet up with them. Don't be too judgmental of me if I simply bring into the light that which you keep hidden.

Perhaps I'm doing us all a service.

i can see the big tree now, and i know i haven't got far to go to get there. i turn the corner by the railings, and i can already picture my little spot where no one can reach me. even so, i look back over my shoulder one last time. he's walking along the path behind me, a long way back. when he sees me looking back, he turns sideways, pretending that he's watching something on the other side of the park. but it's too late. i've already seen him, and i know he's still following me.

i speed up, glancing over my shoulder every few seconds. all of a sudden i've banged into something solid, and my heart jumps. it's a person. i wasn't looking where i was going, and i've walked straight into them. i look up, to discover it's a man. he holds me by the shoulders and looks as if he's about to tell me off. only then do i realise that i know who it is. he's wearing different clothes, so i didn't recognise him at first. it's the vicar. i'm so happy to find someone i know. now everything will be all right.

There comes the point where action requires that your conscience be temporarily disabled. You need to stop thinking about the things you're about to do. I have to let go of the reins. Or perhaps it's more accurate to say that someone else takes them up. I'm present, naturally I am. But I'm no longer in the centre, controlling things. I'm like a passenger, a spectator.

Have you ever wondered what you're representing when you say 'I'? It's not the whole of you, is it? It's that part of your being that you've fenced off from the rest as being safe and familiar territory. The elements of personality that you like, and that you can present to the rest of the world. We have an image of ourselves, most of us, and it's that image that we summon whenever we use the personal pronoun.

But what about the parts outside the fence? What about the voices which don't resonate with 'I'? They live in exile; the cave-dwellers in that dark and unexplored territory. The trouble with outcasts is that they become resentful about their exclusion. They might get together and plot revolution. They might plan an invasion of the 'I'. A quick hit-and-run to get past the defences of the ego. For a short while they may take over the running of the show.

he asks my why i'm in such a hurry, and when i get my breath back, i tell him about the man who's following me. only he seems to have gone. i point to where he was, but the man's no longer anywhere to be seen. the vicar strokes my hair and tells me it's all right now. he asks me what i was planning to do. i tell him that i was heading for my secret place, where i knew i'd be safe. that sounds like a sensible thing to do, he tells me. i offer to show him where it is, so long as he promises not to tell. he says that vicars are very good at keeping secrets, and that he'll feel rather special to be shown my hideaway.

i keep looking round, but there's no sign of the awful old man. so i take the vicar by the hand and lead him toward the spot. we chat a little on the way. i feel all right about it because he's not a stranger. mummy and daddy wouldn't mind me talking to the vicar, i'm sure.

After the incident in the Philippines, I was shattered. I thought I was going to be charged. The police held me for an hour or so, and then the captain of the ship turned up and spoke with them, and I was released into his custody. He drove me back to the ship. Neither of us spoke, apart from a few words of acknowledgement. He was an old seafarer, and had only a functional relationship with the mission. I got the feeling that he'd had plenty of experience bailing errant seamen out of similar situations. It was just a task to be done.

It was a different story when we got back to the Evangel. The director of the mission was waiting for me. He asked for an explanation. What could I tell him? I started to tell him how I'd been entrapped, and how I'd lost control. But everything I said sounded hopeless and pathetic. He was particularly horrified by the violence, by the fact that I'd beaten the girl. Strange—I would have thought that would have been the easiest part to understand.

He surveyed the options open to him. He could hand me back over to the police, and I would face charges in a Filipino court. The ship's captain could discipline me, and hold me in the brig of the ship. Or, he said, he could deal with it all in a Christian way, and seek the good of my soul. It was this latter course he was always intending. He asked me to repent of my sins, and I had no trouble doing so. I was genuinely sorry for what had happened.

Then he read from the scriptures while I knelt before him. I re-

member the passage well. It was from the Sermon on the Mount, the part about adultery. 'I say to you that everyone who looks at a woman with lust has already committed adultery with her in his heart.' My actions, he told me, were because of the sin which I harboured in my heart. Then he read the next verse: 'If your right eye causes you to sin, tear it out and throw it away; it is better for you to lose one of your members than for your whole body to be thrown into hell.' I understand it so much better now than I did then.

He prayed over me, renouncing evil and the works of the devil, and praying that God would forgive me and restore me to righteousness. He was very moved by it all. Afterwards he hugged me, and said there was no need for anyone else to know about all this. When we confess our sins, they can be put behind us, he said. He would be sending me home, of course. But as for the rest, it was a matter between God and me.

he asks me what i do in my hiding place. i tell him how i watch the sky and the birds, and sometimes write poems in my head. he says he's very interested in poems, and that it's good that i'm writing things. the vicar seems a lot friendlier when he isn't dressed up in his costume and speaking at the front of the church. it's funny because i always thought he wasn't much interested in children before now.

as we're walking along, there's a sort of icy feeling that runs down my back, making me shiver. like when the sun suddenly goes behind a cloud and makes you feel cold. it's probably just getting over the fright i've had from being followed. we reach the edge of the shrubs, and i have a look round to make sure no one's watching. it's all clear. i don't want people seeing me go in here, or i may get into trouble. except for the vicar, of course. that's different.

I'd been watching her earlier. Sitting making that daisy chain. I spotted the old tramp as well of course, but he was obvious. I felt I should protect her from him. Strange, isn't it? Though even a ravenous dog is protective of its own kill, I suppose. The first time I saw her at church she caught my attention. It was the hair; that same straight black hair

as the Filipino girl. The smell of it had lodged somewhere in my memory.
Smells are much more evocative even than images, I suspect. Yes, the
hair and the vivaciousness. The zest for life that shone in her eyes.
Something in me was hungry for that. Something deep within, and
separate.

And now she's leading me by the hand in pure innocence. She
knows I'm on the side of good; of God. She feels grateful because I've
rescued her. She wants to show me her special place, as some sort of
reward. Here I am chatting to her like a favourite granddaughter. For
a fleeting moment I remember the story of Little Red Riding Hood,
and it makes me smile. What happens when the woodsman is also
wearing a disguise, a mask?

here we are. the small circle of bare earth, surrounded by greenery. it's my favourite place in the whole world. i watch the vicar's
face, to see if he will be as thrilled with it as i am. but he looks
strange, as if he's frightened about something. no one can see
us here, i tell him to set his mind at rest. maybe he's worried
that we shouldn't be there. i always look after the place and
clean up after i've been here, i say. i don't think it's terribly
naughty. he smiles at last, and tells me it's a lovely spot.

is it really a good place to watch the sky from, he asks? oh
yes, i say. you have to lie down on your back like this, and then
the whole sky fills your eyes. come on and try it. i move over a
little so that there's room for him to lie down as well. i'm looking up at the patchy little clouds which are moving across the
blue sky. you have to try to see things in the clouds, i tell him.
see that one over there? i point. it looks a bit like a turtle, don't
you think? oh, it's moving. now it looks more like a tiger. can
you see it?

the vicar doesn't say anything.

I'm lying on my back next to her. She's talking to me but I can't hear
her any more. It's the pause before the action. That moment of time
after the orchestra has tuned and the conductor is standing with his
baton raised, and there's that vast silence. Oh, I suspect it's not an apt
analogy, but it's the anticipation I'm talking about. The little gap

214

between intention and execution, when there is still the possibility of some different outcome. A hiatus taut with portent. I feel supremely powerful at that point, utterly untouchable. I am the master of history, holding destiny like some small toy. The image of my father's angry face comes to me, and shrivels under my gaze. I stand on the top of a cliff, and draw a deep breath.

You want to turn away now, I imagine. You don't want to hear the rest. You're repulsed. But you can't help being interested. Do you recognise it there, under that layer of revulsion? The faint spark of prurience? You pretend it's so that you understand. But it's more than that. You're participating, even as you listen. I warned you it's not as easy to keep your distance as you might think.

The baton falls.

a shadow falls across my eyes which frightens me. and then a hand clamps over my mouth. it must be some sort of game he's playing, but i don't like it. i can't breathe properly. he's holding me down with that hand and it's hurting. i try to wriggle but he's far too strong. i'm frightened, really frightened. what's happening? what's gone wrong? he's on his knees now, looking down at me. his eyes are strange, as if they belong to someone else. he's putting some sort of tape across my mouth. and then he turns me on my side and tapes my hands together.

he puts a hand under my blouse. the ground is hurting my back because of his weight. this shouldn't be happening, should it? mummy says no one should be able to touch me without my permission. it must be true even for vicars, mustn't it? i try to shake my head to let him know i don't like it, but he's holding me too tightly. mummy, daddy, god, anyone—please help me. please please help me.

The skin is so smooth, you see. So deliciously smooth. Young and fresh. I slide my hand over it and feel it like satin. She's struggling now, and I can see the terror in her eyes. But it's no trouble to hold her. Such a small child; there's no strength in her arms. There are no nipples to speak of. Just little bumps under my fingers. I'm being gentle, you understand, very gentle.

There's a fire raging in the back of my head. A small bead of dribble forms at one corner of my mouth and threatens to run down. I must be salivating. I wipe it away with the back of my hand. I don't want to appear uncivilised.

he's pulling at my blouse and now he's ripped it. i'm crying because i know that mummy will never forgive me for it being torn, and i'm so scared. i can't get enough breath because the tape is blocking my nose as well as my mouth. and now he's taking down my leggings—taking them right off. i try to kick, but he holds my ankles so that i'm helpless. this is wrong, this is so wrong.

i can feel his hand down there and he's touching me. he's looking at me all the time. his face is quite close to mine now. his eyes are seeing something else, as if i'm not here. and in the middle there's blackness. an awful empty blackness.

She comes back to me, that Filipino girl. It's her I'm seeing. It's her who's led me astray, her that fondled my testicles and got me aroused and started all this. Her with her filthy mouth licking and sucking. There's only one thing to do, then as now. I have to fuck her into silence. To push my way into that tight little entrance and destroy what lies inside it. To thrust and push and conquer. I have to enter her darkness, enter her flesh, enter her power to defeat it. She thinks I don't know that. She thinks she can seduce me and capture my soul, but I'm too smart and powerful. I'll slaughter the dragon between her legs. I'll spear her and destroy the evil. I'll put a stake through the heart of the demon, and have an end to it.

the pain is too much. it's burning, burning. i have to find a way out. i have to find the door, the gate. i've got to escape, i've got to fly.

and there it is, burnished in gold. my magic doorway. i can feel myself lifting into the air and flying. i pass between the doorposts and on the other side there's nothing but clear blue skies, and something like music. i'm through and free and flying. behind me there are horrible noises and sights, and i know that i can't look back, that i have to keep flying off away from it all. away into the sky.

You can't know what the victory is like. You have your little experiences of orgasm, but you have no idea. It's like every nerve in your body exploding simultaneously. No, you can't know, and you won't ever. But it happens to me, and I call out in the terrible pleasure of it.

And now I'm looking down, and the Filipino girl has gone, and my whole world has collapsed like a tent in the wind. There's this tiny broken child who I'm pinning to the ground, and she's gone very still. I'm crying then, for her and for me, and I don't know what to do. The loathing comes. It creeps over my skin and slithers into the back of my mouth.

I begin to beat her, to purify her of what she's done. I don't know if she's dead or just unconscious, but she rocks back and forwards under the blows.

i don't know why but i find myself turning back. i can see a man hitting a girl, over and over. the child is white as if she's cold, with no clothes on. there's something wrong with the man, as if he's broken. they're so far away, the two of them, that i don't feel scared at all. i'm safe at last, here in the sky where i belong. no one can touch me here.

i can't understand what that man is doing to the girl, or why. there's something wrong with it, i'm sure. from here it seems as if there's something wrong with the whole world that needs fixing.

I'm thinking again now. There's work to be done. I fold her clothes into a small bundle. I put on the rubber gloves and begin to inspect her body. It's distasteful, I know, but you'd be surprised how many people are caught on the evidence of one stray hair. I have to pry into all the nooks and crannies to make sure, even turn her over. At last I'm satisfied and can leave her be. The soggy condom I wrap in her panties and put in my pocket.

I leave her lying there while I inspect the ground, brushing over footprints and picking up any fragments which might be incriminat-

ing. You need to be so patient and careful. Finally I'm satisfied.

I kneel over her body and arrange her hair. I wipe the tape to get rid of fingerprints. I make the sign of the cross on her forehead, and pray silently for her. It's not her fault that she's got involved in forces outside her control.

i feel very peaceful now, as if there's nothing at all to worry about. i'm as free as a bird, and all the sky is mine to play in. it's not the first time i've been through this door. but this time i'm not sure if i'll go back or not. the air is so clear, and all the colours seem somehow to be brighter than they were.

I dress her again, as best I can. It's not easy when there's no co-operation. Then I lift her body. It's so light, as if there's nothing inside it. I make my way through the bushes. I know a track through the trees to where the car is parked.

I'm startled to see an old man crouching in the bushes as I make my way along the path. It's the tramp who was following her round the park earlier. I don't panic. I just look him full in the eyes as I'm carrying the girl. We see each other. There's an understanding. Two of a kind. He looks into my soul and sees himself.

I don't say a word, and neither does he. He watches as I disappear into the greenery.

I make it back to the car without any other encounters. I lay her across the back seat, tucking her into a foetal position so that it looks as though she's sleeping. And then I drive her to the cemetery. I want to put her on consecrated ground, you see. Not just in a ditch some-where out in the countryside. I'm not a barbarian.

I know all the secrets of the cemetery. How to get in and out with-out being seen. How to avoid people walking the paths. My own hidden clearings like the one she led me to. I lay her gently on the ground. I remove her clothes once again, decently and reverently. Bruises have come out on her white body, but I ignore them. I place her where she's partially concealed but visible enough to be found. I inspect the scene for clues, and leave. On the way home I dispose of the clothes in a bin, emptying some rubbish from the glove box on top of them.

I drive home breathing easily. And then I remember the tape, which is at my feet in the car. I don't want to go out again. So I place it outside, on the footpath near the side gate. Someone will pick it up, I'm sure.

And then I go inside and change into my clerical clothes. It makes me feel different, a completely new man.

when i was very little, mummy bought me a balloon. it was red with big green splotches on it. it always wanted to climb into the air, and i had to hold on to the string tight so that i could keep it. i've never seen a balloon as beautiful as that one. it was sleek and shiny, and i was the happiest girl on earth holding on to it. mummy kept warning me that i'd need to hang on to it or it would float away, so i concentrated very hard on gripping it tightly. when i wasn't looking up, staring at it, that is. we took the balloon up to the park, and i walked round and round, wanting everyone to see me with my red balloon.

after a while, daddy arrived. we'd agreed to meet him there. i was so excited that i ran across the grass to meet him, trailing my balloon along behind me. i was nearly there when my foot caught on something and i tripped and fell flat on my face. the bump jolted my hand and i let go of the string. i tried to catch it again, but i was too late. it was soaring off into the sky, looking more beautiful than ever. i cried and cried, and daddy held me in his arms and helped me to see where the balloon had gone, high into the sky.

you can't always hold on to beautiful things, he said to me. sooner or later you have to let them go, so that they can be free.

> **dissociation** (dɪˌsəʊsɪˈeɪʃən, -ʃɪ-) *n, Psychiatry.* the separation of a group of mental processes or ideas from the rest of the personality, so that they lead an independent existence, as in cases of multiple personality.

So it was never me, you see. I, Alex, was innocent of the whole thing. I can't see why 'I' should be held responsible for things that were not of my doing. I'm a clergyman; a husband and father. It's inconceivable that I could even consider a crime of that nature. What would I have to gain? And I had so very much to lose, as events proved.

I don't expect you to understand it. You've never had to suffer the torments which I have; never been the victim of sirens such as that girl in Manila. But I'm not that much different from you, Kevin. We're both men of the cloth. We fight evil in the name of God. Have you ever wondered where the evil which we resist goes? Does it simply dissipate into thin air? Or does it lodge within us?

Perhaps it's the cost of doing the job. It may be that we are like filters to clean the world of contaminants. But who will purify us? How are we to be cleansed? We act in the name of God, so perhaps some small part of the blame should be sheeted home there.

To this day, I feel no connection with the person who committed the crime. I'll bear the punishment now, without hope. But I'd like to do it with a clear conscience, and so I've written down this confession for you. I find it easier to write than to talk about these things.

I will have been transferred by the time you read this, and so you won't have to face me. I should remind you, chaplain, that even though this is written, it is bound by the confidentiality of the confessional. I know I can trust your integrity on that score.

Kevin returns from the lavatory, wiping small flecks of vomit from the side of his face. He begins preparations to burn the contents of the metal wastepaper bin.

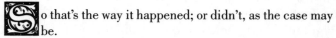o that's the way it happened; or didn't, as the case may be.

Some people turn to the back of the book in an effort to discover ahead of time what the resolution of the story is. I suppose it's a human tendency to want to have things resolved, and not to have to live in tension for inordinate amounts of time.

However, we both know it's an attempt to circumvent the process, and ultimately illegitimate. Those of you who have arrived here ahead of time are wanting to know who was responsible, I imagine. It would certainly help to clear matters up, and make it easier for you to navigate the rest of the text.

So, I have some sympathy—and a suggestion for you. I'll

let you know who's responsible, so long as you undertake not to spread it around. Here's what I suggest you do. Find a mirror, and place your face very close to it. Look intently into the pupils at the centre of your eyes.

What is it you see there? A trick of the light?

Or perhaps a shadow.